Summer in SOFIA

JANE GOLDEN

iUniverse®

SUMMER IN SOFIA

iUniverse books may be ordered through booksellers or by contacting:

iUniverse
1663 Liberty Drive
Bloomington, IN 47403
www.iuniverse.com
844-349-9409

Because of the dynamic nature of the Internet, any web addresses or links contained in this book may have changed since publication and may no longer be valid. The views expressed in this work are solely those of the author and do not necessarily reflect the views of the publisher, and the publisher hereby disclaims any responsibility for them.

Any people depicted in stock imagery provided by Getty Images are models, and such images are being used for illustrative purposes only. Certain stock imagery © Getty Images.

ISBN: 978-1-6632-0895-8 (sc)
ISBN: 978-1-6632-0896-5 (hc)
ISBN: 978-1-6632-0894-1 (e)

Library of Congress Control Number: 2021909556

Print information available on the last page.

iUniverse rev. date: 05/07/2021

Dedicated to diplomats deployed around the globe in the pursuit of human rights, democracy, and the rule of law

PREFACE

SOFIA'S FORTUNE IS A WORK OF FICTION. I CREATED THE CHARACTERS AND THE plot but tried to faithfully describe Bulgaria as a country and the specific places to which protagonist Jeni's curiosity compels her to travel.

While living in Eastern Europe, I explored Bulgaria from top to bottom, from the Black Sea to the borders of Serbia and Macedonia. The beauty and majesty of Bulgaria cannot be overstated, with its ten UNESCO World Heritage sites. I have attempted to bring to life Bulgaria's grand and sometimes tortured history but balance it with scenes from its vibrant present-day culture. The people are warm and the country is safe, which made it the perfect place to roam with my American visitors, especially with my good friend Ruth, whose father really was a US prisoner of war in Shumen, Bulgaria.

I hope this book will whet your appetite for travel to a country that native son Yordan Radichko describes as "stacked, twisted, and shaggy ... this twist and shyness make our land picturesque. In our country, we are stepping, prairies, savannas, deserts, and everything is in a wonderful mess, where nature has played as a young child and has scattered all its toys around us."

Back to what is true and what is not in *Sofia's Fortune*, I should mention that Baba Vanga really did exist, and I have traveled several times to her tiny village of Rupite. And Cyprus continues to struggle with its identity, still painfully divided in half after Turkey invaded it in 1974, when I was a sophomore in college and admittedly a little distracted at the time. As of this printing, President Erdogan of Turkey has pledged that "Cyprus will always be part of Turkey." Go figure. Perhaps one day, diplomacy will make a comeback.

All books need readers to point out when the wrong person dies or a character appears, never to reappear, vanishing like a ghost. To my readers, Cheryl, Jennie, Jay, Kim, and Karen, I give my heartfelt thanks for what is often a thankless job.

I also thank Jennifer Fisher of JF Editing for all her sage advice.

On what slender threads do
life and fortune hang …

✕

—Alexandre Dumas,
The Count of Monte Cristo

CHAPTER
ONE

WE STARED AT EACH OTHER, ONE SET OF EYES GREEN AND THE OTHER BLUE, like boxers before a fight. Both of us were lying prone on the pavement underneath a decades-old Lada, an iconic and tiny Russian-made car, parked near my apartment. The spontaneous and now-intense face-off had begun a few minutes earlier, and the ball of gray fur between us was the cause.

I was walking home from the embassy in Sofia after getting my mail when plaintive meows filled the residential street, which was lined with stately white-stone homes, periodically interspersed with massive apartment buildings, some holdovers from Bulgaria's Communist past and others newly built. The occasional leafy trees, flowering plants, and dark-green grass in random parks softened the sharp corners of the stark concrete walls.

It seemed an easy thing to save a kitten, once I found its hiding place. And it would have been—but for a small girl with curly blonde hair, dressed in a worn sundress, her bare feet poking out below the long hemline, who came upon the scene. Earlier, I had watched her winding herself tightly in the ropes of a park swing and then releasing quickly, like a rubber band, to turn in fast circles. The dizziness she experienced must have been intoxicating, as once the swing's twisting slowed, she began wrapping herself again in anticipation of an even more exhilarating uncoiling.

However, now she had abandoned her play and, like me, appeared intent on rescuing the kitten.

Perhaps it was the heat of the midday sun, but something told me, by the time of her arrival, that I had put too much into the rescue to walk away without anything to show for my effort. Ignoring the child, I called, "Here, kitty, kitty," trying to coax the kitten to come within my reach. The kitten apparently knew as little English as I knew Bulgarian.

Not to be outdone, the little girl—she couldn't have been more than five years old—lay on her stomach so she was eye to eye with the kitten. She began saying, "*Kote, kote*," which I assumed must be the Bulgarian version of "kitty, kitty," with a mesmerizing singsong voice.

The kitten quieted, seemingly confused at the dueling entreaties. In fact, it no longer looked scared, just curious.

So, we stood off—me, an American ex-pat in now-dirty clothes, kneeling on the ground, talking gibberish to a pound of fur, while the tiny Bulgarian girl spoke softly in her language, using her big blue eyes to implore the kitten to trust her.

It should be a surprise to no one that the kitten eventually wobbled toward the little girl, who scooped it up, the kitten nuzzling into her hair, and disappeared with the small creature before I was fully erect and had brushed off the dirt from my knees.

"Oh well," I murmured to myself.

To be honest, it bugged me a little—this kitten thing. I should have been happy for the two of them. I didn't even want a pet, much less a cat. Yet I couldn't help wonder what had suddenly caused a pit in my stomach. It was that gnawing feeling, like something significant had happened. But what could it have been?

After a few minutes, I gave up the elementary self-analysis and decided I was probably only hungry. I shook off the uneasy sense as best I could and adjusted my backpack. Only then did I perk up, recalling that I had mail from home inside that black leather bag, waiting to be opened.

Small things take on an added meaning when living in a foreign country.

As I often did when I received mail, I sat down on my favorite well-worn concrete bench under an old shade tree on the edge of the park, where I had seen the girl play, close to the apartment where Zach and I were temporarily assigned. Only one letter was personal, and I opened it like it was a Christmas present, not sure what was inside.

When I finally realized what I held and its meaning, I didn't know whether to laugh or cry. I glanced at the rectangular piece of paper in my hand, in perfect condition, in spite of its lengthy journey. It was a slightly wrinkled, customized personal check from a small bank in the States, made out to me in the amount of $12,000.

Ordinarily, that definitely would have made me happy. I would have been dancing with joy, waving it in the air like a flag, screaming out to strangers something like, "I won the lottery!" Instead, I just sat there, dumbfounded. Unfortunately, the pretty little piece of paper was about as worthless as the crumpled grocery store receipt at the bottom of my purse.

No bank in Europe, especially Bulgaria, would deposit the check, much less cash it. I couldn't even have it deposited in the United States and then request the money be wired to me from my home bank. The banking systems were totally incompatible. The embassy did not cash third-party checks, and even if it did, it had a limit of $3,000 a week—and then, only if the cashier had that much cash on hand. As I sat at the edge of the sweet little park, my mind quickly sifted through all the potential ways to access this windfall, but I was stumped and ultimately turned my attention to the letter accompanying it.

I knew from the perfect penmanship it had come from Aunt Estelle—her monthly missive to me sent across the ocean through the US embassy.

It began as many of her letters did:

My dearest Jeni,

I hope this finds you well in Sofia …

She went on to tell me that the money was from my great-uncle, whom we all referred to as Uncle Bob. Both my cousin Andy and I had received the same amount. My sister Sue was bequeathed Uncle Bob's Cadillac, which she had always wanted.

She finished her letter by saying that her son, Andy, was on his way to visit Zach and me.

Immediately, my brow furrowed. The frustration over the useless check in my hand paled in comparison to the severe anxiety I felt about a visit from my cousin Andy. Perhaps the pit in my stomach was there for a reason after all.

CHAPTER
TWO

Aunt Estelle, my mother's only sister, lived on a farm a few hours away from my childhood home. Warm and kind, she consoled my sister and me when our parents died in an automobile accident many years ago, while I was in college and Sue was a newlywed with small babies.

Andy is her only child and our only cousin. He is almost my exact age, and we have a strong family resemblance—same slight build, sandy-colored hair, and green eyes. I say that not in a good way; I loathed being referred to as the "twin" of my cousin. We had a fragile love-hate relationship that began in the crib and escalated during the long, hazy summers I spent in the country as a child.

We attended the same college, and our relationship became outright frosty after he broke up with my best friend in order to date a cheerleader. Granted, my friend turned out to be a traitor when she sought revenge and deliberately went out with my ex-boyfriend—like that was going to really hurt Andy. In fact, it hurt me more. Anyway, it was a mess, and I had trouble forgiving Andy for the chaos he created over a decade ago.

And now he's coming to stay with us in Sofia, when we've barely arrived ourselves. A sudden small cloud covered the sun for a second, as if in concert with my now-gloomy mood.

Not being able to think my way out of the visit or useless check, I stood up, put the check and letter in my purse, and began the short walk back to the modern state department apartment where my husband, Zach, and I were staying for four months while he worked on a special detail in Sofia, the capital of Bulgaria. Zach was a US adviser to the Eastern Europe region on law enforcement and rule-of-law matters, sometimes wearing many hats at once. While he traveled a lot, I was usually at home in our apartment in Bucharest, Romania. Due to the length of the detail, I'd chosen to go with Zach to Sofia, rather than be separated from him for four months.

As in Bucharest, the gate to our apartment was opened with a code that I always seemed to have trouble remembering. In fact, I had way too many passwords and codes, all of which I was required to memorize because the government forbade cheat sheets. I wasn't so sure they wouldn't catch me if I tried to hide them in my purse, so I was constantly in a state of confusion. Is it 1234## or 4321**, and how many times do I get to try some variable of it before I am locked out? This time, it was try number two that worked.

Once in the apartment, I fixed a fresh tomato sandwich and sat at a small desk in a chair optimally situated next to a window with a pleasant view, overlooking the neighboring tile rooftops. It took but a second for me to type an email to Andy.

Please call me at 8, my time.

Jeni

It was a typically warm summer day, so after I finished my sandwich, I spent the remainder of the afternoon rearranging the plants and chairs on the balcony and set the outside table for an alfresco dinner later that night, when Zach arrived home from work.

"Andy is supposedly coming to see us," I told Zach several hours later, after he changed out of his suit and came to join me at the chrome-and-wicker table and chairs.

His hazel eyes lit up, and he smiled at my dismay. "That's wonderful news!" he said. Zach had been friends with Andy in college, and they seemed to have maintained a tight bond since, no matter how much I objected.

"Well ... I don't know. You're working all the time on some project that I don't understand, and I'll be left with him twenty-four hours a day."

Zach looked over at me, somewhat bemused by my reaction.

"I'm sure he'll do something to make my life miserable," I added for emphasis.

"He might, but think how much fun it'll be to have company from home," Zach said. "Plus, he's grown up now. Don't worry." Then he added, "What's he doing over here, anyway?"

I told Zach about the letter from Aunt Estelle and that it included a check from Uncle Bob's estate. When Zach didn't express curiosity about the check, I didn't bother to tell him the amount. He seemed unusually preoccupied, juggling his already full position in Bucharest and the new tasks in Sofia. Conversations about money could wait for later.

For the next few minutes, we sat quietly, watching the sun set over the city and drop behind the dome of an Orthodox church a mile away.

"You might be right," I finally said. "It'll be good to see him. I'm getting lonely."

"I think so too," Zach responded, and once again we lapsed into silence.

I started to tell him the story about the kitten, but it fell flat, and I dropped it. Ultimately, the silence was too much for me, and I restarted the conversation. "Rosa told me that a local charity that helps raise funds for refugees meets near here. It has mostly international women on the board." I quickly added, "I'm thinking about going to their meeting tomorrow. I think it's called something like AIC—Aid to International Children."

"That's nice," Zach said absentmindedly as he reached for his phone to read a work email. When he finished, he glanced up, realizing that he had been too dismissive of my news. He smiled an apology and said, "I don't know much about it, but that sounds like a good thing to do—you can meet more people. I'm sorry. I have to go handle this. Can we talk later?"

I sighed. He barely had time for dinner most nights. We had only been in Sofia two weeks. I wondered how long he could go on without rest.

"Sure. I understand," I said, as he was already out of his chair and heading inside.

"I bet you'll have fun tomorrow at that meeting," he said. But before he reached the hall to his office, he stopped and turned back toward me. "I know I don't have to say this, but just remember we're only here for a few months. It'd be nice if you didn't get overly involved."

"I know," I replied, almost wincing. I had a propensity to do everything at full speed, and we both knew it.

"And you realize you have to watch out for some organizations. Be wary of what you're getting yourself into."

He wasn't telling me anything I didn't know. Nongovernmental organizations, or NGOs, usually charities, often could be rife with drama and misuse of funds, especially in emerging democracies.

"You can trust me. I won't volunteer for a thing, especially if anything looks wrong or dangerous."

With that, Zach came back to my chair and kissed me on the cheek. "Promise?"

"I promise," I said and really meant it. I would just go for the coffee.

As I sat alone in the quiet living room, I fully understood something that the government had taught me. When you go overseas, at first there is a honeymoon period that can last for months, but eventually, there will come a time when you begin to see the faults, the cracks in the sidewalks, and loneliness can envelope even an optimistic person like me. You won't feel the same for a while afterward.

Maybe, I thought, *that time is here.*

The sun had barely set when the strange ring of my computer phone startled me from my musings about what I would do the next day. Andy's call came right at eight.

"Hey, Dinky," he said. "I guess you got Mom's letter!"

I was immediately irritated, rising to his bait like a hungry trout. "Why do you have to call me that? I'm a *grown* woman, married for years—unlike you, by the way—and you know I hate that nickname. I'm not even going to talk to you unless you call me Jeni."

I heard him laugh; he'd achieved his goal. "OK, Jeni. How about this for a deal: you don't mention my lack of a wife, and I won't bring up your rather cute nickname. I think it's your loss." Then, before I could argue more, he skillfully changed the subject. "So, did you get the letter? The money was supposed to be a surprise."

"Yes, I never expected anything at all. He's been gone almost a year."

"I know," he said. "You know, it was hard on Mom to lose him. He was a big part of her life."

We were both quiet, letting the memory sink in. Uncle Bob was an adored larger-than-life character in a small family and left a deep hole when he died. His death was hard on all of us.

When I finally spoke, I mentioned how happy was I was to be included in the will, and only then did I remember my dilemma. "You know I can't do anything with the check. No one will take it here."

"Are you sure?"

"Yes." Then I thought of something. "Are you really coming to Bulgaria?"

He told me that he was planning to spend most of his time in the Greek countryside and come to Bulgaria for a day or two. He also planned to rent a car and drive around Athens.

I had a brainstorm at that moment. Perhaps he could ask Aunt Estelle to write another check, cash it in the States, and bring the money when he flew to Europe.

He laughed. "Only if I want to go to jail. You, of all people, should know I can't carry a suitcase full of money into Bulgaria."

He was right; I knew better. Civilized countries had prohibitions against people carrying large sums of money across borders or depositing cash in banks without a lot of paperwork. For the next thirty minutes, we discussed all the options we could think of to access the money, finally deciding that he would get another check from Aunt Estelle but merely deposit it into my personal account in the States.

If I wanted, I then could access the money by $200 daily ATM withdrawals and/or larger weekly checks to the embassy. The weekly checks seemed the better choice. Then, I thought, for safekeeping, I could deposit the money in the bank on the corner, just a few blocks from our flat in Sofia. From there, I could draw it down as needed.

Banking was a strange thing in Europe for Americans. Basically, we kept our US bank and direct-deposited everything into it and direct-paid bills out of it, using an ATM/debit card, when needed, in Europe. In the almost two years since I'd been in Eastern Europe, I only needed to open a foreign account once, in order to buy a car. I closed it immediately afterward.

All in all, the conversation went better than expected. I was especially relieved that Andy wanted to spend only a day or two with us and devote most of his time to Greece.

"I hope you aren't coming here in order to get a mail-order bride," I teased as the conversation grew to a close.

"And I hope you don't think that your handsome and charming cousin would be forced to resort to that," he bantered.

"You never know," I said, much happier now than when the conversation had begun. "Really, Andy, thanks for calling. Tell your mom hello and that I love and miss her."

I thought about the call for a few seconds after I ended it. I concluded that it was good to hear from Andy—family is family, and I missed them, even Andy. Maybe Zach was right. Andy might spice up life for a while, even if only for a short visit.

CHAPTER
THREE

THE NEXT MORNING, I GOT DRESSED IN MY BEST GO-TO-A-COFFEE-MEETING outfit, with the mandatory fitted dress and high heels that everyone in Eastern Europe wore. It was important that my first impression be a good one.

The NGO offices were housed in an older building near the downtown Hilton. It was a bit grungy but incredibly cool. The once-ornate stone exterior had grayed due to years of soot and grime, and the windows needed fresh trim paint, but I was mesmerized by the exquisite lion heads and elaborate stone vases carved on the facade. Two full lions also flanked the small set of steps that led to the entrance and a small foyer. Given the grand scale of the building, I was surprised to be greeted by an old elevator with brass expandable gate, right out of the 1920s. The only other structure of any kind in the lobby was a set of worn marble steps that circled the elevator to the top—perfect for those who like scaling Mount Everest. I took the elevator.

As the elevator began its slow, noisy ascent, I observed that at each landing, there were a few large, brown metal doors with multiple locks for tenants, past and present. Most likely, they led to large apartments with tiny balconies. And I guessed that many of the apartments were now offices. I got off the elevator at the fourth floor, once more admiring the quality of workmanship that had gone into the creation of the building.

The setting was appropriate for our meeting, I thought. Money should be spent on good causes and helping the economy, not wasted on fancy new offices.

Close to a dozen women were there—a miniglobal coalition. According to the paper name tags, they were from France, the UK, Turkey, Bulgaria, Kenya, Serbia, Italy, and Russia, among a few other, smaller countries. I introduced myself and was relieved that Rosa had told them to expect me.

"Thanks for joining us," said a somber older woman with steel blue eyes and a short haircut, her coarse gray hair undyed. She sat at the head of the table and introduced herself as Lucia from Sweden. I assumed she was president or whatever the person in charge was called. "Some of the members are glad to have an American on our board at this critical time." Her pursed lips and lack of warmth were off-putting, and, to me, it sounded like she didn't agree with their assertion that I would be an asset. But then I became more gracious—it probably was just the gravity of the refugee program weighing heavily upon her. Why wouldn't she like me? We'd just met.

As if on cue, the others around the table solemnly nodded in agreement with Lucia's comments that I would be welcome, but no one spoke to me. Instead, they turned and waited for her to speak again. Baffled, I too turned my attention to the leader, with the feeling something of importance must be coming.

"I guess we have to face the facts," Lucia began. "I have not heard from Zlata in a week, and the bank won't give me access to the account."

"*What?*" I said, before I could stop myself.

"Zlata is the treasurer of the group. She has left the country with her husband, and we don't yet know where she is or when she will return," Lucia said matter-of-factly. "We have almost 100,000 euros in the bank but we cannot get access without her signature." It was only a problem, she insisted, because they had promised a 5,000-euro donation to a refugee program by the end of the month, and the bank wouldn't release the money until she signed paperwork allowing cosigners.

I was dumbfounded. Not about the lack of signatories—that happened all the time. *But how could the treasurer be missing?*

Lucia looked to the rest of the group. "We don't have any choice but to come up with that payment among ourselves. Can we all chip in a little bit today and cover this amount?"

The room was quiet for a minute. No one even glanced toward another member.

"We'll all be repaid when she returns or when we can get access to the account." Lucia looked at everyone in turn. "Come on; it isn't that much, and it's for charity. I know you can do this."

After a considerable pause, a striking, tall Kenyan—I would later learn her name was Paka—said yes, and then, one after another followed suit. Initially, I thought that everyone agreed, but upon reflection, I wasn't so sure. Maybe three said nothing. But not me.

I enthusiastically joined in with a *yes*, like someone with no common sense. Uncle Bob's bequest made me feel rich. It wasn't a large donation—just a few hundred dollars—but with the other donations it meant there was 5,000 euro for our obligations.

The fact that I was so quick to offer money was so appreciated that I was immediately nominated as the chairperson of the newly created fundraising committee. "Just in case the treasurer takes too long to return," they told me. I quickly accepted the role. It was an honor to be chosen—or at least I felt that way for a few seconds.

It was only after I said yes that Lucia informed me that the board had less than six weeks to either break into the charity account or figure out how to raise an enormous amount of new money—as in tens of thousands of dollars—if Zlata did not return soon. "We have other larger commitments we must honor," she said.

With nothing left to say, Lucia abruptly ended the meeting. The metal chairs scraped the tile floors as they were quickly pushed back amid quiet goodbyes. There was no social conversation and, worst of all, no coffee or pastries. A few murmured a sincere thanks to me for helping, but others said nothing at all, not even to each other.

I wanted to take back everything I had said about helping, but it was too late. In a matter of minutes, I had gotten myself involved in a financial mess.

"But it's for charity," I told myself. "Surely, Zach will understand." Or so I hoped.

The problem was that in my former life in the States, I had been a lawyer, and I knew that none of this treasurer stuff made sense. Someone should just go find the previous treasurer or call the police. But, for once, I decided to hold my tongue until I could ask Lucia some direct questions. Rosa had told me AIC was a serious organization and had been around for decades, enabling it to accumulate large annual donations and do much good. Surely, there had to be some logical answers.

I hung back, watching everyone leave, other than Lucia, who would be last, in order to lock up. I gently tapped her shoulder to get her attention as she was walking out the door directly ahead of me. She jumped at my touch, seemingly on edge.

"I'm sorry, but I'm curious. Who is this Zlata woman, and why does she control the organization's bank account?" I asked. Lucia slowly turned toward me. Once I had her full attention, I continued to rattle off questions. "Don't you have more signatories on the bank account? Shouldn't we notify the authorities that Zlata is missing?"

Despite clearly knowing English, Lucia slightly raised her shoulders and then looked at me with a blank stare before turning to head back to the door. That only made me more inquisitive.

"Lucia, what is going on?" I asked, my voice now firm and demanding, as a parent might speak to a rude child. I stood with my hands on my hips, my eyes boring into her back, as I waited for a response.

Lucia paused for a moment. I watched her eye the exit and pull the keys from her purse. She turned to face me, her lips so tight they almost didn't move. "Look, Jeni, this is none of your business."

Then she slammed the huge metal door shut, the echo reverberating loudly throughout the building, and turned the large skeleton key to lock it. I stood in the hallway, stunned, as she walked away and hurried into the elevator, closing the old-fashioned accordion-gate door before I could enter behind her.

What have I gotten myself into? And how can it not *be my "business" if I'm on the board?* I'd never experienced this level of rudeness from a new colleague and was frustrated enough to quit before I was further involved. But I knew I wouldn't quit. I'd told myself I'd at least stay until I knew what had happened to the missing treasurer.

My first instinct was to call Rosa for advice on the NGO, but I was embarrassed to tell her what a mess I had jumped into. Rosa was my only friend in Sofia. Both she and her husband, Leo, were Bulgarian, and he worked for an international law enforcement agency in Sofia that sometimes overlapped with Zach's job. Over the years, the couple had periodically lived in other countries, including two years studying at Georgetown University in the States.

Rosa understood Americans like me and the ex-pat experience in general and had offered to show me around Sofia. We hit it off immediately. She told me that I had great timing; ordinarily, she would still be overseas, but Rosa and Leo had returned to the capital city earlier in the year in order to care for her husband's ill mother.

When she offered to serve as my translator, when needed, and act as my skillful cultural adviser on all things Bulgarian, I readily accepted her help. I needed her badly. Although both countries were incredibly beautiful, Bulgaria was very different from Romania on a cultural level, from its Cyrillic lettering to the unmistakable Russian and Ottoman influences. Yet there were also similarities: most educated people spoke English in both countries, although Russian was still taught in school in Bulgaria. And Bulgaria was very safe; random violence rarely occurred.

Like many other countries in the region, however, corruption was rampant, especially in politics and finance. One young man told me they changed politicians as often as they changed clothes. But politics did not interfere with my life in Sofia, and so far, for the most part, I found Bulgaria sunny, inviting, and peaceful, like an outdoor yoga class.

But now, this NGO—or AIC, as they called it—was upsetting my karma, and my gut instinct was telling me that something was very wrong.

Why, oh why, didn't I say no before I offered money or to chair a committee?

Zach was at a conference that night and would get home too late to talk about my day. The more I thought, the more I worried, until I decided that, as much as I hated to bug her, it was the perfect reason to call my trusted adviser Rosa.

"Rosa?" I asked into the phone as soon as I heard the other end engage.

"Hey, Jeni," she said loudly, over the sound of dishes rattling around her. "How did it go today?"

I told her the gist of the news and asked what she knew about Zlata.

"Zlata is a very common name," she said. "What is her last name?"

"I don't know anyone's last name—they weren't on the name tags," I said, kicking myself for not picking up the member list. "I guess you can't help without more information. You told me about its history, but it there anything else you know about the charity?"

"Not really," she said. The sound of washing dishes stopped; I assumed she was thinking about the question. "Now that I think about it, I know hardly anything. I overheard Leo talking about it one night last week and looked it up on the web. Its website mentioned it was looking for new international board members, and it came to me that you might like it."

"What did Leo say about it?"

"Nothing to me. He was speaking to a guy from his office about charities and said the name AIC. We've been out of Bulgaria so long that I couldn't recall what it was. That's why I looked it up." The sound of the water in the sink ended. "You will laugh at this, but I think I may have heard the word 'interesting' used by one of them."

"Well, that would be an understatement," I said with a laugh.

We talked for a few more minutes before she had to hang up and dry her dishes.

Zach was still not home so I turned on the computer to read the daily news in English. While I could follow Romanian news on TV, the language difference in in Bulgaria was too hard for me to understand the details of local TV news coverage. Computer translations, as bad as they were, worked the best for me.

This time, it would have been better not to read the news at all. In a rare and truly depressing story, the charred body of a man had been found floating off the Bulgarian Black Sea coastline. Police said they were stymied as to his identity—there were no clothes or identifying features on his remains, and the fingertips were decomposed. In addition, there were no missing persons reported. Given the unlikelihood that he had killed himself by burning and drowning, they assumed it was murder and vowed to find his killer.

I clicked on the comments, and there was only one—it said something silly, like he was probably swimming in bad politics and banking. It was the kind of thing people write when they want to be cute. I smiled ironically. Isn't that almost always the case when dead bodies are found floating in the ocean? Money or power.

CHAPTER
FOUR

For once, Andy shocked me and did as he promised. A few mornings after our call, my bank account in the States had $12,000 in it. A smile crossed my face for the first time in two days. Things were looking up.

I could only imagine the shock on my local bank officer's face when he saw the deposit. Normally, I called the bank officer on a regular basis to cover an automatic draft out of my account when the unpredictable automatic deposit for Zach's overseas assignment failed to beat the totally predictable credit card bill. I envisioned my banker, with his disapproving face glowering each time I called.

My first thought after the bank's confirmation was to contact Zach to celebrate, but he was in meetings all day. By the time he got home, my glow would have worn off, so I decided not to tell him yet—it would be my secret for now. I would use the money to buy him something, but what? Then it hit me—maybe it was time for a honeymoon, the one we never really had. We could take it after the Sofia assignment ended.

"I'll go to the travel agency after stopping at the embassy," I said to the plants in the living room.

I was almost skipping when I headed out of the apartment. The cashier's office at the embassy, much like the one in Bucharest, was small, with random hours and days of operation that frequently changed without rhyme or reason. As usual, according the posted sign, I was there at the wrong time but, luckily, the right day. I didn't know many people at this embassy, so I simply took a seat in the front lobby on one of those government benches with nice upholstery and wooden legs but terribly uncomfortable for sitting. A glass coffee table held magazines like *The Diplomat* and *Foreign Service*. No fashion or travel magazines to flip through here. The time on the wall clock seemed to crawl.

The sole person near me was a marine, who was encased in a bullet- and bomb-proof office with tons of camera surveillance screens. Only he could let you through the heavy doors to the other side. His shelter separated the interior lobby, where diplomats and their families could enter, and the main lobby.

When I knew it was time for the cashier to open, I passed my badge to the marine, who inspected it carefully and, without comment, released the doors to let me enter. I walked past the same offices that were at almost all the embassies—small diplomat offices for people in political, economic, cultural sections; DEA, FBI, Secret Service, etc.; endless cubicles with support staff; and then, corridors that held medical, travel, post office, etc. The really secure spaces were upstairs, and only those with the highest clearance could access them, and then, only after leaving their cell phones in outside lockers.

I followed the lower-level maze until I reached the cashier. She was not happy to hear what I wanted to do.

"You do realize that we only have a set amount of cash for each week."

I wasn't sure if it was a question or rhetorical statement.

"Yes, but I need the cash," I said.

She glowered. I knew she wasn't paid enough to deal with the headache of paying me a lot of cash each week and then risking the wrath of another diplomat who needed money for travel or to buy a car. She didn't care what I wanted; she just wanted to keep her bank till as full as possible.

We finally agreed I could write a personal check for $2,500 in Bulgarian money (lev) and $1,000 euros every week for the next several weeks. I would forego any American dollars, the hardest item for her to stock. I decided to leave several thousand dollars in my account in the States. She reluctantly handed me the first $3,500 that day as if it were from her own personal account.

It was an exhilarating moment. I had never had that much cash on my person with no practical purpose for its immediate use. It took approximately two Bulgarian lev to convert to one US dollar, and as a result, the wad of money the cashier had disbursed to me was almost twice the size of $3,500 in dollars and barely fit into my purse.

Not surprising, though, the sheer size of the bulky cash made me uneasy. Once outside the secure embassy, I immediately began to fear I would be robbed in a city that had few robberies. I found myself holding my purse close to my body with both hands and with my body bent over. No matter how hard I tried to act normal, I looked like a person who was begging to be robbed.

So this is what it's like to be rich and always worried someone will take your stuff, I thought. I wasn't sure that was such great a way to live.

By the time I reached my apartment, I was sweating. I knew I had to hide the money, but where?

A good hiding place was hard to find in my sterile apartment with its mostly empty closets. After an hour, I was resigned to stashing the money in a shoebox in the bottom of the one closet I was using. I knew it was a stupid place, but it was only temporary. I was more worried that if the hiding place was too good, I would never find it again.

Once I closed the closet door, I opened the curtains covering the large glass doors to our bedroom and filled the space with bright afternoon sun. I couldn't resist walking out on our third-floor balcony, turning my face upward to soak in the sun. My mood lifted even higher, and I decided to stay outside to water the plants and indulge in an afternoon espresso.

When I turned to grab the watering can, I saw a man emerge from behind the one tall bush outside our apartment and hurriedly walk away. He must have thought I didn't see him.

"Now that is creepy," I said out loud. Was he a Peeping Tom? That didn't make sense. If so, he would have stayed when the curtains opened. That only left one explanation—someone was watching our apartment building. I wondered who it could be and why he was there. There were only eight apartments in this building, and most occupants, other than me, were at work. *Sofia is turning out to be a most unusual assignment*, I thought.

Later that evening, I told Zach about the incident, and he said it was probably the Bulgarian authorities checking in on us. It was not that unusual for diplomats to be followed. But I didn't think he was Bulgarian. He'd worn a polo shirt and khaki pants, and, if you asked me, I'd say he was American.

Ordinarily, I would have pressed the issue, but for the first time in weeks, I was in a great mood, one that even a weird guy behind a bush couldn't erase.

The next two weeks fell into a pattern of cash withdrawals and weekly coffee meetings of the fundraising committee for the NGO that I now simply called AIC. I had three key people on my fundraising team—Bella from Italy, Natasha from Russia, and Paka from Kenya. Finally, a board with common-sense names that I could pronounce.

The treasurer was still missing, and the bank still unwilling to grant access to the 100,000 euros, but Bella, who had been on the board for a few years, assured me it was no problem. She had spoken to Lucia. "Surely," she said, "it'll all work out."

I never really believed her, but I couldn't get her to tell me more.

"Don't worry so much," she would say each time I asked and then would walk away to signify the conversation had ended.

Bella recommended that we hold a summer bazaar, with each embassy donating a table of its country's products for sale; we would keep the proceeds for the refugee program. There would be a children's talent show and some celebrity singers on stage. I thought it sounded like a lot of fun and enthusiastically began planning it.

Only Rosa warned me to be careful. When we met for coffee that afternoon, she said they had done something similar with all the embassies in another country, and it was a political nightmare.

"They had talent shows with children—how could that go wrong?" Rosa asked and then proceeded to answer herself. Apparently, children from one country performed an elaborate dance, with guns that looked like assault weapons—I think they are called Uzis—that they tapped on the floor and held in the air, like some ISIS video. Then, before that shock wore off, another country had their children sing a disrespectful song to a neighboring country, at which point everyone picked sides and left angry, before the bazaar ended. "Now," she said, "they have rules that the children in talent shows can't carry weapons or provoke fights."

I didn't know what to say, so I shook my head and took a sip of coffee.

"Can you believe it?" she asked me, knowing by my expression that I couldn't. "And that doesn't count all the diplomatic protocol and saving face of whatever country performs first or who has the best location in the bazaar."

This was not good news, but I was stuck. I knew all about protocol but had not factored it into this event. "I'm sure everything will work out fine," I finally said, sounding every bit like Lucia discussing the disappearing treasurer.

Rosa rolled her eyes. She knew better.

"By the way, I found out that the missing treasurer Zlata's last name is Petrovia. Do you know her?" I asked.

"Zlata Petrovia? She was the treasurer?" Rosa asked, looking a bit startled.

"Yes. Well, I'm not sure if it is Petrovia, but it sounds something like it."

Rosa's face scrunched up, and she took a sip of water before she spoke again. She told me she thought it was odd that Zlata was on the board. Her husband worked for the government, and she wasn't the type to be a volunteer.

"Why?"

"It sounds mean, but she is more in the trophy-wife category—trades upon her looks." Rosa brushed a lock of hair from her face as she contemplated her words. "I've only met her once or twice, and she wasn't friendly to me, which I assumed was because I was just an ordinary Bulgarian."

I smiled. Rosa wasn't in the least ordinary—tall, with long brown hair and large brown eyes to match—but she preferred to be considered for her brain rather than looks, using only a touch of mascara and insisting on wearing glasses, not contact lenses. She had an advanced degree in fine arts, and her interests were in the local museums, where she volunteered, rather than modeling in fashion shows. We had agreed a long time back that we were a good team—she was artsy, and I was analytical.

"What do the other women say?" she asked.

"Nothing. It's like they want no part of her—or, perhaps more accurately, want no part of discussing her with me."

Rosa bobbed her head in that way that told me she agreed with them.

"Do you think she took the money?" I asked.

"It would be a huge scandal if she was arrested, so I would say no. Her husband works with powerful men he wouldn't want to upset. No, the more I think about it, I would be shocked if she took the money. She's probably just a flake, getting a facial at a spa somewhere."

I laughed. Rosa had lived in the States long enough to pick up our more nuanced terms to describe one another. We agreed that I'd continue to keep her informed of goings-on at AIC, for her entertainment, if nothing else.

It didn't take long before I decided I wouldn't waste any more time thinking about Zlata Petrovia—or whatever her last name was. I was busy with brochures for every type of honeymoon on the market—and there were lots of them. It had been hard to wait for all the money to be available, but I finally had $9,000 in euros and Bulgarian money in my box in the closet. It was time to find a bank, and I felt sure this was something I could do on my own.

The Vorbank was at the end of my street; I passed it almost every day. Occasionally, I used its ATM, and once, I had converted dollars to euros for shopping. It was constructed like most new American banks, with lots of tinted glass windows, ceramic-tile flooring, and bank officers at modern desks with computers. It seemed perfect for my needs.

I took out the shoebox, stuffed my overflowing wad of bills into a large brown envelope, and then placed the envelope into a nondescript shopping bag, which I held tightly under my arms. I walked down the sidewalk to the bank, with my body protecting the package as if it were a small child in the rain.

When I arrived at the bank, I introduced myself to the guard at the entrance. He ushered me through the oversized revolving glass doors, which, in turn, emptied me in front of the first desk, where, conveniently, a young man sat ready to open accounts. The plaque on his desk read *Oleg, Novi Smetki* (Oleg, New Accounts), and another said he spoke both French and English. It was meant to be.

"*Zdrasti.*" I said hello. "I need to open an account."

He smiled broadly at my request. "Of course. It is easy. I just need a copy of your passport."

I gave him my passport, and he filled out a long, single-spaced, tiny-print, triplicate form, all in Bulgarian. I signed it, figuring that I never read the ones in English at home, so what difference did it make here, if I was only opening an account. Within minutes, I handed over the contents of the envelope to be deposited.

Oleg wasn't in the least impressed by the sheer volume of loose bills or even curious about the source of the money. I was glad the amount was just under $10,000. Once over $10,000, certain kinds of international banking forms might be required. I didn't want to invite that type of government scrutiny.

Oleg methodically put the bills into a money counter, verified the amount and conversion rate, and then gave me a receipt, banking instructions, and debit card.

I watched him as he worked on my account. He was youthful and handsome, with dark brown hair and brown eyes, clearly intelligent and destined for greater things. Opening accounts like mine was probably routine and monotonous for him. It was almost like his mind was somewhere else while he entered the answers to each field on his computer screen. When I heard the familiar sound of a printer in the background warming up, he smiled and said, "Two minutes."

That was all it took before he returned with my final set of papers to sign. I scribbled my name without comment.

"*Blagodarya*," I told him as best I could when we finished. The Bulgarian word for *thank you* was ridiculously long and hard for me to remember.

He flashed a beautiful and genuine smile in return. "*Dobra dosti*," he responded—Bulgarian for "my pleasure."

It was so easy. I stood and walked out of the bank, breathing a sigh of relief that my money was safe. Now I could begin to plan how to spend it.

CHAPTER
FIVE

THE NEXT MORNING, WHEN I GLANCED AT THE CALENDAR ON THE KITCHEN wall, I found it hard to believe that we had been in Sofia a little over a month. So much had happened since the early unhappy weeks; my boredom had lifted, my savings account was full, and Andy would soon be on his way. I almost skipped out of the apartment on my way to the AIC weekly meeting.

I was still gleeful when I arrived at the office, but my mood soon changed.

"I have news."

Much to my dismay, Lucia began this meeting the same way as the first one I attended. Immediately, my shoulders drooped, as did others in the room.

"Zlata is in Cyprus and not likely to return any time soon," she said. Then, through reading glasses, she peered at a piece of paper with handwritten notes on it. "Her text, sent at 11:10 last night, said that she 'had an emergency' there. I texted her back, asking that she call me, but I have heard nothing yet."

We all sat quietly until I spoke.

"Then, in that event, we need to go to the police." I said it more forcefully than I'd intended; my words echoed across the cavernous meeting room.

"No, *you* have *nothing—no proof.*" Lucia's immediate and angry reaction startled everyone as she muscled up indignation to defend Zlata. She stood and glared at me, leaning forward with both hands on the table. But when she moved her eyes away from mine to the shocked women around the room, she seemed to know things were not going well. If she wanted support, she would have to soften her tone and try to reason with them, if not with me. "We must first try to find out if the money is in the account. That is *all* we need to do." She stood tall with her hands at her sides and a wan smile on her face. "Does anyone know a contact at the Vorbank, an officer who might help us?"

The Vorbank? My bank? I didn't know what to say.

"Oh, I know people there," Natasha quickly said, much to everyone's relief, including mine. "I'll see if I can get some verification that the money is there or not."

I ultimately agreed with the rest of the women that we would wait for Natasha to get information on whether all the money was still on deposit before we took drastic action. We ended our meeting with a rather terse agreement to meet again the next day, when we hoped to know more.

Just as our gathering ended, Natasha asked if we could meet in my apartment rather than the office on the following day. It was closer to everyone's home and the bank, she said. That took me aback for a moment, but then I recalled that I had placed my address on the sign-in sheet for the first meeting.

"Of course, I'd be happy to have people over for coffee," I replied without hesitation. It was true. I loved my role as the wife of a diplomat and had all the paraphernalia that was needed, down to a Nespresso machine and enough porcelain coffee cups for large groups. Hosting a meeting would be right up my alley.

Zach arrived home early that night in order to pack for a long trip to Brussels. He was happy to know I was busy with the AIC and would not be bored while he was away. I didn't mention the missing treasurer, hoping Lucia was right and that Zlata would be home soon.

"It's good news that Leo is traveling along with me," Zach said. He was going with Zach to Brussels to work on ratification of a regional law enforcement agreement. "Rosa will be in Sofia, if you need help. Even better, you'll have sole possession of the BMW if Andy arrives early and you want to show him the sights," he added as he threw me the keys.

We loved our ten-year-old gray BMW X-5, despite the fact that it was beginning to show more than a few signs of age. BMW X-5s were made in South Carolina, and it was crazy that the model was one of the major imports to Germany. But don't even think about buying one in Europe and bringing it home—you have to be fluent in German to read the dashboard, and those pesky emissions requirements are for Europe, not California.

When Zach gave me his itinerary and we discussed how much travel money he would need, I remembered the bank issues that day.

"By the way, Zach, do you have any friends who work at the Vorbank?"

"You mean the Russian bank on the corner?"

"Oh … I didn't know it was Russian." I almost choked on learning that information.

"Yeah, of course I don't know anyone. Why?"

"I just was wondering," I said, trying to act nonchalant. "The NGO might have an account there, but the treasurer—" Before I could finish about the AIC problem and muster up the courage to tell him about my account, Zach's phone began to ring.

He shrugged his shoulders and whispered as he covered the mouthpiece, "Sorry, I can't help." He wandered away from me before I could say more.

"Thanks," I said while my mind was whirling. It only made sense that Natasha from Russia knew people there.

How, out of all the banks in the world, did I pick a Russian bank to open an account?

In Romania, I only banked at the BancaTransylvania when we bought our car. I loved that bank because I loved its name. Sadly, that decision represented the extent of thought I put into my choice of a financial institution, not that I could ever understand Romanian banking in a lifetime. It was made even harder because while there might be other Romanian banks, I eventually realized that most large banks in Bucharest were from nearby countries, such as Austria, Italy, Germany, Switzerland, and, yes, even Russia.

No American banking institutions were in Romania or any other Balkan country, as far as I could tell. *Still,* I told myself, *couldn't I have found an EU bank?* I needed to find a honeymoon destination soon and close that Russian account. Once again, I'd need to get Rosa to help.

The next morning, I prepared the apartment with a red woven tablecloth made by hand in Bulgaria, traditional blue-and-white pottery dishes, and an overflowing vase of colorful flowers that I picked up at a vendor on the street corner. I found that lots of things happened on street corners in Europe, including everything I needed for brunch. Pastries, deviled eggs, and a tray of olives, pickles, and cheese were on the table when I ran upstairs to add some last-minute makeup.

I heard the bell ring and dashed back down to see that Natasha had already arrived. It surprised me at first. It was a huge faux pas for any self-respecting European to arrive early, but her smiling face and hostess gift of flowers quelled any irritation I had for my not being completely ready.

"Oh, your apartment is so pretty!" she said as she looked around the room. "I love the windows and the hardwood floors. It is perfect!"

"Thanks, but we just rent it," I said, a bit surprised because it was, in most respects, quite ordinary.

"But you have done such a nice job making it a home. Can I have a tour of the other rooms in the back? *Please?*" That took me aback—she was so infectious and sincere. "I think this would be a nice place to live."

"Certainly," I said, although a bit haltingly. It caught me off guard. I thought that asking to see our private rooms, especially the bedrooms, was a bit odd in Europe, but she was Russian, after all. Maybe these requests were normal for her country. I went with it. What was there to hide?

She was an enthusiastic guest, asking about my travels and my work in the States. She even studied some pictures of my family on the wall in our bedroom.

"I love this room so much and the way it is decorated. Did someone help you?" she asked, looking around my bedroom.

"No, it's all me," I said, smiling with an almost childish sense of pride. I thought I'd done a good job as well, given the temporary nature of the stay. Right when I was going to say more, she snapped a picture with her phone, startling me.

"I hope you don't mind," she said with a broad smile. "I just love the bedspread and want to get one like it."

What could I say? How could I be mad at someone who flattered me so much?

"No problem. I'll tell you where I found it." Although I tried to shrug it off—imitation is the sincerest form of flattery—it still seemed weird that she took a picture of my entire room. That's why I was relieved when she passed Zach's office, just briefly stopping at the door to look inside. She really was only interested in the bedspread.

The other women arrived at my apartment fashionably late. Only two board members said they couldn't make the meeting.

Lucia was in an uncharacteristically happy mood and began by thanking everyone for coming and me for the food and coffee. All in all, a good start. Then she got to the reason for the meeting.

"Did you find out anything about Zlata and the bank account?" Lucia asked Natasha.

"Yes," Natasha responded in her almost flawless English, but then hesitated for a moment as we all watched her intently. "I am afraid I was told that the account has no money in it. However, I am sure there must be a computer error." She shook her head of stylish, short dark-black hair from side to side in order to emphasize her dismay. Her long gold earrings continued to swing back and forth, even when her head stopped moving. Between her perfectly proportioned body and her sometimes exaggerated movements, I wondered whether she had been a ballerina at an earlier age.

There were moans throughout the room. Lucia's smile dissipated.

"At this point it doesn't appear to be a mistake," I said and slapped my hand on the table. "It's time to go to the police."

No one spoke for a few moments.

Lucia just looked at me with disdain.

"Lucia, *you* must be the one to go to the police," I said. "You know all the details." I rose and stood before my chair to see her at eye level across the conference table.

"No, not really. I don't know very much about any money, especially this," she said rather comfortably, settling back into her seat, almost daring me to say more. Her unusual demeanor and incredible pretext that she was ignorant about the money threw me off. But before I could respond, she added, "I have other news that I am sure you will not like. My husband is being transferred to Spain, and we are leaving immediately. I can't continue on the board." Turning to the other members, she told them she was sorry to be leaving. Then, for maximum effect, she added, "Today is my last day."

Ordinarily, her departure would not be that much of a surprise—it was a given in the ex-pat world that you could be recalled or moved on a moment's notice. More worrisome was the news that she was jumping ship, right as we found out the banking account was dry and the treasurer was AWOL—and Lucia was the only person who seemed to be in contact with Zlata.

The remaining members instinctively turned and looked at each other in shock, putting down cups and saucers in order to concentrate. No one spoke. I am sure the others felt like I did. Perhaps if we were silent long enough, Natasha would tell us she was just kidding about the empty bank account or some new woman would walk through the door with a solution to all our woes.

I sank back down into my seat.

Lucia finally broke the silence. "Jeni, if you are so determined, then you go to the police." She stared into my eyes, almost daring me to agree to do so. As she talked, I was already shaking my head no, which, crazily, in Bulgaria means yes. I was already too involved and had no intention of doing more.

When I didn't readily agree to report the loss of money, Lucia changed tactics. I could tell she had her next lines planned, and I saw a slight smile as her voice sweetened, as if in a fake show of respect.

"Think about it. You are an American. *You have to go.* Surely, there is no one else on the board who can do something this important."

Lucia then surveyed the room for approval of my selection, seeking an affirmation from everyone there that they were all too incompetent to handle such a simple task as a police report.

Amazingly, everyone smiled in relief and nodded yes. They agreed that, for the good of AIC, I was the chosen one to go to the police.

I continued to argue against Lucia's suggestion for another five or ten minutes until I decided it was true—no one else was a lawyer, and no one was willing to go except me. They wouldn't even volunteer to accompany me. I felt sure some of them had legitimate reasons that they kept to themselves, but most were just cowards.

"Fine. Just give me all the information you have, and I'll go tomorrow," I said to Lucia and then turned to look at the Russian with the dangling earrings. "Who'd you talk to at the bank, Natasha?"

Natasha only gave me a blank stare.

Maybe she hadn't heard me right.

"Natasha, who told you the money was gone?"

She certainly heard me that time but paused before answering. "Oh, I didn't get her name. I didn't think I needed it." She smiled sweetly to the others, shrugged her shoulders, and played dumb.

"Well … well … what did she look like?" I asked, totally floored by her answer.

"She looked like all the rest of the women in a bank uniform—brown hair, Bulgarian. I don't remember her. I thought you just wanted to know about the account." When her perfectly made-up eyes began to tear up as her answers faltered, she looked away from me and asked the group for forgiveness for not keeping notes. All the board members, except me, smiled back with compassion and told her it was OK.

I was beginning to wonder who had extracted everyone's brains. How could Natasha not remember the name of the employee she had spoken with? Which raised an even more troubling question: did she speak to anyone at all? When she offered to go back to the bank to get the name of the woman, something in her voice told me not to expect a name any time soon. No one wanted to deal with this mess. I had no idea what I was getting myself into.

"Ignore Lucia," a voice behind me whispered into my ear. I turned to see Paka leaning in close to me. "She was Zlata's friend, and she is worried she may be blamed if something is wrong. I heard someone say that is why she and her husband are leaving for Spain. She is afraid."

My eyes widened and my jaw dropped. *Lucia, afraid?*

Paka then shrugged her shoulders and held her hands in the air, as if anticipating my next question. "Who knows?" She smiled genially, stood up, and walked away, leaving me uncharacteristically speechless.

CHAPTER
SIX

As soon as the group left my apartment, I called Rosa, caught her up on the situation, and asked her to accompany me to the police station, just in case I needed an interpreter. I also mentioned that I might need her to assist me in finding a new bank. Without hesitation, she offered to help the next day, after her art class ended. I then began to review the AIC checkbook, bank statements, wire transfers, and deposit slips that Lucia had given me to see if, in fact, only one person could have taken the money—the treasurer. In the end, it was clear to me that Zlata had removed the money from the account and transferred it to another account. The only question was to whom that new account belonged.

Along with the account registers, there was a file of random loose papers, including a memo with a partial account number and the name Durres or Durrell in poor handwriting. It had been carefully torn in half. It didn't seem to have anything to do with the charity's accounts, so I put it aside. There were also restaurant receipts and petty-cash disbursements but nothing that was extraordinary. I found no justification for any transfer of funds.

Rosa and I both thought alike, and the next morning, we dressed in professional suits to go to the police station. As a result of the clothes—or

Rosa's introductory statement—we were immediately granted an audience with the superintendent.

"How can I help you?" asked an earnest young policeman. He sat up straight in his rolling desk chair, with a pen in hand, ready to take notes.

Although he spoke English, Rosa told our sad story in the Bulgarian language so nothing would be lost in translation.

"Ah," he said as he reviewed the paperwork from the AIC with the few bank statements we could find. His face never changed its stony façade. "Let me go speak to my colleague." With that, he stood up and left the room for a few minutes.

"I am sorry, madam, but we cannot help you," he said as he returned to the room and took his seat, not looking up at me but rather looking down at the pen in his hand. "We are certain this woman has stolen no money."

"No, she has the money or knows who has it. Look at the paperwork," I said, standing up and pushing the sheets of numbers and names back toward his hands. "The money is missing. It looks like she withdrew it." My hands began to slightly shake as I spoke, rattled by his use of the words *this woman*, as if he knew her.

"Again, madam, I cannot help you. Now, I must ask you to leave." This time as he spoke, he looked back at the closed door from which he'd come and then at me. He sat up higher in his chair, as rigid and unmoving as a palace guard, saying nothing more and almost daring me to question him again.

I started to argue, but Rosa grabbed the back of my jacket to pull me out of the room.

"Thank you ever so much," she told the police officer in English. "I am sure we must be mistaken."

He nodded his acceptance of the apology and returned to twirling his pen as he watched us exit the room.

"What do you mean—*surely we are mistaken?*" I asked Rosa, my voice low but full of anger.

"That's the way the game is played. We got what we needed to know. He wasn't surprised or curious about the theft."

I tried to control my anger. "I don't understand."

"Think about it—he is a policeman, but he asked no questions. To, me that means they already know something about Zlata and aren't going to tell us."

"So, what now? We can't just walk away!"

"Now," she calmly answered, "we have to find out what it is that they know and why it looks like they are protecting her. This is *so* interesting. I'm glad you asked me to help you."

I looked at her happy face in amazement.

She laughed. "It's a long summer, and I'm bored. It'll be interesting to see where this leads."

"You know what? I want a cold drink," I said. "Let's stop by the ATM, and I'll get some cash to pay for your drink as well."

"Sounds great. We can sit and brainstorm what to do."

Less than five minutes later, I put my shiny new debit card in an ATM ensconced in the wall of the nearest bank, expecting to see a thriving balance ready for my withdrawals. I hit "English" for the language and entered my PIN.

Invalid account.

What? It had to be a mistake, so I tried it again and again, thinking that multiple attempts would change the outcome. We tried another ATM—same results. Finally, Rosa said we just needed to go to the Vorbank and use its ATM or speak to the man who had opened the account.

Unfortunately, the Vorbank ATM also rejected my card, and Oleg, the man who opened my account, was not inside. His desk was now occupied by a pretty young Bulgarian girl who looked to be barely out of college.

"Do you know where Oleg is? I'm sorry I don't know his last name. He opened my account, and I need his help with some problems I'm having," I said.

"I'm so sorry. He didn't come in today," she said in perfect English. "They relocated me to this office on a temporary basis because I'm fluent in English. Is there any way I can help you?"

I showed her my debit card and asked her to check for an account in my name. She studied the computer screen intently through her pair of stylish horn-rimmed glasses and punched a variety of numbers and buttons in an attempt to access the information. After ten minutes, she stopped and sat back in her seat, moving the glasses to her forehead. The answer was, "There is no account."

I almost passed out.

"Are you absolutely sure?" Rosa asked.

The girl nodded *yes*, left and right, Bulgarian-style.

I was too stunned to speak. We sat in silence for a few minutes until it was clear we could gain nothing further from the account clerk.

"But I have a card and a receipt. How can there be no account?" I said in agony.

"Perhaps it was accidentally voided out, but it will take a while to determine if and why that happened," she said with compassion. "I will send in a request. Please give me your name again and phone number."

My mind was reeling out of control as I scratched the requested information on a sheet of blank paper and handed it to her. It was impossible for me to formulate a coherent sentence, and once again, it was Rosa who handled the situation.

"Thank you," Rosa said and then quickly asked, "Do you happen to know where Oleg lives? Perhaps I can ask him if he remembers my friend's deposit."

"I'll see if his address is still in the system." The young woman pulled down her glasses after she had glanced around to see who might be watching her. Then, she gave us a sly smile as she looked back at the dark screen with its tiny print. She appeared to care more about helping me than protecting some unknown banker's personal information. "Yes, it's here. I'll write it down for you."

I could barely breathe when we left the bank. Over my life, I had lost many things, and there was always a moment when I believed that if I had just done something differently—no matter how slight the change—then I might not have lost anything. That moment came upon me again. Why hadn't I just left the money in the Unites States? Why did I have to carry it around like some minor-league thug? What did Oleg do with my money? *Oh my gosh, what have I done?*

Without my saying a word out loud, Rosa seemed to feel my pain.

"Jeni, we can talk about this over a real drink. I'll pay. Just relax, if you can. Breathe." She repeatedly told me that we would find the money. She insisted that I was very analytical and would be able to figure this out.

The only problem was that I didn't believe her. I didn't even speak Bulgarian.

"All we need is a plan to find out where the money is," she said. "And the good news is that our husbands are out of town, and we have some time to work it all out before you have to tell Zach. OK?"

"OK." That was all I could say. I couldn't talk, as I had to use all my concentration to hold back tears that would have embarrassed us both.

The closest bar was totally new and European. Its walls were made of angular bright-blue glass, interspersed with flowering vines in a crisscross pattern. The tables were clear plexiglass with matching molded seats and blue vases of white lilies. It all sat on a raised platform of teak wood, which surrounded a pool of water with more white flowers—this time water lilies. It was called—predictably—the Blue Lily.

I asked for a table away from the water, as I knew I was the one person who would get up from her chair and then promptly walk into the knee-deep artificial pond—drink or no drink. I was that distracted.

"Two scotches on the rocks, please," Rosa ordered, stronger drinks than either of us ever drank. "I think the first thing we need to do is go to Oleg's house and talk to him," she said. "It has to be someone at the bank who took the money—maybe even him. He may have taken it and intended to put it back—you know—embezzled it. Or maybe he was not that sharp and sent it to the wrong accounts. Maybe he was fired for incompetence. Or maybe he is covering up for someone else."

I stopped staring at my drink and looked at Rosa, nodding. I knew no possibility that didn't involve Oleg. "But he seemed so honest ..." I still couldn't match Oleg's face to that of a criminal.

We thought of questions as we sipped on our drinks. Ordinarily, I loved to investigate matters, even though sometimes those investigations got me into troubled waters, but not this time. It was just missing money, not human life, yet it was very personal—Uncle Bob's bequest was gone. Given that factor, I decided it would be prudent for me to let Rosa interrogate Oleg. Her simple plan was to nicely convince him to return the money or tell us who took it.

"Carrots," she reminded me as we finished our drinks and stood to leave, "not sticks."

We took a taxi to Oleg's home. It turned out to be a modest house with typical white-stone walls, red-tiled roof, and a square front garden with everything from flowers to lettuce and cabbages to trellises covered in grape vines. From the outside, it looked like a happy, idyllic home, but that all changed dramatically when we knocked on the front door.

Rosa spoke in Bulgarian, as it was unlikely the woman who opened the door knew English. It didn't take a translator for me to understand that the listless woman with swollen red eyes who met us was in distress.

"Oh no," Rosa said as the woman began to explain what had occurred. Rosa looked shocked and unnerved, something I had never seen happen with her. Their conversation became almost rapid-fire, with me understanding nothing other than Rosa's occasional outbursts of "oh no!"

It ended with the woman writing a name and number on a sheet of paper that Rosa folded in half and placed in her purse. She then hugged the woman goodbye as I awkwardly stood to the side and murmured my farewell.

"Oh, my goodness, Jeni," Rosa said. "This is all so bad. I don't know where to start. Let's walk to that coffee shop before we get into the car." She pointed to a small mom-and-pop operation with some pastries and two small bistro tables on the sidewalk.

I watched as she gathered her thoughts and ordered two espressos. When she was composed, she said, "Oleg was hit by a car two days ago."

It was my turn to gasp.

The woman had told Rosa that the driver left the scene of the accident, and Oleg died before the police arrived. His mother was very upset and didn't understand what had happened. Oleg had been on a street in another neighborhood—one that he had no reason to be visiting. She said he was a good boy, but he had been very serious lately and moody. But even then, he continued to come straight home from work. Now, she was worried that he had gotten into some kind of terrible trouble.

"Did he have any other family or friends who might know more?" I asked.

"The mother mentioned she was a widow, and he was her only child. However, she did say that he had a girlfriend who left a few weeks ago to go back to university, but she has not heard from her."

"Maybe it was a bad breakup, and he wanted money to get away …" I started to wildly speculate before I realized that was preposterous. Why, then, did he die on a bicycle?

"It was so hard to listen to a mother in such pain. I'm completely distraught over the news, and I don't even know the family," Rosa said, her eyes watering as mine did. It had been such an emotionally wrenching day.

I pictured Oleg's face in my mind and still couldn't see him as a crook. So, why was he dead? Then a chill went through me—*what if he was murdered?* It was possible. Maybe probable.

The one thing I knew about Bulgaria was that corruption was rampant, and often, the Russians were involved. It looked pretty bad that the charity money in a Russian bank—as well as mine—was gone. *Now, on top of that, a banker is dead, and the treasurer who deposited the AIC money in Vorbank is missing.*

And just that quickly, in a matter of seconds, I spiraled so far down that I was envisioning an evil world closing in around me.

But the world wasn't all evil. The reality was that no one thought Zlata was dead—she had texted from Cyprus. The only other dead body I had heard about lately was the washed-up, charred remains of an unknown man on the Black Sea coast, far from Sofia.

A rational mind would successfully argue that no one was dead because of me or my honeymoon money. My money was gone because I had been careless, and Zlata was probably careless as well. I had done something stupid, which allowed someone in another country to steal my identity.

It all was totally depressing, but just when I decided to head home and sleep on it, Rosa spoke.

"I have his girlfriend's name and number, if you want to call her." She pulled the folded paper from her purse and laid it on the table.

"Do you think she speaks English?" I asked. "Do you think she knows anything?"

"She probably speaks English because he did," Rosa responded. She suggested the girlfriend might have overheard Oleg talk about the bank—maybe he mentioned something about lost accounts. Or maybe she knew he was a criminal.

"Wow," I said softly under my breath, not expecting this opportunity. "Let's give it a try."

I called the number on the paper and asked for Maria.

A young woman answered in English. I told her I knew her boyfriend from the bank and wanted to talk to her about him, if she didn't mind. She was hesitant at first, and I thought she might hang up the phone, but instead, she simply responded in a hushed tone that we could meet. She didn't seem to worry about who I was. It was almost as if she knew my name.

"Can you come to Veliko Tarnovo?" she asked.

"Yes, of course," I said.

"I will text you where and when to meet tomorrow afternoon," she said and then hung up the phone.

I put away my phone and looked into the face of a very curious Rosa. "Are you up for a road trip to Veliko Tarnovo?" I asked her.

She smiled and nodded *yes*, American-style.

"She may have information as to my account and possibly the AIC."

"When do we leave?" she said.

CHAPTER
SEVEN

THE REGION OF VELIKO TARNOVO WAS ONE OF MY FAVORITE DESTINATIONS in Eastern Europe, just a half-day drive from Bucharest and only 221 kilometers from Sofia. The actual city of Veliko Tarnovo was perched above a craggy wall of rock that towered above the rushing waters of the Yantra River, which snaked its way around the mountain in an S. Sitting up high on one side of the S was the historic village of Arbanasi, and on another side were the steep cobblestone streets and old homes of the original Veliko Tarnovo city center and former capital of Bulgaria.

The equally unique and enchanting towns of Arbanasi and Veliko Tarnovo were divided by a mere four to five kilometers—easy to drive but far harder to walk, as a steep gorge separated them. The original old city center of Veliko Tarnovo was forged out of rock thousands of years ago and was occupied by many of history's great civilizations, including the Thracians, Romans, Byzantines, Ottomans, Slavs, and Bulgars.

Arbanasi, on the other hand, was more recently developed in the sixteenth and seventeenth centuries as a trading post and was now known for its fine arts and crafts. Its white-stone homes had terra cotta rooftops and ornate fences and chimneys.

Overlooking the shared valley and the surrounding mountains was the imposing Fortress Tsarevet, perched high on the end of the rock and looking as ominous as it had in all its incarnations for almost two thousand years. The river below and the winds above continued to hone its dramatic point into the shape of an Indian arrowhead, providing an impenetrable location in a rather harsh landscape.

Rosa and I were already close to Veliko Tarnovo when I finally received the text from Maria—we were to meet at the fortress near the sixteenth-century monastery at three in the afternoon. She said she would be dressed in blue, and I told her I was in a red shirt and white shorts.

"She doesn't expect two people. I might scare her away," Rosa said and pointed toward the fortress looming in the distance. "You can see there isn't much open space for me to hide."

I had to agree, as much as I would have preferred company, in general.

"Do you know what you want to say?" Rosa asked.

"I'll have to wait and see if a grieving girlfriend or cold witch meets me. I won't know until then." I smiled ruefully, now dreading what seemed to be a clever idea just a day ago.

We both knew I had to find my money before Zach came home, and time was running out. Maria was my only option at this point, and the key was asking the right questions.

I paid my six-lev (three-dollar) entrance fee and then tossed the BMW keys to Rosa. Our plan was that when I was finished with Maria, I would walk down the hill and meet her at a small inn, precariously situated on the side of the steep hill in Old Town.

The arched entrance to the fortification opened up to a long, wide walkway that led up to the ruins. At first, there was a gentle upward slope, but it narrowed and became rocky and rough, the higher I ascended. The path I was on would lead first through the monastery remains and then open up to the famous outcropping—the Cliff of the Executioner, where, as the name indicated, criminals, heathens, and political prisoners were likely sent to their deaths.

Actually, it was a bit unclear who did what on Executioner's Point. In the eleventh to fourteenth centuries, traitors supposedly were the ones who unwillingly took the fall. Then, in the sixteenth century, the monastery was built at the site. According to some, the fact that the path went first through the monastery and then to the cliff was not an accident of the medieval times. It was the court of last chance for those accused of heresy or crime. I doubted that once they entered those stone walls that many were found innocent.

Once condemned, the man or woman was immediately taken out the back door of the monastery to the edge of the cliff and promptly pushed off with the pointy end of a stick. If they lived, it meant they were really innocent, and the decision was reversed by God. If they died, their guilt was affirmed. It certainly saved on the costs of prison and lengthy appeals.

Or so legend said.

I decided that if I were prodded off the ledge of the steep cliff with a stick and fell toward a sure death, I would prefer that God let me die rather than live. I hate pain.

I was huffing a bit from the heat and walk when I reached the meeting place that Maria had texted to me, and I became aggravated with myself over my sudden lack of stamina. I sat on a stone boulder on the outside of the monastery site. It was far closer to the edge of the cliff than I wanted, but it was a good vantage point for me to see Maria approach.

As I sat under a scrubby shade tree, I surveyed the area. No one was dressed in blue anywhere in my line of sight, much less a woman. I began to check my phone every few minutes for a message or call. The time crept by, but no Maria appeared. So far, only one young man wearing a black soccer jersey from the local university, with a camera hanging around his neck, was anywhere near me. When he jogged in the opposite direction, I tried to text Maria, but it appeared her phone no longer worked, or perhaps I was blocked.

Finally, after an hour had passed, it was too uncomfortable to stay in my current position any longer. I stood and stretched my legs.

"It's all a hoax," I said to myself. "I fell for her ruse—no telling where she is. Shoot."

Just as I pulled my phone out to call Rosa and tell her the bad news, the young man with the camera approached.

"Jeni?" he said in a deep voice. He didn't smile or lift his hand for a greeting. His eyes were hidden by dark sunglasses.

I froze, mid-dial. "How do you know my name?" I asked, unable to process who he was and why he was there. I instinctively looked around for help in case this young, extremely large man intended to hurt me. My heart began to beat faster, a fear borne from both the uncertain circumstances and my unfortunate close proximity to Executioner's Point. As unfriendly as he was, he looked clean-cut enough—but so had Oleg, the banker, before my money went missing.

"Maria is not coming," he said, ignoring my question.

My sense of impending trouble heightened. His answer was too cold. He had to have done something to Maria.

"Oh no, please tell me she's not dead," I sputtered, unable to contain my thoughts and words. "What happened?"

Suddenly, fear of being alone with this strange man who knew my name took over reason. I began to panic and instinctively walked backward, away from his scary sunglasses, baseball cap, and black clothing. With each step, I felt myself closer to the edge. I wasn't sure what I feared the most—the chance of a fall or what he might do to me.

I wished he'd say something—anything—but he just continued to quietly observe me.

Finally, he broke the quiet. "No, she is not dead, but she did not come."

I breathed a sigh of relief but only momentarily.

"She does not know if we can trust you," he said as he slipped the camera off his neck and returned it to its case that was strapped to his side. He was so … casual, but at the same time, not. It was like he enjoyed seeing me squirm.

I stared at him and couldn't help but get angry. All this effort for nothing?

"What do you mean—*trust* me? And who's '*we*'? The truth is that I'm probably the only person anyone *can* trust." My voice began to elevate and echo as I lost control of my emotions. "This is insane. I don't know even who you are." As I looked into his face, all I wanted to do was get out of the fortress. "Please, just leave me alone. If Maria is not here, I'm leaving," I said boldly, throwing my arms in the air as if to dismiss him—until I realized he was blocking my way out.

He just stood there, appearing scarier by the moment, eyes hidden by sunglasses.

"*Look*, you have to *move*," I instructed him through gritted teeth. "I can't walk back much farther." This time, when nothing happened, and I could sense him considering his options, I lost my bravado. "Now you're scaring me," I barely whispered. I gave in to full panic, forgot my precarious position, and retreated backward toward the edge of the cliff, eventually standing on a large, flat stone that almost elevated me to eye level with the man.

It was then that things went terribly wrong.

The large rock was not flat at all. I lost my balance and began to wobble, my body tilting toward the ledge next to the abyss. Before I could process what that meant, a scream caught in my throat, my right foot slipped in the same direction, and the fall, which started out slowly, increased in velocity. I was in panic mode and could do nothing to stop my momentum. No trees to grab; nothing to stop me from certain death if I plunged to the bottom of the gorge.

But just when I had lost all hope, I saw an enormous right arm sling out as fast as a baseball pitcher, and then the hand grabbed a wad of my shirt to help keep me balanced. Momentarily, it stopped me, but I was still leaning backward toward the abyss. Both of us held our breaths to see if the flimsy shirt would rip.

It held—only for a second. The horrifying, maddening sound of the fabric tearing an inch at a time filled the quiet space we occupied, and there was nothing I could do but hold my breath and try to stay still, praying I could regain my balance.

I didn't.

That caused the young man to make a calculated decision. Without warning, he loosened his grip on the shirt, and I saw my entire life pass before my eyes.

But it was not my day to die. Before I could fall backward, he deftly grabbed both of my forearms with his free hands and yanked me toward him and to safety. Neither of us could keep our footing at that point, and we landed on the worn ground beneath the path. I fell upon him, and his body took the brunt of the hard, rocky ground underneath. Had we hit a foot or two in any other direction, he would most likely have suffered a broken back—or worse, a broken camera.

"Oh my God, thank you, thank you," I said in gasps. I sat up on the ground and tried to control my breathing.

"I'm sorry I scared you. I just wanted to make sure you were not one of them," he said, still lying prone with his back on the ground, like a downed football player, and breathing heavily.

"Them, *who?*" I was so tired of his ridiculous pronouns.

"Never mind that. I was worrying over nothing," he said. He took a few more deep breaths and then added, "Maria is somewhere safe. She'll text you when I tell her it is OK. You can't text her. She has a new number." He then sat up, and his voice returned to its normal deep cadence. "Madam, I don't know you, but you seem OK. If I were you, I would stop looking for information about Oleg."

"But why stop?"

He looked toward his camera, checking it for damage, as he contemplated the question. The silence around us was only interrupted by a distant echoing of voices on the canyon below. Then he sat up.

"Because … because Oleg is dead because he knew too much. And because Maria is now in danger. Because ma'am, you may be next if you don't stop—no, you *will* be next." He took another deep breath. "They will come after you, just like me …" As he spoke, he punched a nearby mound of loose dirt with his closed right fist, as if to release the anger he was building inside.

Then he abruptly stopped, sprang up from the ground like an athlete, and shook off the leaves and debris on his back, as if shaking off the dirt under his shoes. Then he mumbled goodbye, looking past me toward the fortress exit.

"Don't leave yet—please. I have more questions. What did Oleg know too much about? Why is he dead?"

He stopped, leaned his head to the sky, and took a deep breath. When he turned to me, he raised his sunglasses to look into my eyes. For the first time, I was able to see his tired, soft brown eyes. The face that once looked formidable now looked sad and kind. "The money. It's always about the money and power."

Then he smiled ruefully, once again said goodbye, and began to jog back down the slope before I could ask anything else.

"Where are you going?" I yelled to him as he started down the hill.

"Away," he said. "Away. Far away from here."

I yelled questions at his back—"What is your phone number. Will you please call me? Was Oleg killed?"—but he was long gone, turning only once to wave another goodbye. I lost track of him before he reached the exit.

CHAPTER
EIGHT

By the time I recovered from my near-death experience and was walking along the road back down to the inn, Rosa had already checked us into our rooms and left a happy note for me to meet her for a glass of wine on her balcony and watch the sunset. I headed to her room after I took a long shower and dressed for dinner.

"OK, what happened?" she asked as soon as she opened the door to her room and saw my solemn face.

"A glass of wine first," I said.

She smiled sweetly, poured a glass of chilled white wine, and handed it to me.

I walked to the balcony, took a sip, and intently stared at the bottom of the hill, which was so far below that people appeared like ants. I quickly pushed a chair away from the railing, as close to the room's walls as I could, and sat down to regain my composure.

Rosa listened in shock as I proceeded to tell my story, still unnerved by the experience.

"I almost died a horrific death, just one more person to add to the list of bodies that have hit the rocky river below. *It was that close.*" I held up my thumb and index finger an inch apart. Granted, I was probably exaggerating, but it *felt* that way. "The young man in black caused my predicament, and then he saved me—how weird."

"Do you know his name?"

"No," I said, hitting my palm against my forehead for an omission I had now made twice. "I didn't think to ask. I was fixated on falling."

I was finding my years of legal training in questioning witnesses did not train me well for interrogating someone in Eastern Europe. On the other hand, the daily challenges of living in a foreign country meant that my analytical skills were even sharper.

"Why do you think he told me to stop looking for information on Oleg? I know *we* think Oleg is a criminal, but maybe he's not. Do you think it is possible that maybe he really did know too much about someone else? But it makes no sense...Oleg died in a bike accident."

"What about your money?" Rosa said. It was, of course, why we were there. "How would that fit in? And the charity account?"

"They didn't come up." I could feel my face turn red with the admission that I had failed in asking yet another direct question, but something told me at the fortress that the meeting was never about my losses or even the charity. "He didn't seem to be focused on me personally in that way."

I put my glass down, rubbed my face, and thought hard as to what had transpired and how to explain it. Then I picked up my wine glass, twirled the liquid around, and looked at Rosa. "I know this sounds crazy, but it was more like there is some deep, dark, criminal conspiracy that is lurking out there and that he was warning me that I might accidentally fall into it by asking the wrong questions. And ... I think he was telling me that Oleg knew about it, whatever *it* is."

"Well, I hope not because you'll never stop asking questions!" Rosa said as she poured another ounce of wine in my glass. "I think he's a bit off in the mind."

I raised my glass to her and nodded my agreement. Enough said. I wasn't one to waste time on vague conspiracy theories. It was time to unwind and watch the flickering lights begin to appear across the valley and mountains beyond. We both sat quietly until the sun totally set, both lost in thought.

"Do you feel up to dinner?" Rosa asked, jolting me into reality as she stood up to put a sweater on for the cool mountain evening. "I made reservations here in the inn." It was surprising to see that several hours had already passed since the incident at the fortress.

I smiled. "I'm always hungry."

I'm not exactly sure if what I experienced that night was sleep—it was more fits and nightmares than anything related to rest.

When I awoke the next morning, I lay in bed for a while, looking up to the white plaster ceiling with its tiny Communist-era light fixture. I wanted to be home so badly that it almost immobilized me, and I wondered if I could ever enjoy Bulgaria again.

Less than an hour later, I waited on the balcony terrace, drinking Nescafe from my in-room service—a hot pot and instant coffee—until I heard a knock from Rosa, signifying she was up and ready. It was merely granular coffee, but the Nescafe helped me recover enough to face the day. Over the past few years, I had grown used to the ease of the simplified method of caffeine infusion.

"Ready for breakfast?" she said.

"Sure. I'm already packed to go back to Sofia."

"I have an idea. If the guy at the fortress was wearing a jersey from the local university, maybe that is where Maria went. We ought to take a chance and stop by there," Rosa said. "Maybe someone will know who she is."

After a quick breakfast, we drove out of the inn's tiny underground garage, onto the street, and headed to the university area.

The University of Veliko Turnovo, St. Cyril and St. Methodius, was established in 1971 by the Communist Party as Bulgaria's second university. In typical local fashion, the year was *symbolic*. Just about everything in Eastern Europe was symbolic. In this case, it purposely opened exactly six hundred years after a theologian named Euthymus left the all-male Mount

Athos in northern Greece and established the Turnovo Literary School on the same site.

In any event, it only confirmed that Bulgarians like their history very old and not forgotten.

"Excuse me, can I help you?" asked an older American man who passed us on the bridge to the campus after we parked the car, causing both Rosa and me to look at each other in surprise. "I heard you speaking in the parking lot, and there are very few Americans here. I couldn't help but notice you."

He explained that he had moved to Bulgaria when he retired in order to have a culturally interesting lifestyle. He said his pension went further in Bulgaria than the States. His wife now worked part-time at the university.

I told him we were looking for the student activity building on campus in order to find a student.

"I think you probably want the building over to the right."

Once we entered the activity building, a woman in a nearby office directed us to a room full of bookshelves and small tables, where only one student was working. School wasn't in session, but this man was a class officer and supposedly knew everyone. He gave us a slight wave to come in.

"Hello, my name is Jeni," I said. "I'm looking for a man who might have been here today, wearing a school jersey and carrying a nice camera. He's really tall—"

The young man working at the table heard us and replied over his right shoulder. "I know him. You must want Stephan, but he has already packed and left."

"You mean he has left permanently?" I hadn't considered that possibility.

"Yeah, he finished his paper and is gone—backpacking across Asia."

I was disappointed but not surprised. "Well, we didn't really need him. I know this is a crazy question, but do you know a couple, Oleg and Maria?"

"*Why?*" With that one-word question, he turned in his chair toward Rosa and then to me. He leaned back and crossed his arms on his burly chest.

"We know Oleg's mother," I said, hating myself for implying more than was true, but I could tell that I had to get his trust.

He considered my answer and looked us over for a moment before he spoke. We did look like the kind of people who would know a student's mom, dressed nicely and carrying purses instead of book bags.

"Yeah, I know them—or mostly knew Oleg. He graduated from here last year," he said. "I guess you know that Oleg died in an accident. It is very sad; everyone liked him." Then he eyed me to see if I was surprised at the news.

Only when I said how sorry we were about how upset Oleg's mother was did he lower his crossed arms and relax.

"What about Maria?" I asked.

"Don't know much. Someone told me that Maria left before she finished her final paper." He stopped to think and then added, "She was in economics. I think the paper was about banking or finance or something complicated like that. Oleg must have been helping her—probably even writing the paper. He was like that."

"Do you know how to get in touch with Maria?" I asked.

"No, I don't even know her last name." He began to pull his papers toward him to begin work again. He had heard that she went to Nessebar, but lots of kids went there to work at the beach in the summer. He wrote down my phone number and agreed to call if he saw her. He was already back to writing when we said our goodbyes.

"I guess I will have to rethink what to do about my lost money," I said, once we were back in the car. Zach's return home was looming in my mind, and I wanted the money back before then.

"We aren't giving up," Rosa said. "Let's just think about it some more and try to come up with a different plan. There has to be an explanation."

There was not much else to do in Veliko Tarnovo after that, so Rosa and I headed back to Sofia. It was a beautiful early summer day, eerily juxtaposed against the sad news about Oleg. It was almost as if the rolling hills were indifferent to the drama of human life around them. They teamed with fields of yellow sunflowers with their black eyes turned toward the sun. Vineyards were heavy with full clumps of red and white grapes, and small tables with boxes of fruit and vegetables for sale dotted the roadway. The sky was so cerulean blue that it appeared to be straight out of a Van Gogh painting.

Everything we saw portended hope and a bright future, while my mind was full of theft and death.

When I arrived at the apartment in Sofia, I forced myself to sit at the desk to check my emails. I had about a hundred, but only two were important.

The first was from Zach. He would be home in three days and said he had some free time for a short trip to the beach. I smiled—what a wonderful, refreshing idea.

The second was from Andy, and he wanted me to call him in Greece. Something sounded wrong.

"Hi, Jeni," he answered, with none of his usual self-confidence.

"Hey there, how's it going?" I asked.

"Where do I start?" He then proceeded to talk nonstop. I wasn't sure he took a breath. "My rental car reservation was on file, but there are no cars. They have told me they don't have any left, and no one else does either. So I'm stuck in this town and can't drive to Athens." He paused and took a deep breath before unleashing the rest of his news. "Part of my villa is under renovation, but that's only when the workers show up. It's a mess, and on top of everything, the pool is temporarily out of commission until they make upgrades. The owners are really nice and try to make up for it by giving me lots of olives and homemade ouzo, but then I drink too much while they tell me about Greece's recent financial crises, and I get depressed because I can't escape.

"To top it off, the garbage collectors went on strike this week, so the streets are piling up with garbage. And the nearest beach is beautiful but crowded and all rocks—not like the white-sand beaches at home. I fell twice on the slippery rocks in the water and now my knee hurts."

I stifled a laugh. "You should have asked me to help you plan your trip. Greece is amazing; you just got bad advice."

"I'm going to ignore your I'm-always-prepared lecture for the moment. Look, the point is that I'm ready to leave here. I can get a flight to Sofia tomorrow." He then added tentatively, "Mind if I come early?"

I felt sorry for him. Apparently, his self-esteem had taken quite a blow in order for him to call me for help. Still, I wasn't sure how he intended to act in Sofia. "Are you going to leave a negative review after you stay here?"

"That's mean," he said, and it was. I began to feel bad even before he spoke again. "No, I won't complain—and for the record, I'm not whining. I'm just stating the facts."

"Fair enough. It sounds like it wasn't what you hoped for. Please, yes, do come. I mean it." And I did. "Just email me the time of your arrival."

I realized how much I had missed sparring with Andy. It would be good to have another face around the house, even if it looked like mine. Andy could definitely stir things up a bit. The nagging question was whether it would be for good or bad. After a lifetime of familial togetherness, the one thing I could predict about Andy was his unpredictability, and that might prove to be dangerous in Eastern Europe.

CHAPTER
NINE

ANDY'S CONNECTING FLIGHT THROUGH ATHENS—AT LEAST HE SAW THE great city and some of its ancient ruins through the windows of his airplane—arrived right on time at the Sofia airport.

"Food first or head to the apartment?" I asked as he threw his bag into the back of the Beemer.

"Food," he said. "And, by the way, nice car."

I smiled, glowing with a childish sense of pride that Zach and I had been able to negotiate the levels of bureaucracy in Romania enough to own a car, even one not so new. I also wanted to impress Andy with lunch, so we drove into town to a well-known restaurant near the Hilton Hotel, a sign of staid westernization in a renovated building that stood in the middle of the old downtown. The restaurant was popular for its seafood, although I usually preferred to eat anything other than seafood in Europe. It was one of those few foods in Bulgaria that paled in comparison to the Gulf estuary shrimp and fish I devoured back home.

I asked for a nonsmoking table.

They obliged by putting a NO SMOKING sign on our table. The fact that the table of businessmen seated next to us was anchored by an overweight and by all appearances wealthy man holding court and smoking a cigar didn't seem to bother our waiter. After all, it wasn't a cigarette.

Andy started to argue, but I stopped him by holding up my hand like a schoolteacher.

"Welcome to Eastern Europe," I said.

"This is ridiculous. Let's go to another table," he said.

"No, just ignore it. I would much rather listen to their conversations and inhale second-hand smoke than sit at that table by the bathroom door—which is where we would end up." I pointed to option number two. "The food is great. Just get a drink and enjoy yourself."

It took a second, but Andy did as I instructed and relaxed as he consumed the wine and food, especially the traditional dishes recommended by our overly attentive waiter. Andy's stories about Greece were hilarious, and in no time, it was like we were back in high school, laughing and enjoying one another's company.

Andy told me how surprised he was that I had only been in Sofia for six weeks and yet was already comfortable.

At times during the lunch, however, it was hard to ignore the loud men at the table next to us, boasting about some business deal they had made. When I heard the name of Vorbank mentioned, it momentarily brought me down.

The loudest man, who was also the largest man in the room by a hundred pounds, boasted that he had made a big fee on something that sounded shady to me.

When one of the men mentioned taxes, he bellowed in English—as one of the men at the table appeared to be from Australia—"Taxes? You must be silly. I put it in the Vorbank, and it will be in Cyprus in no time at all. Taxes? Who pays taxes?"

I wanted to yell that I paid taxes, but I just glared at the men. Their gloating made me so angry that my hand shook, and I almost spilled my water. It hurt more that it was an immediate reminder of my lost money. I swore to myself that as soon as I could, I was going to resume my investigation and figure out what Oleg did with my money. He had been up to something.

But for the time being, I had Andy to deal with.

"Wasn't Uncle Bob in Bulgaria for a while? Do you remember the whole story?" I asked.

"Yes," Andy answered. "Mom filled in the blanks before I left for Europe." Then he sat back to recount the tale.

Uncle Bob was a pilot in World War II. After Italy fell, the Allies were finally able to refuel our bombers in Italy so they could reach the valuable Romanian oil fields that were supplying Hitler's armies. The problem was that in order to get to Romania, pilots like Uncle Bob had to fly over Bulgaria, which was hostile territory. At some point near the end of the war, Uncle Bob's plane was shot down over Sofia, and he was sent to a POW camp in a city named Shumen. The war ended a few months later, in large part because of the bombing of the oil fields.

While they were waiting to be returned to the States, Uncle Bob snuck out of camp with another pilot to celebrate. They went to the closest bar over the train tracks and ordered a beer to toast the Allied victory.

It was a bad move.

The locals, who were understandably upset about losing the war, didn't take kindly to them and began to form a drunken plan to fight.

"According to Uncle Bob, a pretty barmaid warned him of the impending attack and urged him to run back to the POW camp, all the while speaking in French so the Bulgarians couldn't understand her." Andy rolled his eyes. "I'm not sure I believe that coincidence—that Uncle Bob and the barmaid both knew French—but that's the story. Anyway, Uncle Bob and his friend hightailed it out of the bar, with the local men chasing them like bloodhounds the whole way back."

"That's some kind of story," I said.

"Yeah. Uncle Bob said he never got that beer, and he never got over the woman," Andy said, waving to the waiter for our check. Then he crossed his hands over his heart and looked upward, as if searching for an angel. "These are Mom's words: no one else was ever as brave as she was so he never married."

With that he leaned toward me, raised his eyebrows, and cocked his head. "It's crazy, I know, but while I am here, Mom wants us to see if we can find the place and take pictures and see if we can find any of the French-speaking woman's family. Mom wants to write them. Frankly, I want to find out if the story is true. I tried to find some information before I left, but it was a nightmare. Any article about the place was in Bulgarian." With that, he finished the last of his glass of wine.

"That's a great story, if it actually happened," I said. "I only knew he was a pilot and a POW. Maybe Rosa can help us find out where the POW camp was located."

I saw Andy look around, clearly absorbing the atmosphere. He was just beginning to understand the world into which his uncle Bob had parachuted. It could be far more sophisticated yet decades behind the States at the same time. Bulgaria was a contradiction on almost every level.

My apartment would most likely confuse him even more. Stylish, roomy, and well appointed, it was the antithesis of the Communist-era concrete block apartments a few doors down. While our front entrance was tall glass with wood double-doors, the neighbor's entrance was a cold steel door, once painted bright blue, that bore the scratches of every occupant for the past few decades. Concrete stairwells with exposed piping connected the neighbors' apartments to each other, while our walls were Sheetrocked and steps were tiled. Our park was pretty and well kept, while the other was full of 1950s-style children's outdoor playground equipment in unkempt grass. Truthfully, I liked their park better, but I could see that not everyone would agree. Bulgaria was changing, but sometimes it was important to remember the past.

"I'm really tired, Jeni. Do you mind if I hit the sack early?" Andy said after I'd given him a tour of the apartment.

"That's a first with you! Getting old?"

"Jet lag. Thanks for the great day. I'll see you in the morning." With that, he almost fell into his room, ready to get a good night's sleep.

My phone rang a few minutes later, and I walked out on the terrace to watch the city lights and take the call. It was Rosa.

"Did your company make it?"

"Yeah, he's fast asleep."

"What are you doing tomorrow?" she asked.

"I have no plans—Zach doesn't get back for another day, so I am trying to decide where to take Andy."

"He'll have plenty of time to see the usual sights," she said, "but I have a fun idea I thought about today that might help you see your money. Are you OK with taking about a thirty-minute ride out of town?"

"Sure. Where to?"

"It's a surprise, but I promise it's one of those famous places that you would never think about visiting."

"What do you mean by *see* my money?" I asked.

"You'll find out tomorrow!"

There was nothing I could say other than, "Sure, it sounds like fun," even though I had no idea what awaited us a mere thirty minutes from my apartment.

It is embarrassing to admit, but I sometimes hated surprises and often lacked cheerful flexibility when I contemplated the unknown. Traveling had loosened me a bit, but it was only because I lived by my Girl Scout motto of "Be prepared"—or perhaps that was the Boy Scout motto. I don't really recall, but I adopted it, regardless of the origin. I was the queen of planning for contingencies that would never happen. All anyone needed to do for proof of that was to look at what was in my car trunk—water, first-aid kits, fire extinguishers, emergency food, blankets, extra oil, rain ponchos, and more than a dozen small tools, including a can opener and a corkscrew.

I wondered what could be so great that might help me find my lost money. After an hour with no answers, I went to bed.

"Where *exactly* are we going?" Andy asked as he downed coffee and devoured a chocolate croissant that I had picked up from the corner market.

"I'm not sure, but I feel certain that if Rosa is taking us, then it must be something that we have to do before we leave Bulgaria. The only thing I don't understand is how it will help me find my money."

"Your money? What do you mean, your money?" Andy asked, looking at me with a puzzled expression.

"Oh, I don't want to tell you the whole story right now; it's too embarrassing." I started clearing the table. "I'll tell you later, when we have time. Now, we have to leave and meet Rosa. I have some coffee cups for the car and another croissant, in case we get hungry."

"So you're still like that? Preparing for a sudden croissant disappearance?" Andy was back to teasing, having gotten a good night's rest and the requisite amount of caffeine.

"I'm going to run to the ATM next door for some money, and then I'll meet you after you get out of the parking garage," he said before I could respond.

I didn't tell him not to use the Vorbank ATM. The ATM was not the problem—or at least, it wasn't my problem.

It was a good fifteen minutes before he returned, making me worry that the machine had swallowed his bank card.

"Sorry," he said as he jumped into the car. "I met a friend of yours at the bank entrance. She asked if I was your cousin."

"Who would know you were here, other than Rosa?" I asked Andy, not really expecting him to know the answer. I didn't have any other friends.

"Her name was Natasha. She looked like a Natasha—kind of mysterious and cool; short black hair," he said in a way that concerned me. His next words didn't help. "We really hit it off."

"Oh," I said, prepared to dismiss what was probably a momentary flirtatious affair. "Was she at the ATM?"

"No, she was coming out of the bank, and she seemed to know who I was and that I had arrived to visit you," he said. "Then we started talking, and you know how it goes."

I was quiet for a second or two. I was confused. Did I tell Natasha from AIC about Andy? I didn't think so, but the truth was that sometimes I talked too much. I might have told someone else and she overheard me.

"Yes, if it's the Natasha I know, she has short dark hair and is on a charity board with me."

"The good news is that she offered to take me out for drinks tomorrow night, and I agreed," he said, his face already lighting up with anticipation. "This is already better than my time in Greece."

That threw me. For some reason, I thought Natasha was married, but then, I realized I must have assumed it. I needed to stop worrying about Andy and his girlfriends. Given that Natasha was single and ready to entertain him, I took a deep breath and relaxed. It might be a good thing if they spent time together. Andy wanted exotic, and he was going to get it.

Let everyone witness how many
different cards fortune has up her
sleeve when she wants to ruin a man.

✗

—Benvenuto Cellini,
The Autobiography, 1956

CHAPTER
TEN

ROSA ARRIVED AFTER LUNCH TO PICK UP ANDY AND ME. AFTER INTRODUCTIONS and after we loaded into my car, Rosa asked both of us, "Do you know anything about Baba Vanga?"

"Vanga?" I repeated. "I think I've heard the name, but so much of the history of Bulgaria is confusing to me."

"Great—you don't know. This will be a wonderful surprise," she said. "We're going to her home. It's in the Rupite area of the Kozhuh Mountains."

She then told us the story of Vangelia Pandeva Dimitrova, also known as Baba Vanga, Grandmother Vanga, and the Bulgarian Nostradamus.

Baba Vanga was born in Macedonia, then part of the Ottoman Empire, in 1911. When she was about the age of ten, she lost her sight in a tornado when sand and debris blinded her eyes. In 1925, she was sent to a school for the blind for three years to learn to read braille, sew, and do housekeeping. After her mother died, she returned to her family to help with the younger siblings.

Over the years, she became famous as a clairvoyant in the Eastern European region and in Russia.

"I don't know if you would call them predictions, but during World War II, people would come to her to ask if their relatives were alive or dead." Rosa then explained that Baba Vanga would also soothsay and heal. They really believed in her during a time of misery. Baba's husband was one of those men who went to visit Baba Vanga to find the killers of his brother. She told him what he wanted to know but made him promise not to seek revenge.

Eventually, world leaders from the region visited her for advice on politics and predictions, including Leonid Brezhnev, the leader of Russia.

Baba Vanga could read braille but couldn't write; that, however, didn't stop her notoriety. Over the years, lots of men wrote books that purported to describe her visions. Her fame increased with those who liked to trade in conspiracies and wild tales.

"The problem is that no one knows whether she did or did not say many of those things," Rosa said. "Still, I think she was a good person."

I didn't know what to say to that. Was Rosa telling me she believed in fortune-tellers?

Andy leaned forward to better hear Rosa, seeming confused as well. "Why would we go there? Are there any predictions that might mean something to me?"

"The most famous is that she predicted that the forty-fourth president of the United States would be an African American, long before President Obama even dreamed about running for office. There are some disputes about what exactly she said, but it is always mentioned by her believers. And that's not all—Baba Vanga also said a messianic—a combination of Jewish and Christian—would follow Obama, and he would be the United States' last president."

When she saw Andy's eyes roll, Rosa laughed. She told us that some people believed President Trump was that messianic, but she preferred to believe it only meant that he would be the last *male* president, given the spelling was in the masculine gender.

"Also," she added, "in 1989, Baba Vanga predicted the US would be hit by 'steel birds,' which some say was a prediction of 9/11." Those were the most famous ones about the US. There are others, predicting the sinking of a Soviet nuclear submarine and Chernobyl, plus hundreds about the end of the world and Russian supremacy.

"Wow," Andy said, staring at Rosa and shaking his head slightly. "I never heard about her."

"Don't get too worried," Rosa said with a laugh. "Baba Vanga never wrote anything down, so no one knows if all the prophecies are actually hers or made up by other people. Plus, some are clearly wrong. For example, she said World War III would occur in 2010 and the earth's orbit would change in 2013. In addition, like many fortune-tellers, most of her predictions are so cryptic that they might mean anything, or they are fairly predictable, such as the fall of Damascus.

"You also have to realize that she loved Russians, Orthodox Christianity, and, sadly, white supremacy." Rosa then turned to me and smiled. "She supposedly predicted that Russia, the mother country, would ultimately 'dominate the world'—at least until the day the world ends, which will be in 3797."

Andy began to roll his head around like he was losing his mind.

"I know—it all sounds nutty, but people revere her," Rosa said. She told Andy that Baba Vanga died in 2008, but she was so beloved that her home was made into a museum, and in 2013, the state-controlled Channel One Russia made a twenty-four–part series about her. Now, she had a growing cult following; all around the world, people deciphered her sayings and her life.

As we pulled into the road leading to our destination, Rosa paused for a second and then said to me, "I know that many things she said will be hard for you and Andy to believe—like the mystical seeing and talking to dead people—but you have to remember that she was blind. She's an enigma for sure—that's the English word, isn't it?"

I reminded myself that Baba Vanga lived an otherworldly life in this small village, where no one disputed her veracity.

"That is why it is special to me, as a Bulgarian, that she has such a honored reputation in Europe." Then Rosa smiled sweetly. "How about if you hold your judgment until we get there?"

I could tell she had rightfully interpreted the looks on our faces as cynical and disbelieving. Andy would never let me forget this.

In the meantime, I was about to be proven right about surprises. They never worked out well.

�֍

The road leading to the museum was inauspicious. We parked in an unpaved lot next to a few other cars. A tour bus was already headed out with a cargo of elderly but enthusiastic passengers, who had finished their pilgrimage and were returning to Sofia.

A path led us past a body of water fed by steaming hot springs, so hot it burned my fingers when I tested it. Beyond the pond were picnic tables and the small, white, peasant-style home of Baba Vanga. It was not all that different from my own grand-aunt's home in northern Florida, except that Vanga's abode was quainter and surrounded by flowers and gardens. Some of the grass was mowed, but in other places, it was a lush, unkempt, deep green.

Baba Vanga had lived a simple existence. There was no gold- or silver-leaf wallpaper. In fact, there wasn't enough to see in her house to justify a tour. The abode was really no different from the surrounding homes in the area.

She has been dead for only a little over twenty years. How historical could the house be? I thought.

After we finished our walk around the residence, we made our way across a small concrete bridge, spanning a rushing creek that moved water down the mountainside. Vanga's house was optimally located for natural resources—hot and cold water.

It was immediately evident that although Vanga's homestead looked much like it had for the past sixty years, the new construction on the other side of the creek was the opposite.

As she had requested before her death, a church was built on that site, so modern that its architecture reflected a mix of Bulgarian, Lutheran, and a bit of Catholic. It could be in the suburbs at home, complete with a modern education facility.

I knew that Rosa could tell we had mixed feelings about the trip, and I couldn't see how it could help me in the least.

"OK, now it's time to find your lost money," she said with a wink. "This should be fun. I have the name of a fortune-teller near here, and I made an appointment with her for us." She glowed with excitement.

"Oh, I don't think so. I hate fortune-tellers," I said, stopping dead in my tracks.

"Jeni, that's ridiculous. It'll be fun," Andy said.

"Remember the time at summer camp when the girl who told fortunes said my dog was going to die, and I spent the whole time crying?" I said, almost tearing up at the memory. "It ruined that summer. And guess what? The dog lived another ten years."

"The supposed psychic was fourteen years old. No one believed her, other than you," he said.

"I didn't really believe her. It's the power of persuasion that works on your mind." I still refused to move, like a stubborn horse. "I'll go, only if the psychic tells me I'm winning the lottery."

"That's ridiculous as well," Andy said as he kept walking. "Rosa, Jeni and I are game. Just ignore her; she'll have fun."

I knew better.

CHAPTER
ELEVEN

IN THE PSYCHIC'S YARD WAS A SMALL SIGN PAINTED WITH OLD IMAGES OF tarot cards—the only evidence of her entrepreneurial enterprise. Like the worn and tired sign, the tiny house was unkempt and dreary, not at all like Baba Vanga's home. There was a ragtag garden and a patch of weeds in the yard. A small dilapidated barn in the back held a goat, an old horse, a cart, and a milking cow, all surrounded by a makeshift fence that had seen better days. On the front porch was a montage of mixed-breed cats, lazing about.

"Are you sure this woman is a 'legitimate' fortune-teller or seer?" I asked. "I mean, who would voluntarily go to see anyone in this house?"

"Mostly locals and the Russians visit her," Rosa said. "No worries. It'll be fine."

She may have said the words, but I could sense concern beginning to creep into her voice.

The woman who answered the door was not so different from the pictures of Baba Vanga or many Bulgarian women in their seventies. Her gray hair was roughly cut and stuck out in places around an unusually taut, angular face for an older Bulgarian woman. I couldn't help but think she must have been pretty as a young woman, but a jagged scar across her cheek and several missing teeth told me those days were long past. Life in the country had taken its toll.

She wore a loose, well-worn, embroidered white shirt of muslin, cinched at the waist with a wide black-leather belt. Her long black skirt was covered with a floral half apron that fell to her ankles, almost hiding the short thick boots she wore on her feet. Those clothes covered a body with a large bust and ample hips on a short frame, making the woman inside them look more like a kindly, overweight grandmother than a psychic-for-pay.

She smiled when she saw us—a broad, almost toothless smile—squinting her eyes at the prospect of a financial transaction. She quickly led Rosa, with Andy and me following, into her main room. A wooden table with tarot cards was centered in the middle, with rickety kitchen chairs around it. The windows were covered with faded flowered fabric in a mixture of browns, beige, and dark oranges, not unlike her apron. The room was dank and claustrophobic, with only a small lamp with a low-watt bulb and no fan. Once my eyes acclimated to the lack of light, I began to observe the home's other contents for insight into our host.

There was a religious icon of Jesus and Mary on the wall by the entrance and some Bulgarian rugs on the floors. Old, heavy furniture was scattered around the room's edges, but there were no pictures or personal effects. A moldy smell was only slightly masked by the aroma of some odd tea or candle. I began to feel uncomfortable and wanted to leave, but I knew I was alone in my desire. Andy and Rosa were already pulling up chairs and eagerly awaiting the psychic's insight.

"You go first," I whispered to Andy.

As I spoke, I noticed the old woman briefly glance sideways at me, her smile suddenly disappearing. The intense look she gave me sent a slight chill up my spine—the only cool moment I would feel that day. But she quickly recovered, turned to Rosa, and resumed the same welcoming smile she'd flashed when we arrived. She held out her hand for the first of the two money transactions.

"OK. Rosa, tell her I would like to know my fortune," Andy said.

"Well, you have to narrow it down to a question."

"How about whether I'll meet the right girl in Europe," he said, laughing at me as I rolled my eyes.

Rosa told the woman Andy's question, at which point she stared into Andy's eyes for a few minutes without blinking. It was creepy. She then began shuffling and moving cards around with the dexterity of a casino dealer. When she finished, she laid them out on the table and studied the pattern, smiling to herself slightly. Rosa translated her words when she finally spoke:

"You will find the right girl, but you will have to overcome distractions before you will find her waiting on you. In the meantime, you must be vigilant, or you will be hurt. It is important." She stopped and shook her finger at him. "You must always think and listen."

"Well, I can live with that. I have no intention of letting another woman hurt me," Andy said, smiling broadly and leaning back in his chair like a rock star. "*Natasha,* here I come. Now, I think I'll go out for some fresh air and dream about the future while you finish." With that, he left the room.

I decided, then and there, that what she'd told Andy was ridiculous. This psychic was clearly a fraud. I was no longer afraid of what she would say; I just wanted my reading over and done with so we could leave the house.

The good news was that I didn't need to say anything. We had discussed it, and Rosa knew what to ask after she dropped the money into the woman's open hand.

"Where is Jeni's money that is missing from her account at Vorbank, and can you tell us what really happened to the banker named Oleg?"

"Wait," I interjected. "I want to ask about Zlata Petrovia as well." Immediately, I felt my cheeks go red in embarrassment—now it looked like I was actually interested in what the woman had to say.

The good news was that no one noticed because just as Rosa replied, "Oh, yes, I forgot," the old woman's hands started to shake, and she knocked over a candle on the table, causing Rosa and me to jump back. As the woman righted the candle before it set fire to anything, she looked at me as if to divine what I meant. Zlata Petrovia's name hung in the air until the psychic looked down at the cards and began her routine.

Now I was really intrigued and watched the old woman intently. I leaned in closer to see her lips moving and hear her murmuring. I could have sworn I heard her mumble *Vorbank* as she looked at the cards, and then she suddenly stopped. Before I could say anything to Rosa, the psychic quickly recovered and turned over another card, clearly mumbling Oleg's name. She then laid out more tarot cards with a heavy hand. She had a good act.

When she was finished with the cards—I knew nothing about tarot cards—she stopped and stared, with furrowed brows and grimaced lips, at the cluttered tabletop.

Something was wrong. There was no smile. She just stared at the cards without speaking and then lit two short, fat, homemade candles that were on the table in front of my face. She shoved them closer to me, presumably to see me more clearly. The smell was noxious—who knew what was in them? At the same time, one of her many cats—this one a gray-and-white mix—began to rub up against my leg. I was suddenly aware of cats everywhere, including a kitten crying in the distance, mewing like the one under the car.

By then it was so hot that the airless room tightened in on me like a noose. I felt faint, even as I tried to concentrate on the psychic. I wanted to leave, but I also wanted to hear her out.

It was then that the old woman looked at Rosa and did the oddest thing. She picked up all the cards, stacked them in front of her, and coldly pointed to the door for us to leave. Rosa's face showed a mix of shock and anger, while mine was confusion.

"*Ostavyam!*" the old woman snarled.

Rosa's once-happy face crumpled with dismay, and she turned to me in confusion. "I don't know what is going on. She's telling us to leave. This is, this is …"

Before Rosa could gather more words, the psychic glared at me with a stony face that was now gaunt and white. From my perspective, she appeared like a ghostly apparition. Mesmerized and unable to move, I sat unmoving as she slid a third candle toward me and lit it.

"*NU Oleg! NU Zlata! NU Vorbank,*" the psychic growled as she slowly and dramatically turned her long, thin, right index finger back and forth in my face, leaning so closely to me that I could smell her stale breath over the candles.

Her slow-motion movements disoriented me. The odd smell from the air around me creeped into my lungs like a sickening, dense fog, and I began to feel dizzy and hot—and then even hotter. Something was wrong, and all I could think was that I had to get out of there—and fast.

I shot up from the chair to leave—or at least tried to do so—but my body failed me, as if my arms and legs were not attached to my torso. When my feet wouldn't move at all, I began to think I was paralyzed. Before I could fully stand erect, my legs crumpled under me. I wanted to scream, but my voice was suddenly locked within me.

My eyes stared into the psychic's face as I made my slow and frightening collapse to her dirty floor.

She didn't seem surprised by my sudden condition.

When I fully regained my wits, I realized that I was sitting on a small three-legged stool on the porch, as Rosa forced me to drink from a water bottle that Andy retrieved from the car. Rosa had a wet washcloth on my head to stop a small bleed from my temple, where I'd apparently hit something when I fell. I assumed by Andy's exaggerated massaging of his back that he had helped me to the stool.

No one spoke while I drank the water and gulped fresh air, all of us now anxious to leave the hellish place. I was still a bit wobbly but nodded that I was able to walk to the car after a minute or two.

"Jeni, I'm so sorry," Rosa said. "I wanted this to be fun."

"It's not your fault. I don't understand why I got so ill. I still feel bad," I said. "What was that awful smell?"

"After Andy left, she moved some of the candles nearer to you. I bet they had something weird in them that made you sick. Plus, it was *so* hot in there. I'm sure you are dehydrated and hungry. We are way past lunch"—she paused a moment and looked toward the house as she wiped my face with the cloth—"but … there was definitely something about you she didn't like."

"What didn't she like?" I said. I held my head, as if it would help me regain my composure.

Rosa handed me more water. "I don't know. Please don't worry about it," she said, "We won't ever do anything like that again."

"But what happened when I fainted? Did she say anything?" I asked.

"Only one thing—and I don't want to tell you because she obviously is a crook, a fraud, or mentally ill."

"Please, Rosa. Tell me what she said … please?"

Rosa hesitated and looked at me intently. Reluctantly, she answered. "She said for me to tell my American friend to stop asking questions."

"She said *American*? Did you tell her I was American? I didn't even speak, other than whisper to Andy."

"Jeni, you look American. She also heard Andy talk. I'm sure that is all there is to it."

"You don't believe that, do you?" I asked Rosa. "You don't believe it was just some random thing, do you?"

"I don't know," she said. "Don't read too much into it. Please? Otherwise, I will feel even more guilty for taking you here." She turned to Andy. "Let's get out of here. Andy, will you drive so I can watch Jeni? Jeni, you can rest in the back seat."

"OK," I murmured, suddenly tired of the conversation. I shook my head to rid it of the remaining cobwebs and smiled ruefully. Maybe I did ask too many questions, and she wasn't able to concoct that type of complicated fortune. But even in my condition, I knew that everyone asked her all kinds of questions. That was her job! So what upset her? Oleg? The bank? Zlata? Or all of them? What did she know?

I still felt nauseated as Andy backed the car out of the parking lot, so I lowered the window and poked my head out of it for some fresh air. It was then that I saw an expensive black Mercedes with a Russian car tag pull onto the opposite side of the yard. A stylish man in a gray suit and white shirt with French cuffs quickly exited the back seat, tugged at his suit jacket to pull it over his waist to button it, and then walked to the old woman, as if late to a board meeting. She opened her arms to welcome him to her home, but all the while, she was peering past him and watching me with a fierce intensity I could actually feel.

Ordinarily, that would have ended the psychic episode, but fresh air and clarity of mind have a way of reviving memories.

"I've seen that man before at the bank," I blurted, startling the quiet in the car.

"What man? What are you talking about?" Rosa asked. "The man who pulled up to her house as we were leaving?"

"I can't remember when, but I can almost swear I saw him at the bank," I said. Then I closed my eyes and folded as best I could into the backseat, exhausted. "It has to be the bank."

Neither of my car mates said anything more. What could they say? I had fainted and busted my head. It wasn't an ideal time for more discussion.

CHAPTER
TWELVE

Once back at the apartment, I fell fast asleep. Andy was due to meet Natasha for dinner that night, so I was able to rest. It was a long night of dreamless and deep sleep, the kind that almost left me as groggy the next morning as if I had received no sleep at all. I saw my reflection in the mirror, and it looked like I had been on an all-night bender.

Zach called just as I was fixing my first cup of coffee. I told him about the psychic and how ill I had become at her house.

"Jeni, do you think you need to get your head checked?" Zach asked, which made me laugh.

"If you mean do I have a concussion—no, it wasn't that bad a hit. If you mean a psychiatrist, you have to make Rosa and Andy go as well."

"No, I meant a medical doctor. It sounds awful. I imagine it was the cumulative effect of the heat and lack of ventilation, plus the bad odors. No telling what she had in the house."

"She was so creepy, Zach. And why did she pick up the cards and ask me to leave?"

He agreed with Rosa that there was a good chance that she picked up the cards because she knew she had that rich Russian client arriving.

"I don't know," I said. "It seemed more personal."

"Jeni, you don't believe in those things anyway, do you?" Zach gently chided me.

"Of course not, but the routine they do … In the moment, it was so convincing that it threw me off-kilter," I said. "She seemed to recognize the names. And another thing—I am sure I saw the man in the Russian car one day at the bank. I can't remember what it is about him—it's still fuzzy—but I know I'm right."

Zach asked a few questions to jog my memory, but it was no use.

"Well," I said, "just so you know, Andy believed her. He was *thrilled* because the psychic told him that he was going to meet the girl of his dreams here in Europe. He already started on his search last night with Natasha, the Russian woman from my AIC."

"Knowing Andy. it went well." Zach laughed. "I'm thinking we need to take a trip to Sunny Beach with him. He'll find lots of opportunities to meet a girl there."

We agreed that when he returned to the embassy the next day, I would pick him up for a late breakfast, and we could make plans.

"Can't wait," I said. "Love you."

Andy was entering the kitchen just as I hung up the phone. He was unusually cheerful for such an early morning.

"I take it you had fun last night," I said.

"It was incredible," he said as he plopped into a chair. "I never knew that I could find someone who had so much in common with me. She even likes the same food as I do." His face almost took on a cartoonish, dream-like quality as he poured a cup of coffee.

"It was your first date. I'd wait before I fell in love." I wanted to be the good cousin, but there was something about Natasha that bothered me. Too much … too fast. And her connections to the Vorbank and bizarre behavior about the bank officer were hard to dismiss. And I was still unsure how she knew Andy was my cousin on the first day he was here.

"No, Jeni. You don't understand. I mean she is *really* my soul mate."

"OK, I'll bite. How is she your soul mate?" Despite my reservations, I was willing to give her a shot.

At that point, Andy began the litany. First, she liked everything he liked and not in the way of "me to"; she would bring it up in conversation herself. For example, every song on her playlist was a favorite of his. He began to hum a verse from one of them. They liked the same movies—everything. She was curious and beautiful and definitely not boring. I almost gagged when he said he thought the old lady psychic was right—he might leave Bulgaria with a wife.

I laughed. "A Russian bride? Don't get your hopes up!"

"You don't know that it won't happen. Just in case, is it OK if I stay a while longer?" Andy asked.

"Sure, I guess. Why not?" I wasn't prepared for that request, especially without Zach's input. But no matter how tepid my response was, Andy took it as an enthusiastic yes.

"You were going to tell me how you lost your money. Now is as good a time as any," he said, sipping his coffee. He lounged back in the kitchen chair so that the chair's front legs were off the floor, and Andy's back leaned against the wall. It was one of those smug, confident moves a man might do while basking in the glow of a potential Russian conquest.

I groaned and began the story of my lost money at Vorbank as simply as possible. Before I finished, he started to chuckle and unexpectedly reached over to hug me.

"Thanks, you've made me feel better. Your story may be worse than mine, but I'm not sure," he said. "I just wasted most of my money."

It turned out that Andy had spent thousands on the villa in Greece, only to want to escape it from sheer boredom.

"It was so stupid. Why did I ever think that I needed a four-bedroom estate way out in the country, vineyard or no vineyard?"

Not only that, but he had prepaid to rent a high-end convertible car, in high season, that he never got and for which he might or might not get a refund since he left before the end of the intended rental contract. Yesterday, they'd sent him a text that said they now had a convertible Jaguar ready for him.

"Of course, I'm here so I can't get it, and now they're threatening to keep my money. Then, I got in such a hurry to leave Greece, I unwittingly agreed to pay huge penalties to change my flight departure to Sofia." He sheepishly smiled at me. "I bet I wasted more money than you lost. Can you imagine what Uncle Bob would say if he knew what we did with the money he left us?"

"Put a curse on us?" I said. "Now I really feel compelled to search out his old girlfriend, like your mom suggested."

Andy promised that he would work remotely from the apartment, at most for a few weeks, just so he could replenish his bank account before he took the trip home.

I nodded my approval. It sounded like a plan that Uncle Bob would have been proud of. I hoped we wouldn't waste all his bequest.

"Mom won't realize what happened as long as you don't tell her I am freeloading off you and Zach."

"I won't tell your mom as long as you don't tell Zach about the missing money. He'd really be upset with me," I said.

"I'm not so sure that keeping secrets is good for a marriage." Then he winked at me. "I'm happy that Natasha isn't like that at all. She told me she doesn't like secrets, and I have to agree."

Andy was right. I needed to be more open with Zach. The problem was that we had very little time together, now that he was so busy with his diplomatic work. I rationalized that my secretive behavior was good for him; I didn't want to waste his free time by endlessly confessing my mistakes.

Just then, Andy checked his watch and jumped to his feet.

He told me that his supervisor was calling in an hour to discuss the company's newest project and then he was going to meet Natasha for drinks. "I'll see you later."

With that, Andy escaped, his computer case over his shoulder. He was in such a hurry that he held a loaf of my fresh French bread in his mouth while he used both hands to operate the double-door locks. Looking at him, I was reminded of our former golden retriever.

I spent the remainder of the day doing chores and occasionally checking social media to see what my friends at home were accomplishing. It was summer so every other picture was about travel to some beautiful or exotic destination. Even Andy had posted a picture on Instagram from our visit to Baba Vanga's home.

It made me jealous, although I realized that was insane. I never posted anything, as my whole life was travel, and it was too hard to choose only one aspect of it to share with others back home. I told myself it was OK—my life was a wall tapestry or a full-length movie, not a still shot.

That night, I had dinner with Rosa—our last before the men came back—and we discussed my next move in regard to the missing money.

"Maybe I should give up and not ask any more questions," I said. "It isn't like I am getting anywhere."

"That's not true. You're only saying that because of the psychic, and she's a fraud," Rosa chided me. "And even though we have known each other less than two months, I know you enough to know you won't let it go."

I had to agree. It would bug me forever if I didn't resolve what happened.

"Let's see what we can learn about the bank and the missing AIC treasurer, Zlata," Rosa said. "This is far more interesting than painting alone at home."

We agreed to meet for lunch in a few days, after we came up with a plan. Rosa loved plans more than me.

It made sense to do more research, and after talking about the bazaar a bit, I went home for the evening and logged onto my computer to follow up on Zlata. But first, I wanted to know more about the woman with Andy that night, Natasha.

I wasn't surprised that Natasha had a Facebook page, but it didn't divulge much about her. It was only a few years old. There were a lot of pictures of scenery around Bulgaria and a few of Russia. She liked some travel websites and one or two clothing products. What was strange was that she had only a few "friends." I saw Lucia was one of the dozen or so women and men, but her posts were nothing at all like I expected for someone who looked and acted like she did.

Her profile stated that she'd gone to college, was single, and liked to ride horses and that her profession was as a business consultant in retail sales. That made sense. I was sure she could sell swampland in Florida. All in all, it wasn't too terribly different from my Facebook page. Due to Zach's admonitions to be selective in my choice of posts while overseas, I rarely shared anything personal and used Facebook primarily to send pictures home to friends. I considered Natasha's reluctance to be too open on the net as showing good judgment and nothing more.

I then googled her. Even less was on the internet. There were some press pictures of her at an AIC event with sponsors and a few with local celebrities or politicians but nothing unusual. It was unusual that she had no pictures with friends or family, but, again, I thought it was a prudent move.

Her AIC pictures prompted me to google AIC itself. I had never really done it before. It was a relief to find that AIC was everything that it was supposed to be. There were news articles about large corporate donations. An EU audit a few years ago confirmed its banking practices, and there were pictures of women and children they had helped. Dozens of other impressive articles filled the web. It made me oddly proud.

The only disturbing thing was that the last article was almost a year old. Either the AIC social media expert was falling down on the job, or the board had stopped disbursing money sometime over the last year. For the first time, I began to wonder why it saved up 100,000 euros in the Vorbank account when the refugee needs were so great. I turned off the computer to digest that thought.

I decided to start afresh with Zlata's pages the next morning. They would still be there.

Unlike the night before, I enjoyed a restful sleep and was eager to pick up Zach at the embassy as soon as he called.

Unfortunately, the call didn't go as I'd planned.

"There's a slight change of plans," he said, his voice strangely devoid of emotion. "Don't pick me up at the gate. You'll need to park in the embassy garage and then meet me in the public conference room outside the marine guard station."

"Why?" I asked. My desire to see him evaporated into thin air upon hearing his solemn instructions.

"It's a surprise," he said dryly. "At least it was to me. You'll find out soon enough. I've got to go. See you when you get here."

The voice on the phone had none of the warmth I had come to love.

I hung up the phone and slowly prepared for my trek to the embassy. There was no need to rush to bad news.

CHAPTER
THIRTEEN

The government-style conference room, often used for handing out awards and proclamations, was anchored on one end by a large, glossy wooden table, around which Zach and two other men sat in black rolling chairs with polished chrome legs and arm supports. I could see the subtle back-and-forth movement in Zach's chair, a sign that he was agitated. A projection screen was at the far end of the table, ready to use.

I knew one of the men—he was the regional security officer for the embassy. He looked to be in charge. I never remembered his name and always called him the RSO. The other man was unfamiliar to me.

"Hello, Jeni," the RSO greeted me coldly. "Thank you for joining us. This is Frank. Have a seat."

Frank looked slightly older than middle-aged—"mature," as they like to say—and probably was retired from some previous law enforcement position on behalf of the government. After retirement, highly skilled men and women sometimes ended up working for the United States in complicated temporary positions in Europe. Frank seemed to meet the criteria—he probably had top security clearance, discipline, and great training. His jacket was rumpled and his tie didn't match, but he exuded a kind, almost distracted demeanor, as if the meeting was more of a bother than a necessity.

I sat down and looked at Zach for some answers. He spoke to me for the first time.

"They have some video you need to watch," Zach said. "They asked me some questions, but frankly, I have no idea what's going on. That's why you're here." He looked at me as if I was a stranger. Then he added, "The truth is that I may be more interested in what you have to say than they are."

I didn't know how to respond. Instead, I sat like a small child beside her parent, waiting for the teacher's conference to begin and worrying about what she had done to get everyone so upset. No one offered me coffee or a cigarette.

The RSO turned on the computer and lit the screen up with a huge picture of me. Actually, it was a series of pictures. They were CCTV pictures from embassy security, showing me furtively carrying the money I'd obtained from the cashier to my car. Other than the fact that I swore never to wear my white pants again because they made me look enormous, the tape didn't look all that bad to me.

I relaxed for a moment. I could explain the money.

The next pictures were from a surveillance camera by my apartment entrance. In these pictures, I was leaving the apartment with the bag containing all the cash. I wore an oversized rain jacket and clog-style shoes. It was a short walk to the bank but painful to watch. Surely that bag lady couldn't be me. When I stumbled forward a few steps on a cobblestone in the road, I heard the RSO stifle a laugh.

That same camera was able to record me entering the Vorbank branch on my street corner and exiting without a bag, looking no better, except that I was no longer hunched over. That whole scene at Vorbank was going to be harder to explain, especially since I knew I had no bank account to prove what I did with the money.

The final clips were of Natasha entering my apartment on the day of the AIC board meeting. While she looked like a model on camera and I did not, her appearance at our apartment still was easy to explain.

"What were you doing, Jeni?" Zach asked.

Slowly, I began the story about the check, deliberately neglecting to mention the exact amount out of embarrassment. When I told them that

I kept the account a surprise because I intended to use the money for a honeymoon, at least Zach smiled. But he just shook his head when I confessed there was something wrong with the account and now the money might be gone.

"How did you pick the bank?" Frank asked

"The bank branch was close to our apartment. I didn't know it was Russian-owned until Zach told me, and by then, it was already too late."

"Tell me about the woman entering your apartment," Frank said, altering his chair position to fully observe me and my answer. Up until that time, he had not appeared terribly interested in my banking preferences or anything about me in general. Suddenly, his demeanor changed to interrogator-in-action, throwing me completely off guard. Now it looked like he was in law enforcement. *Am I in trouble?*

"Natasha? She's on a charity board with me, helping refugees."

"Did she go into your apartment?" he asked.

"Of course. We were having a coffee." What did he think we were doing? I looked toward Zach for comfort, but he was watching Frank.

"Do you remember which rooms she entered?" the RSO asked. Now I was being double-teamed.

"All of them." This was a strange line of questioning.

"All of them? You mean the bedrooms and the room used for an office?"

"Yes, well, most of them. She wanted a tour. She liked the bedspreads and how I decorated everything." I could tell from the RSO's expression how vacuous and lame I sounded, especially since our apartments were part of his territory. With that realization, I went on the lawyerly offensive. "Look, I promise it was all normal. She had lots of questions about the decorating, and I answered them. We only talked for about ten minutes before the rest of the ladies appeared. I don't understand why what I do with my friends is a problem."

"It isn't a problem, Jeni. We just have to ask some questions to clear up a few things. Was she ever alone?" Frank asked.

"Maybe to go to the bathroom and perhaps to the kitchen for more coffee. Is something wrong?" I asked.

"No. You've explained everything. Don't worry about it." Then, almost on cue, the two men—Frank and the RSO—smiled at me, that kind of fake smile a beauty contestant gives when she has won second place.

"Are you sure? Should I be worried about Natasha?" All of a sudden, this sounded exciting. "Do I need to report everything about her to you? I think she had drinks with my cousin Andy. Should I follow them?"

"No, Jeni, nothing is wrong," Frank said and then stood up and looked me in the eye. "You shouldn't do anything. Nothing. Don't question people. Don't follow people. Understand?"

I nodded that I understood, but I didn't understand at all. Who was this Frank man, and why was he here in Sofia, telling me what to do?

With my acquiescence to his rules, he smiled and slapped his hands on the edge of the table to punctuate the end of the meeting. "Thanks for coming. We have to be somewhere else in a little while. Enjoy the remainder of your time here."

I thought it was all over when he stood to leave, but halfway out of the chair, he stopped and touched his forehead, as if he suddenly recollected something important.

"Wait—there is one thing," he said, turning to look at me. "Try not to let anyone go beyond your living room and dining room. There's no need for anyone to be in your personal space, especially Zach's office. OK?"

I nodded yes.

"Thanks again, Jeni. Zach. So sorry we bothered you." Frank slid his notebook into his suit pocket. "We're out of here."

I said nothing as the men exited, still confused as to the meeting's purpose.

"Well," Zach said, shaking his head as he looked back toward me. "That was some return home."

"They didn't ask me anything important. Everything was about Natasha. Don't they want to know about the dead banker who opened my account?"

"I'm afraid to ask what you mean by that, but no, they probably don't need you to tell them more. I feel fairly sure that anything that you know, if it's important, they already know as well."

"Then, I take it they also don't want to hear about the psychic?" I asked.

Zach laughed. "You know better. Of course not. We'll save that one for dinner-party conversation one night." Then he looked in my eyes and said those words that always made me melt. "I missed you."

With all eyes but ours out of the room, except perhaps that of the strategically placed security cameras, I threw my arms around Zach's neck, hugging him tightly. Despite his discovering from a possible federal agent that I hid a secret stash of money in a shoebox in our closet, I knew we were still on the same team. "I'm *so glad* you're home!"

He returned the hug with a kiss and gave a thumbs-up to the watchful glass eye above us. "You're something else, you know?" he said as we walked out, hand in hand.

"Yes, I guess so."

CHAPTER
FOURTEEN

I<small>T WAS A CHEERFUL MORNING AT THE APARTMENT AFTER OUR RETURN HOME</small> from the embassy meeting. Zach fixed a late-morning American-style breakfast and caught up on Andy's life. The early sun streamed through the large windows and filled our apartment with a warm glow. It was one of those perfect moments in time when I was the most satisfied—still traveling abroad with Zach but with a little bit of America around me. Back in the honeymoon time.

As pleasant as it was, Zach had to return to work after our brunch, and Andy left to finish his project at the internet café. I offered Andy our apartment, but he said he was less distracted when surrounded by a roomful of strangers speaking in another language.

It was as good a time as any to plan for the meeting with Rosa. I decided things were getting complicated, and I needed to make some type of chart.

With a black Sharpie, I carefully wrote on one-half of the paper the words, "Where in the world is Jeni's money?"

Then I wrote the names of the people or businesses that might have information about my money in a column, starting with the Vorbank, then Oleg, and finally Maria—with a question mark.

On the opposite half, I wrote the words, "Where in the world is AIC's money?"

Under it, I wrote another column with names of many more potential witnesses, beginning with the Vorbank, and then Zlata Petrovia, the missing treasurer; Lucia, the former president of AIC (and I added the entire AIC board for good measure); Natasha, the Russian; and finally, Zlata's husband, Igor, just because she was with him in Cyprus.

I drew a line across the bottom fourth of the sheet and added a title—"Miscellaneous Weirdos and Other Dead People"—and entered Oleg and the "psychic," only because she refused to help me. For good measure, I added the unknown Russian at the psychic's house, and then, because everyone needs a dead body in an investigation, I decided to add the charred man who had washed up on the beach.

I realized I hadn't heard more about him on the news so I stopped and texted Zach to see if he knew anything. I didn't want to waste time on a random dead body if he didn't matter.

Zach was quick to text back: *Looks like an OC hit job, but a source told the news that they have a tentative ID and are waiting to notify next of kin.*

With that news, and given the unlikelihood that the charred man at the beach was killed due to my bank—after all, it wasn't all that large—I decided to cross out that entry.

In the end, the only common name in the two columns was the Vorbank, so I drew a line connecting the bank's name.

I put the words "criminal or good-guy?" by Oleg's name, followed by Maria and the same question. I added a blank red box to check off if I found anything more about them, which I was afraid was unlikely to happen.

I wasn't so sure what to do with the second column regarding AIC. The reality was that there wasn't much Lucia or Natasha really knew and the bank wasn't helpful.

Finally, I put Zlata and Igor Petrovia, with the words "where are they?" and another empty red box. They might be easier to find.

Once done, I stood back and surveyed the work product. Sadly, it did not meet the criteria for any great reveal on a murder show. It needed more to it—more pictures, more random information. And actual suspects.

Zach was due home soon for dinner, so I rolled up my chart and stashed it in the back of my clothes closet. The paper was not stiff which made the top collapse each time I went to close the door, like one of those creepy inflatable balloon men on top of car dealerships that blow up and then deflate, over and over again. It was as if the chart was attempting an escape from the dark closet. I finally stuffed it behind a heavy coat.

Already, in less than a day, I was keeping another secret from Zach.

Zach brought home Bulgarian sausages. We ate them with fresh French bread, Bulgarian salads, and french fries. It was almost another American meal, except that the bread was right out of the baker's oven, the sausage was homemade, and the potatoes were so new that they still had a sweet, not starchy, taste to them. The salad of tomatoes and cucumbers accompanied everything perfectly. Andy had picked up dessert—a sweet pumpkin pastry known as *banitza*.

The men laughed about the trip to Rupita and the psychic, but I was less amused. No matter what they said, I still didn't feel like it was a laughing matter.

I was happy when the subject changed, and Zach mentioned a possible trip to Sunny Beach that weekend. Were we on board? I nodded an enthusiastic yes.

"I'm going to spend the day with Natasha tomorrow, so I'm sure she won't die if I go out of town after that," Andy said.

"It'll give you the opportunity to break a lot more hearts," Zach said.

It was at that moment that I decided not to break Zach's heart, one lie at a time.

"Zach, do you have time to talk? I need to tell you some more things," I said.

With that, Andy took his cue and left the room.

"Sure," Zach answered. "Should I be worried?"

"No, I just want you to know that I think something is really wrong with Vorbank. I never got the chance to tell you about the man who helped me, Oleg."

I explained that Oleg had opened my account and that not only was the account and money still missing, but Oleg had been run over by a car under suspicious circumstances a short time after I met him. My words spilled out in a rush, but Zach listened intently, slightly tightening his lips, which he only did in the most serious of conversations.

"And then, when I went to meet his supposed girlfriend to ask her questions, before I could find out anything important, I almost fell off Executioner's Point. A huge guy who knew my name caught me, but he left Bulgaria and is nowhere to be found."

"So you went to Executioner's Point in Veliko Tarnovo while I was gone?" Zach asked, his eyes wide open. At least he caught some of what I said. "And you fell off the cliff?"

"No, of course I didn't fall off. *I almost* fell off the edge, or at least it felt like I was falling over," I said, knowing that such a revelation was not going to go over so well. "Like I said, Rosa and I went to meet Oleg's girlfriend, but she didn't show."

"And Rosa was with you the whole time?" he asked.

"Well, not at the fortress," I responded.

Zach looked at me for a second before he spoke. "I'm not sure where to start." He shook his head in disbelief. "But really, Jeni? How would I ever recover if you died in Bulgaria, especially plunging to your death at the exact location where witches have met their deaths?" With that he gave me a quick kiss. "I'm sorry about the banker and your money, but I doubt his death had anything to do with you. Face it; you're not exactly one of their biggest customers."

"Well, maybe not, but I think there's something wrong, and maybe an innocent young man has died as a result. He didn't look like a thief to me."

Zach thought for a second and then offered to mention it at the office. He thought that Frank might be interested. I grimaced, and seeing my discomfort, Zach nudged me in good humor. "He's OK."

"Hope so," I said, relieved to have unloaded most of my tale of woe.

I was ready to tell him even more, but he yawned from his long day of travel.

"Let's get some sleep," he said.

I nodded in agreement. I was ready to welcome Zach back to our home away from home properly.

For lunch the next day, Rosa chose an outdoor picnic table in the main city park, Borisova Gradina, or Boris's Garden. Several restaurants nearby sold sandwiches and wine to go, perfect for an al fresco lunch on a pretty day.

"Did you bring the chart you made?" she asked.

"No, it's too big and not much is actually on it," I said. I told her I hoped to find out more about the treasurer and her husband, since I knew so little about them. I needed to do real research on them.

"And I can go through the newspapers for information on Vorbank," Rosa said. "If you need help translating anything you find, let me know."

"Oh, and pictures of anyone would help—if for no other purpose than to keep us focused," I said.

We finished our lunch early. I decided to forego shopping on the tempting downtown Vitoshka Boulevard, with enticing stores on every block. If we were going to Sunny Beach the next day, I wanted to save my money.

"Start with Facebook; then head to the other sites," Rosa said as we parted.

Good old American Facebook.

At the time, it seemed like a good idea to go home early, but spontaneous ideas often go wrong.

CHAPTER
FIFTEEN

THE SMELL HIT ME AS SOON AS I ENTERED THE APARTMENT BUILDING AND began to walk up the stairs. It was the whiff of expensive perfume.

Once inside our apartment, I rushed straight down the hallway to my room in order to change out of my painful high heels, but the smell followed me. That's when I noticed Andy's door was closed, and I heard a woman's low voice and small laugh. Before I could connect the smell and the sounds, I assumed that Andy was either watching a movie or Skyping on his computer.

"Andy," I said as I made a quick knock on the door. I cracked it open enough to say, "Hello, I'm home."

The TV was off.

Instead, I saw Natasha, beautiful and sexy Natasha, leaning against the chest of drawers. I could also see Andy's crossed legs stretched out across from her, presumably from a chair, with the remainder of his body hidden by the door. The scene looked so … casual and comfortable.

I was at a loss for words and barely squeaked out a muddled apology as I saw her surprised face. I quickly retreated and shut the door behind me.

Knowing that if I hid in my room, it would make things even more awkward, I walked to the kitchen and started a pot of coffee, considering the implications of this new development.

It took five minutes before Andy left his room and sought me out. By then, I was drinking a cup of coffee and crunching on an almond biscotti.

"I'm sorry," I said. "I didn't know you had company." I wanted to be mature about the matter. "Once I saw Natasha, I didn't know whether to stay or go, so I came in here."

"You were supposed to be shopping. How did I know you would come home early?" Andy demanded, no longer sporting the casual and relaxed demeanor I had seen earlier. "We were just talking, and I was tired of paying for coffees at cafés and restaurants."

"I know. I'm sorry," I said, ignoring for the moment that the apartment was mine and not his. Instead, in a lame effort to defend my intrusion, I decided to tell him about the embassy instruction from the day before. "I guess I'm just concerned because we were told not to have guests in our private spaces. Did she go anywhere else in the house?"

"I'm sure she went to the bathroom—what a stupid question." Then, like a bolt of lightning, my words hit him. "An, what do you mean—we can't have guests here? You never told me that."

"Actually, I just learned about the rule." I was already regretting my words and wishing I had stopped with *I'm sorry*.

"Oh, because she's *Russian?*" He clenched his fists and became red in the face.

"No, no, it's anyone," I said.

"Sure, I bet," he said, as he leaned toward me. Then he caught himself, stood up, and took a breath. "What is it about you government types and the Russians? They're not all bad. Natasha's a divorced woman. She moved from Russia in order to get away from her abusive husband. She's trying to start a new life. You don't know anything about her." Then he huffed. "She said you might not be happy if we dated, but I told her you were better than that. Maybe I was wrong."

Just as Andy was ending his defense of all things Russian, Natasha walked into the room. I prayed she had not heard the conversation.

"Good afternoon, Jeni," she said in almost-perfect English. She was ready to leave, with her Prada purse crooked in her elbow like Queen Elizabeth.

Unlike me, Natasha was as cool as a cucumber. "I hope it was OK that I visited Andy here."

"I'm sorry," I said. "I didn't mean to startle you."

Taking that as an OK, she smiled and kissed me on both cheeks to signify she was leaving. She blew a kiss to Andy, and he blithely told her he would see her when we returned from Sunny Beach.

Once Natasha left, Andy turned on his heels and withdrew to his room, frustrated with me for ruining his afternoon. For the next hour, I sat and drank more coffee than I needed and worried about how to make things right, while Andy just slept.

It was a ping on my phone, informing me that I'd received an email from Paka, that made me move from the kitchen. In the email, she reminded me that I had to send out letters to the potential donors for the AIC bazaar. Time was compressed, and the committee needed to know quickly who would be sponsoring the event so they could get the brochures, banners, and advertisement done. She forwarded to me the list of past donors and a form letter, making it a painless task, which I easily completed. Another member was working on inviting countries to participate. Talent could be arranged last-minute.

I welcomed the diversion, as Andy never left his room.

When I finally heard the key in the front door, I jumped up like an expectant puppy and ran to the living room. Zach had a bottle of wine from a new Bulgarian winery, happily intending to celebrate the beginning of a three-day weekend at the beach. Little did he know what awaited him.

"What's wrong?" he said as soon as he saw my forlorn face.

I told him the details of what had happened.

"OK, let me get this straight. Andy was in the room with Natasha, fully clothed, and he was sitting in a chair?"

"Yes, and I apologized for walking in." I told him that Andy was angry when I mentioned that we couldn't have guests in the private spaces of the apartment and that he assumed it was because Natasha was Russian.

"Well then, Jeni, it looks to me that he didn't know he was doing anything wrong, and you embarrassed him." He sounded as if he was sorry for Andy. Then he offered to talk to Andy and tell him we preferred to be here when he had visitors—at least for now.

It upset me that I might be in the wrong, and I wanted to loudly defend my entirely innocent behavior, but Zach suddenly looked very tired. I knew that it was one of those times to change the subject.

"Busy day?" I asked, as tenderly as I could muster.

"Yes," he said but then brightened up as he understood I would say nothing further about Andy. "By the way, I made a reservation for us in Sunny Beach—the last rooms available."

"That's great," I said. Zach usually wasn't the vacation planner, and I appreciated the surprise.

"I hope the hotel is OK," he responded. "Actually, it's a condo with two bedrooms that a coworker recommended. Who knows what it will be like?" He handed me the paper with the confirmation number. "Whatever it is, I'm really looking forward to it."

I couldn't wait to go to Sunny Beach, with its twenty kilometers of white sand on the Black Sea, cool breezes at night, and deep-red wines waiting to be consumed. It was as alluring as either the California wine country or Florida beaches.

Zach had managed to secure the last apartment available in the Fort Nox Golf Resort, which, according to Tripadvisor, had a minigolf course and high marks for being quiet. It also had tennis courts and ping-pong and lots of pools. Fort Nox, despite its misspelled copycat name, sounded every bit like an American resort—at half the price.

When Andy finally exited his room for dinner, he found Zach and me happily discussing our plans for our three-day weekend. Saint's holidays on Monday frequently provided the justification for national holidays in Eastern Europe, and this was one of those occasions.

"I heard you had company today," Zach said upon seeing Andy. With a conspiratorial smile, he nodded his head toward me.

"Yeah, Natasha was here," Andy said. "I didn't realize it was a problem."

"It's not a problem," Zach said, giving Andy a slight friendly punch in the upper arm. "It's my bad. I should have mentioned to you that this apartment is rented by the government, and I have to follow strict rules about visitors. Just let me know when you have guests."

Then he offered a friendly wink to Andy and poured some wine in his glass. "Now that Natasha is more than your 'casual acquaintance,' she is considered a foreign contact, so I also have to report her personal information to the embassy."

"Yeah, I guess she's a bit more than 'casual,'" Andy said, his good humor restored. "Be happy to help."

"For sure. I need her full name, address, and occupation. Her place of birth and birth date would be nice as well, if you could entice it out of her."

"No worries; that'll be easy."

Then Zach added some information that is obvious to most government employees—that there was no classified information in our apartment.

Andy smiled in relief. "I'm glad I haven't botched up government secrets."

It was funny to me that, as men, there were no hard feelings between them, but I could tell Andy had not quite gotten over my earlier intrusion.

"Yes, nothing here to worry you," Zach said. "Any classified work I would do is in the SCIF at the embassy."

"What's a SCIF?"

"Sensitized compartmental information facility, or in layman's terms, a debugged safe room for the handling of classified information. It has limited access, and we can't bring cell phones or other electronics into it."

"Sounds like a spy movie," Andy teased.

"It's not nearly that exciting," Zach replied with a tired smile. "So—are you going with us to Sunny Beach?"

"Can't wait," Andy said, throwing me a sideways glance to see my reaction.

I wasn't so sure he was sincere, but as a financial captive, he had no other choice.

CHAPTER

SIXTEEN

We left early the next morning in order to beat the traffic, but even then, the roads were jam-packed. It turned out we weren't the only ones looking forward to a long weekend at the Black Sea.

Finally, I thought, *I am on my way to Sunny Beach.*

Sunny Beach, Bulgaria, sat at the fullest part of a crescent-shaped cove about twenty kilometers long. When we arrived, I found it was not what I had expected, which was an old, dilapidated port city. Instead, it was new and glitzy, with giant hotels, which were built haphazardly after the fall of Communism. Some of the five-star hotels were on the beach or just off the beach, with more elaborate lay-outs and alluring pools. There was a sameness to the concrete architecture. Sunny Beach was meant to—and did—conjure up an image of a modern American movie set.

The seemingly endless buildings with similar façades made directions more complicated. Even with GPS, we twice drove the entire width of the area, counting down the minutes we were losing at the beach, until we hailed a cab for directions.

Fort Nox had about a dozen or more blocks of apartments and multiple pools scattered about a large tract of land. I actually lost count of the pools. One side of the property was on the Ring Road, and the other side opened up to a wide expanse of undeveloped land with an incredible view of small mountains beyond.

Rose bushes lined every sidewalk, and we could tell a lot of effort went into the green spaces, with children's fun pools, play areas, and restaurants. At first sight, other than being away from the beach scene, we agreed that it might be OK. We were tired and hungry and just wanted out of the car.

The Fort Nox front office also served as a car rental agency. It was manned by two earnest-looking young men who had been waiting all day for us to appear. Incredibly, they had never met an American guest.

They had all kinds of questions, such as "What do you do?"; "How is your weather?"; and, best of all, "Why are you here at Fort Nox?" I didn't have a ready answer for that one.

They wanted to practice their English. They wanted to discuss politics. We, on the other hand, wanted to check in and go to our rooms.

Once Zach agreed to talk to them later, we were led to our apartment. It was by the "golf course," and we were assured we had a golf course view. We walked past one building and then another into the deep recesses of the resort. Finally, I could see the three-hole course emerging in the back.

Our apartment was indeed "quiet," as Tripadvisor said—the very last building in the back and up on the fourth floor. The area surrounding us was almost as desolate as the moon's surface. There was no elevator and no parking inside the complex. No beach, no real golf course, no bellman, and we couldn't operate the TV (the satellite boxes were from China and were all broken, according to the cheerful desk clerk).

By dinnertime, I was pretty upset about the whole thing. I did not like Sunny Beach, and I did not like Fort Nox. Things were not going well.

But then, we discovered that in addition to renting cars, the guys at the front desk sold local wine.

An hour later, we were sitting in white plastic chairs on a deck that we observed was twice as big as the others, with a killer view of the sunset over the mountains and stadium seating over the mini golf course, where children rode bicycles on the fairways and families picnicked on the greens. We mellowed as we drank our wine and devoured the tomato-and-cucumber sandwiches I had brought with us. Once the night fell and only the stars were out, we all agreed that maybe Fort Nox wasn't so bad after all.

After a wonderful night's sleep, we were ready to hit the beach early. A shuttle dropped us off at a boardwalk area that was crowded with umbrellas and chairs, lots of vendors, and myriad places to eat and drink. We immediately nabbed the last three chairs at the water's edge—the winner's prize for people who went to sleep early. There were rows and rows of chairs, thousands of them, so getting one in the front also meant we were much more likely to find them again if we went for a swim.

Finally, we were able to relax in the sand in our bathing suits and baseball caps. With sunglasses pulled down, we began to people-watch in earnest.

The people who paraded before us were not like Romanians—tall, thin, sultry-looking women with shiny dark hair and eyes. At Sunny Beach, the women were primarily blonde or light brunette, with rounder bodies. Everyone wore the smallest bathing suit possible—if they wore one at all. It did not matter what their figure, shape, or age was; grandma or not, they were either topless, wore a string bikini, or were covered in a sliver of a thong. In fact, I was the one who looked like a freak of nature in my one-piece purple bathing suit.

The men were even rounder. In fact, a huge percentage of the men appeared to have swallowed watermelons, with stomachs so large that their tiny black bikini bathing suits seemed to disappear under their immense bellies.

"Who are these people?" I asked Zach. For sure they were not African or Asian. Only Caucasians walked on this beach.

"They're mostly Russians and Ukrainians and a smaller mixture from other countries including Israel. They like the location and the cheap cost to visit. Many can take a bus here. That's why they aren't friendly to us—they probably only speak Russian, and we obviously look foreign."

It wasn't long before Andy left us for a stroll down the beach. I watched with amusement as the girls' heads turned in his direction, his American looks obviously an interesting departure from the men they usually saw. I felt sure that he was returning gazes behind his Ray-Bans.

By early afternoon, he was back, and we all agreed to leave the beach, grab something to eat, and head to the hotel before we were totally fried. I decided to order a hot dog, which was topped with the vintage weak and watery ketchup and mustard that all of Eastern Europe must endure, and a Coke Zero, while Andy and Zach trudged off in the sand to find the food vendor of their choice.

I couldn't contain my excitement when the cook passed my lunch to me over the counter. The fact that the hot dog was almost tasteless and the drink warm didn't matter. I was eating an American meal on the boardwalk of Sunny Beach, basking in the bright sunlight. Who needed Malibu?

While I was finishing my hot dog at a small, standing-only table and sought to erase any errant drops of mustard on my face and clothes, my eyes were drawn upward to a small TV screen on the wall above the cook's station of the hot dog vendor. There, on the regional "breaking news," was a film clip of the police removing a handcuffed man in a suit from the Vorbank offices in Sofia.

It took me a second, but then I realized that it was the branch next to my apartment. The arrested man's head was down, while another man yelled at the reporter. I became fixated on the TV, with the remaining half of my hot dog suspended in air and my mouth wide open.

Maybe that guy is the key to finding my money.

I was once more determined to get to the bottom of whatever was going on when I returned to Sofia.

As I watched the TV, the man yelling at the reporter became even more agitated, speaking in a loud and brusque way, and then he turned his back dismissively and walked away. He had a large, pointed nose; ruddy skin tone; and large eyes that were very close together. He waved off the reporter's questions with the back of his hand, almost daring anyone to question him.

I believed that this was potentially an important development, so I tried to get Zach's attention, but he was twenty feet away, headed to the restroom, and before I could even yell his name, the station was on to another story about northern Greece.

There was no use in calling Andy—he was engaged in conversation, as best he could, with a topless woman sunning on a blanket. I had to give him credit; he had managed to find one of the few flawless topless sunbathers to ask for dinner suggestions.

By the time Zach and Andy finished their respective errands, the news was featuring the weather—sunny, sunny, sunny. What else did we expect in Sunny Beach?

It wasn't until the shuttle trip from the beach back to the hotel that I had the opportunity to tell Zach about the news story. He was quiet for a few seconds and then began to question me like a lawyer.

"Was either of the men the man at the psychic's house?" he asked.

"No. The man in Rupite looked more sophisticated than the men on the news." I recalled his fancy suit, and, for the first time since I'd fainted, I recalled the glint of a cufflink as he buttoned his suitcoat outside the psychic's house. "No," I said again, shaking my head. "I'm sure they were different men."

"I'm sure it will be on the news again," he said. "You'll probably find out more when we get back to Sofia."

We took a cool dip in the pool when we returned to the apartment and voted to order a pizza for dinner. It was another peaceful evening on the terrace, listening to the sounds of children playing in distant pools and watching the sun set over the mountains. Zach went to bed early for much-needed sleep, and Andy watched a show on his computer.

I was alone in the living room, reading a magazine, when my cell phone rang. I wasn't expecting a call, and I didn't recognize the number.

"Jeni, this is Maria," the hushed voice said—the same voice she used in her first call. "I was told you still want to talk to me."

"Yes, I do," I said, lowering my voice to match her hushed undertones. Something about her led me to be quiet and cautious.

"I have something for you," she said.

"For me?" I felt a touch of unease.

"Yes. Oleg did most of it … his paper on banking … maybe his bank," she said haltingly. "I don't understand some of it. Maybe you can look at it."

"Sure, I'll help if I can. Maybe I can get it to someone who will know what it means," I said, already thinking of possibilities and no longer reticent to meet with Maria. "Where are you?" I jumped up from my seat and ran to get a pen.

She said nothing for a while, as I stood, pen in hand, listening to her breathe at the other end of the call. Just when I thought she would hang up, she spoke again. "I can't tell you where I am, but someone has agreed to mail you the paper if you tell me an address. I left it in Nessebar."

"*Nessebar?* I'm near there—I can pick it up." Once again, I couldn't contain myself. I was too loud—too anxious. I glanced toward Andy to see if he'd heard me, but he was wearing his headphones and was intently watching his computer screen.

The problem was that my proximity to Nessebar was apparently not what Maria wanted to hear.

The sound of her breathing became deeper, and she hesitated once again. "I'm … not sure. It's not safe to meet. I don't know everything, but I know it's not safe."

"*What* isn't safe?" I asked, plopping back down on the couch.

"I don't know," she said plaintively. "I don't know what I should do. I'm scared. *Watch the news*—you'll see what they can do."

Before I could ask what news, she hung up the phone. I dialed her number, but it just rang.

I sat on the couch with the phone in my hand, knowing that I had blown it. She would never give me an address. She was too frightened, and I didn't think it had to do with being arrested.

"Who was that?" Zach mumbled as I crawled into bed.

"I'll tell you in the morning. Go back to sleep." There was no reason to keep him awake when the odds were stacked against my receiving any further information.

It was about three in the morning when I heard the distinctive beep, notifying me that I had a text. I jerked the phone off the bedside table and fumbled around on the screen in my half-asleep mode until I could read what had been sent.

Church of St. Stephen. Tomorrow. Inside. 1600.

It was from "number unknown." which meant it was a different phone than the one Maria had used either time before, but it had to be her. Once I committed the text to memory in the event of my phone dying, I lay back down. To my dismay, sleep eluded me for the remainder of the night as I considered what I should do, what I should say, and how much I should reveal to my two traveling companions.

CHAPTER
SEVENTEEN

"Can we take a taxi to Nessebar, just to see what she has?" I asked Zach after I told him the story over coffee. "Please?"

I knew it was probably nothing, but if the paper was about Vorbank, surely we should be interested. It was a long shot but worth the effort.

"I have no idea what you have gotten yourself into or what you're thinking," he said, leaning toward me and tapping my forehead for emphasis, "but going to Nessebar might be interesting. I've had enough sun, and the truth is that I really wanted to go there before we went home." With that, he smiled as broadly as I did over my hot dog purchase.

"Why didn't you say anything?" I asked, surprised by the excitement in Zach's voice.

"Because I didn't want to take you and Andy away from the beach. But if you're OK with it—"

"*Of course*," I interrupted. Even without Maria, I would never have denied Zach the opportunity to see Nessebar, had I known it mattered. I felt more than a twinge of guilt that I had never even asked what he wanted to do on this trip.

"That's great," he said with a quick smile before he took a sip of coffee and pushed his chair back to be more comfortable. He took on his professorial posture. "So what do you know about Nessebar, other than this paper conspiracy you have constructed?"

"Not much—it's old and on the water," I said, ignoring his gentle and deserved jabs about Maria.

"Well, I know quite a lot about it," he said and gave me a brief travel lesson.

Nessebar probably was one of the most significant ancient cities on the Black Sea, with a history that rivaled great cities anywhere in the world. Bulgaria might have ineffective political leaders, but it was not so with the rulers who placed their mark on the region in the past.

Located on a privileged piece of land at the end of a rocky point, which was once an island, it was high, green, moderate in climate, and rich in seafood. As a result of its natural assets, the militarily strategic Nessebar hosted all the greats of the past millennia—Thracians, Romans, Greeks, Christians, Turks, and the mighty Bulgarians. Each left its characteristic architectural mark. Ruins from every period existed, including ancient churches that dotted the landscape like gems at every road crossing, some dating back from the earliest period of Christianity.

"Bricks and columns from government buildings, public baths, fortification walls, and city gates—they're all there for the interested observer, layer upon layer. I can't even imagine how fascinating it will be," Zach said.

He told me that even the more recent Bulgarians had left their indelible mark. Two hundred or so years ago, they'd begun to build homes—moderate dwellings consisting of a white-stone first story and a brown wooden second story that protruded from the first. The small-paned windows with shutters and window boxes look like they were from a children's storybook image of a seaport town.

We decided that, given the four o'clock meeting time, we would spend the morning lazing about the pool and then head to Nessebar after lunch. Something told me not to tell Andy why we were going, other than as tourists, and Zach didn't object. He thought nothing would come of it anyway.

But I could barely wait, and the time passed slowly.

As soon as we walked through the old city gates, Nessebar enthralled me, one ancient site after another in a fairy tale setting. There was no need to talk. Just being on the water's edge reenergized us.

The midafternoon breeze off the water fanned my red skin and pushed my hair gently off my neck as we wandered the narrow streets. We ambled first around the waterside perimeter in order to get our bearings and periodically peaked through the small alleys and doors to see the restaurants with terraces, long stone stairways, and flowers flowing downward along the rock walls. We strolled along the small, narrow cobblestone roads, stopping for cheap trinkets and visiting church after church. We climbed down old stone steps to the water's edge and back up worn wooden steps, never tiring.

Before we knew it, time had passed so quickly that we had to rush toward St. Stephen's in order to make the scheduled meeting.

Once there, we checked out the sign outside the church to make sure we had the right place. I was glad we took the time to read it—it informed us that construction had begun on St. Stephen's in the eleventh century, and it was increased in size in the centuries thereafter until the city fell under Ottoman rule. The church and a small courtyard were surrounded by a wall in a distinctive red-brick-on-plaster pattern and a large carved wooden gate. The place was now a museum.

I told Andy that a friend of mine from Sofia said she might be here at four, and it would be fun if we could meet up and perhaps have a drink afterward. I rationalized that I wasn't really telling Andy a lie. It was just a lot of misdirection.

We three entered the gate together, gaping at the ancient hand-carved entry. I was startled to find that the museum was closing at four on this particular day and pleaded with the attendant to allow us to take a quick look around.

Once in the door, it took just a second for my eyes to adjust to the dark, and I quickly saw an envelope on an old wooden chair in the corner. You couldn't miss it. I rushed to grab it and put it in my purse.

"*What are you doing*? Why are you taking that?" The words echoed across the stone walls of the tiny interior, sounding almost as loud a boom.

I jumped two feet—a thief caught in her tracks. I held my breath and turned to see the figure of a man silhouetted against the bright sun at the church entrance. It took me a second to realize it was Andy.

"That's not *yours*," he said, pointing to the envelope in my hand and looking at me in disbelief.

"Oh, I know that," I said, as if I had a ready response, although, in truth, my mind was furiously seeking an explanation. When it finally came to me, I felt emboldened and brilliant. "My friend just texted me that she was sorry she missed me—her cruise ship left early. She said she was pretty sure that she forgot an envelope she intended to mail on a chair in the church. I told her I'd pick it up and bring it back to Sofia. Uh, I recognize her handwriting on the front." I momentarily lost my confidence on the last lie. Andy stared at me in disbelief, but then I quickly regained my steam. "So that's what I'm doing," I said, daring him to challenge my story. I added, for good measure, "You scared me to death, accusing me of being a thief!"

Andy stood in the doorway for a second and seemed to think about my response.

"Only you," he said, "*only you* would have a friend who wandered into an old church and left an envelope she intended to mail on a random chair, after telling us to meet her there at four, when the museum was actually closing at that time." He rolled his eyes. "It's almost like she wanted to ditch us and then get free postage for her envelope to Sofia."

Before I could form a retort, I had a chilling feeling that we were being watched. It was confirmed by the sounds of a heavy footsteps, those most likely of a man, which could be heard from the back recesses of the altar, a private place I would never enter as a visitor and that I thought had been empty. I turned and looked around the church for a sign of a priest or any other person but saw no one—just the sound of the metallic scraping of a door bolt sliding shut with a click on a side entrance. I stood immobilized, debating what to do, when I saw Zach enter the church.

"I'm hungry. Let's leave so they can close on time," he said.

I told myself that I was imaging things and agreed. But as I turned back to join the men and leave, I could see, in the shaded small patch of ground between the church and the walls, the outline a man who looked eerily like the man outside our apartment. He was walking away, his back to us, but there was something awfully familiar—perhaps the cut of his clothes. I would have to tell Zach about him.

CHAPTER
EIGHTEEN

We were all quiet as we walked in the late-afternoon sun toward a restaurant that Zach's colleague had recommended; occasionally, we meandered into a shop to buy a souvenir. It took longer than expected, but we eventually found the charming little restaurant overlooking the harbor and with a view toward Sunny Beach. Sunset was fast approaching. We devoured a feast of mussels, clams, and great wine. Along with the calories, our good humor returned.

That is why it surprised me to hear a loud groan from Zach as we strolled back to the car. Andy and I turned toward him and stopped in our tracks to see what caused his unlikely outburst. His eyes were focused on the man I had seen earlier outside the church—or his twin. He was approaching us, waving for our attention, and calling out Zach's name. I looked at Zach, eyes wide with surprise.

"I guess I have to be polite," Zach said, almost under his breath. "Excuse me for a second. I'll be right back."

Andy and I stood in confused silence, watching him speak with the other man but unable to hear them. It was so unlike Zach to walk away and not make an effort to introduce us to the person he was talking to. Although they shook hands goodbye, it was very stiff.

When Zach returned to us, his face had a slight scowl, and he let out a deep breath as if to regain his composure.

"What's going on?" I asked. "You know, that looks like the guy I told you about outside our apartment."

"Huh?" He threw up one hand into the air. "Might be. He had been asking if they had vacancies in our building because he is still in temporary quarters."

"This is bizarre, Zach. Why didn't you introduce us? Who is he?" I asked.

"He's the new guy in my office. I didn't introduce you because we won't be around long enough to socialize. You know our stay is half over."

"You don't seem to like him," I said, suddenly sad that our four-month trip was two months done and that this new guy might be a problem. I took hold of his hand as we walked, in a show of solidarity. If Zach didn't like him, neither would I.

"I hope I'm not that transparent," he said, squeezing my hand to reassure me things were OK. "Let's just say he's not one of us. He came here on a political appointment as an attaché right after a divorce—at least, he told me he was divorced. For sure, though, he is living high here. Already bought an Audi, which, you know, he probably can't even take home."

I nodded in agreement. A new Audi was very expensive in Eastern Europe. "What's his name?" I asked.

"Don Dorlyn. I made the mistake of telling him we were coming to the beach, and he must have decided it sounded like a good idea. I need to be more careful about that in the future. I don't want to get mixed up with him without knowing how he suddenly has money."

I had to agree. Something didn't add up. His polo shirt and khaki pants cried expensive resort golf more than embassy picnic clothes.

Later that night, when we were back at Fort Nox, I separated from the men, who were on the porch, having an after-dinner aperitif of plum brandy.

Sitting cross-legged on my bed, I pulled out the envelope from my purse and emptied its contents, expecting a trove of salacious information.

Instead, my shoulders dropped. I'm not sure why I didn't anticipate it, but it was a shock to see that everything was handwritten in Cyrillic lettering. What a let-down. I'd have to wait until our return to Sofia before I could have it translated, so I quickly stuffed the contents back into the envelope.

In an effort to speed up the translation, I sent a text to Rosa that I had some papers from Maria, and we should meet as soon as possible. Although it was only a five-hour drive home, I suggested that we schedule the meeting for the day after we returned. With that call done, I fell sound asleep.

"I'm thinking of stopping for a bite to eat in Plovdiv," Zach said the next day as we reached the midway point home to Sofia.

"That's a great idea." I'd been to Plovdiv briefly once before and was happy to return, if only for lunch. Plovdiv was the second-largest city in Bulgaria, with such beautiful topography that it was called the City of Seven Hills. It was a vibrant, modern place in the heart of Bulgaria, but it was one of the oldest cities in the world and still possessed an original Roman theater, Roman aqueducts, and a Roman stadium.

Because it was cool in the hills, eating lunch outside on a patio was in order. The glass of chilled white wine and chicken was refreshing.

I used the time to check my emails and saw that Rosa had written back with an OK for lunch when I returned. She also forwarded a newspaper article about the Vorbank arrest that I had seen on the TV in Sunny Beach.

It had been auto-translated by computer into English; thus, it made almost no sense and would have been comical, if not so serious. From what I could tell, the nameless branch manager had been arrested at the bank for stealing money, but the man yelling at the reporter on the news that I'd seen in Sunny Beach told the paper that the manager was wrongfully arrested and would be vindicated. The angry man was a politician, so his picture made the front page.

His name was Radko Volkov, which I thought meant that he was likely a Bulgarian of Russian descent. Volkov meant *wolf* in Russian, an appropriate name, given the man's facial structure, eyes, and nose. The connection between the politician, Radko, and the bank manager was not made clear.

What I could understand was that the politician said it was a hacker who stole the accounts. I stopped reading and took a breath. *Ah, so that's what might have happened to my money—a hacker.*

But it didn't appear the police agreed. The manager had been arrested and released on bail. I was finally relieved that the answer to my missing money was most likely under lock and key.

What made no sense was why the politician was taking such a stand on the lowly bank manager's behalf. I decided that I would have to check that out.

The rest of the trip back to Sofia was uneventful. I found that having Andy with us all the time curtailed Zach's and my normal road-trip conversations about our future, finances, and life in general. I wondered if Zach was relieved or concerned about how long Andy would be in our lives.

The day after we returned to Sofia, I unpacked, washed clothes, and watched the clock. Promptly at twelve, Rosa and I met at a restaurant near my apartment. She reached out her hand and took possession of the envelope containing Maria's paper.

"Oh," she said with a hint of dismay as she scanned the contents. "Maria was right. This just looks like an ordinary research paper on money laundering." She flipped through the papers, looking for anything out of the ordinary that might give us a clue to its meaning. "Other than some bad typing and irregular fonts, I don't see any names or numbers that look odd to me."

She sighed and put the paper down. "It *has* to have some meaning," she said, frustrated.

"Maybe not," I said, "if it really was the bank manager who took my money. I should know soon." Still, Maria had gone through the trouble to get the paper to me. Rosa was right—it had to have meaning. "Let's say it might tell us something about the bank. I don't even know who to ask to decipher it. Zach can't read this, and I can't ask his colleagues. Do you think you can ask your husband?"

"Maybe, but Leo's out of town for a day or two, visiting his mother near Sandanski."

Sandanski was a popular old spa town in the mountains, just north of the Greek border. In addition to other health problems, Leo's mother recently had hip surgery and went there to soak in the mineral baths. Rose offered to look more carefully at the paper until Leo returned.

We were both quiet while we contemplated our next move, so I was caught off guard when Rosa started talking about a totally different topic in a voice I had never before heard—her pitch higher, eyes averted, and body tense. My years as a lawyer had taught me how to catch those signals, and they were flashing red.

"How is the bazaar going?" she asked, looking toward me but not into my eyes.

"OK, I guess," I said, not sure what she wanted me to say about it that I hadn't already told her in past conversations.

There was an awkward silence that we had never before experienced until she spoke again.

"Jeni," she said, drawing out my name in affection, like a parent ready to address a concern with a child, "the other day, I mentioned to Leo that you were involved in the AIC fundraising and that I had recommended it to you." She stopped, took a breath and assumed a faraway look, as if reliving the conversation with Leo. "Anyway, you know Leo is always really understanding ... but this time, I may have messed up when I told you to join the charity board."

I could only look at her in confusion. "Why?"

"I thought perhaps it was because he wanted me instead of you on the charity board for work relations—stuff like that—but it wasn't that. He realized that I had overheard him talking about the charity, which I did, and I'm not supposed to listen to his work. I thought it was no big deal …" Her voice trailed off as she turned her eyes back toward me.

"I hope I'm not causing any problems," I said, almost frozen in place over the news that Rosa and Leo might be having problems at home due to me.

"No, no, it's fine," she said, but then almost immediately let me know her answer wasn't true. "I'm sure this sounds odd, but can you quit the charity—like, now?"

I almost choked. *Quit?* I gathered my thoughts before I answered, looking at her closely for more information and finding none. "It's almost time for the bazaar. If I quit today, what would I tell the others? Did Leo tell you to ask me to quit? Is there something wrong with AIC, other than the missing treasurer? I'll do it for you, but questions will be asked." I didn't want to ask if Leo was working on a case involving AIC, as that would clearly cross the line, and she would never answer.

"No … no, it's just that I know better than to repeat anything he says to a work colleague, no matter how innocent it is. That's why he's upset. I'm sure he doesn't want you to quit; it was my idea." Rosa shook her head, as if to dismiss the thought. Then she diverted her eyes to the right and fixated on a picture on the wall for a second or two, until I saw her shoulders heave as if she'd taken a deep breath. When Rosa looked back at me, her voice returned to normal, as if we hadn't talked about my quitting the board.

I reached over and grabbed her hand. "You know I'd do anything you asked." Then I assured her that, in any event, I would quit after the bazaar. No one would be happier than Zach, other than, perhaps, a few of the board members.

Until I quit, just to be sure Rosa did not feel uncomfortable, we both agreed not to talk about the charity board anymore. We'd focus on my lost money and our growing curiosity about the workings of the Vorbank.

And that is what we did.

"I think I'll do some research on the bank manager and the politician," I said, "as best I can in a foreign language."

"And remember Zlata and her husband. They are more visible," Rosa said, finally relaxing. "Maybe they are all connected through the bank—you know, it can be a small world, even here in Bulgaria."

At home, I used a local bank that most of my friends used as well, so it wasn't all that outlandish a thought. But the people we wanted were not all from Russia, and they weren't similar in the least. And this bank didn't seem to be a community fixture, intent on doing good while making money.

"I'm not so sure about a connection, but I agree that researching their bios sounds like a super idea. In fact, I can't believe I keep putting it off. Who knows what we'll find?"

With that, we toasted to the plan with our glasses of mineral water, two co-conspirators back on a mission.

"Let's meet day after tomorrow," she said. "How about we take a proper tour of the cathedral?" Then Rosa tilted her head and smiled at me, as if she were a child with a toy hidden behind her back. Like the child who can't keep a secret, she surprised me once more. "I also have some great news that I can't wait to tell you. I haven't told a soul so far!"

"You won't tell me today?" I asked, wondering what the news could be. I knew they weren't ready for children, so I was stumped.

"Nope, I am forcing you to wait until tomorrow," she said. "I know how you hate secrets, but I'll know more when we meet."

Once again, I was grateful for the deep relationship that I had been able to form with Rosa in two short months. It would have been dreadful to live in Sofia without a true friend.

CHAPTER
NINETEEN

I DEFINITELY COULDN'T CALL MY FUNDRAISING COMMITTEE MEMBERS *FRIENDS* yet. There was an early-morning meeting scheduled at a coffee shop in order to hash out the logistics of the bazaar, and I knew that any minute, one of the members could cause trouble.

Paka from Kenya was the nicest and most agreeable, but she was wary of making too much of a commitment on anything. Bella was intensely aware of her Italian heritage and pushed her country's visibility in all aspects of the bazaar. We would sell nothing but pasta and chianti, if she had the choice.

Then there was Natasha and me.

No, I couldn't say we were all friends.

It was a pleasant surprise when I received a report during the meeting that we had ten major sponsors, for 5,000 euros each, and two top-tier sponsors for 10,000 euros. In addition, I was told that twenty-eight countries had offered to have booths at the festival. Upon reasoned consideration, I realized that it was an easy and perfect way for both corporations and countries to have a visible diplomatic presence in the country, but I sighed in relief that it had occurred.

I congratulated the group over a job well done and ordered a double-espresso to celebrate. The waitress in the coffee shop had barely put her pen back into the pocket of her slim black skirt when Bella spoke.

"I wouldn't be so happy." Bella ground out a cigarette and sipped on her espresso. "This is definitely not good news." Her dark eyes narrowed, and her brow furrowed as she talked.

"Why?" I asked. "We could make a lot of money."

"Let's see—one, we need a larger place; two, these countries can be difficult at best; three, we don't have a big enough committee; four, we don't know what we are doing—"

"OK, got it. Can't we make the entire board help?"

"Did I miss something? To the best of my recollection, I didn't see anyone else volunteer for this committee," Bella retorted.

"I guess not."

"Right. Most women—and men—on boards like this don't volunteer to do the dirty work. They just like to give money—preferably, someone else's money." Bella was in a very cynical mood.

We all sat looking at the list of country booths as if an answer would magically appear.

Finally, I spoke.

"OK, I think we need to look at this in pieces. First, we need to find a large enough location where we can hold the event and then firm up the date with the embassies."

They nodded in agreement.

"Maybe the date will be inconvenient for some of the countries, and they'll drop out. It also may be that we can't find an adequate place, and we will just have to plan a different fundraiser," I added.

"The place has to be free, you know. We can't use up all the sponsor money for a room," Bella said and then scraped her chair back and headed to the restroom.

I slumped in my seat as I saw the much-needed funds from the bazaar slipping away. Natasha said she had no ideas and headed outside to take a call on her cell phone, leaving me deep in thought.

Paka pulled her chair closer to me. "There is a man here who has worked in the oil industry in Kenya with my husband, and he has a vacant warehouse that has power, lights, A/C, and bathrooms. It is empty and ready for a new tenant who will be occupying it at the first of next year." I was all ears as she continued. "Now, it has nothing at all inside, other than concrete floors, and we would have to decorate it, but I bet he will lend it to us for the costs of power. He's a very close friend."

"Do you really think it is possible?" I was afraid to be too optimistic. "If so, then please ask him."

"OK, I will, but only if you don't tell anyone else how you got the space," she said intently.

I immediately looked at Paka in a new light and saw that her normally curly black hair was pulled into a fashionable, slick bun, and her wide black eyes were made up with a touch of glitter. Not just that, but her dress was form-fitting and revealed the golden-brown skin on her shoulders—odd for a woman I had considered so demure.

I'm sure I gulped before I responded, wondering what I should do. I felt like something was off about Paka's deal, but I was too desperate for a solution to ask any questions. The truth was that I was beginning to see nefarious actions in everybody and on every corner, and I needed to stop before I went crazy. Paka had done nothing to make me doubt her intentions.

"Of course," I said, finally convinced that I was reading more than I should into her words *close friend*. Paka was probably dressed this way for an event later in the day. "I can't thank you enough for trying, even if it doesn't work out." I gave her a brief hug.

When Bella and Natasha returned, we all agreed to continue to think about solutions to the problem and to stay in touch. I never mentioned the space.

When Paka warmly kissed me goodbye on each cheek, I thought that maybe I finally did have a friend on the committee.

After a quick trip to the market after the meeting, I went home to my empty apartment. Andy had texted me earlier. He was at the corner internet café, doing work on his computer. I sent back a text reminding him that Zach needed the information on Natasha to send to the embassy.

I unlocked the security gates around my apartment and then the secured front doors, and because my arms were full, I took the tiny elevator up to my floor.

It was taken aback when I saw a wrapped gift, about the size of a shoebox, with a bow on top of it, sitting directly outside the apartment door. I was not expecting a gift, and it was not my birthday. There were three holes on the side of the box, facing me.

The sound of me approaching must have triggered something because suddenly, the mews of a kitten emanated from the box.

Well, I thought, *at least it's not a bomb.* It was also probably meant for someone else.

Without touching it, I ran down to the basement where the property manager had an office.

"No, it is not a mistake," he said. "It is for you."

"I don't understand."

"A woman came here today and asked me to give it to you," he said. "She said you wanted it."

Oh no, I thought, *the child with the kitten!* I couldn't believe someone would take it from her. I turned and ran back upstairs to the box, intending to return it to the rightful owner.

Sure enough, as I tore through the wrapped package, I saw a tiny gray kitten with blue eyes.

However, it wasn't the child's kitten. It was a different kitten, a bit calmer and cleaner, with short fur. I put it back in the box with the top on and went down again to talk to the property manager.

"What woman?" I said, winded from all my running around in high heels.

"An older lady, but I didn't ask her name," he said, glowering at me. "I didn't pay her any attention. I just thought you would be happy." He could tell I wasn't happy, and I could see he thought I was a jerk.

I pondered the package as I retreated back upstairs. Maybe Zach gave it to me. No, he wouldn't wrap it in old paper. Rosa? No, it would be wrapped beautifully. Andy? That thought was laughable. Maybe Natasha? It could be a hostess gift in some weird way.

I finally gave up trying to figure it out and took the kitten into our apartment, and then left again for food, litter, and a box. When I returned and fed the kitten, it fell asleep on the rug in front of a sunny window—no angry cries or scratching of furniture, which was good news because it would have to stay with me until Zach returned home from work.

CHAPTER

TWENTY

While the kitten slept, I decided it was past time for me to dig up some information on Zlata, the treasurer, and her husband, Igor. The search engine–suggested sites were in Bulgarian, so I auto-translated them into English. The often-bizarre translations always entertained me, even if they didn't educate me. I assumed it was the same humor, or most likely aggravation, that those people in Europe felt when I spoke in French.

There were many men in Bulgaria with the same name as Igor, so I put in a limited query: *What position does Igor Petrovia hold with the Bulgarian government?*

Two men called Igor Petrovia immediately popped up. One was listed in a government roster as working in the janitorial department, and other one was employed in the recently created Department of the Interrelation of International Economics.

It only made sense that the Igor I wanted wasn't a janitor, so I focused on the midlevel bureaucrat. The best I could tell, his job description involved overseeing international corporate finance activity.

I scrolled down the page of names in his department and gasped when I saw the name of Radko Volkov, the politician with the large pointed nose who had protested the arrest of the bank manager. He was directly above Igor in the supervisory chain. I couldn't tell much about Volkov's—or, the Wolf's, as I now called him—position, only that he outranked Igor. What a strange coincidence—both men in the same office.

I returned to my search into Igor's past.

Igor's LinkedIn biography—yes, he had one—stated that he'd gone to the university in Sofia for two years and had been in retail before he went to work for the government five years ago. His position, like Volkov's, was a political appointment, and all political appointees had some power, but I didn't know what his job entailed. If anything, his slim and unimpressive biography cried low-level politician for life. His picture wasn't any better—he looked into the camera, much like a sad Eeyore from *Winnie the Pooh*—large sloping eyes and stooped posture to match. This was odd in Eastern Europe where "puffing" was taken to new heights, and men took great effort to look powerful in business photographs, throwing their shoulders back and glowering into the camera.

In addition, there were no news articles about Igor, which emphasized a fairly unremarkable career.

The only other public information about Igor was on his Facebook page, and it had only a few posts, one of which was a glamour shot of him and his wife, clearly taken by a professional photographer, and another picture of them on the beach in Cyprus.

This was my first glimpse of Zlata. She was far more beautiful than I expected, even with Rosa's description. She was a full three or four inches taller than Igor and wore her tiny bikini on her tanned body like a pro. She looked right at the camera, a cover-girl smile and sorority-girl stance.

Igor, on the other hand, wore an ugly brown Speedo. He didn't smile into the camera and didn't even try to pose. I thought that perhaps if he appeared more confident in the photograph and stood upright, maybe had a shirt or tan, some sunglasses—perhaps if he tried *at all*—he might have looked like he belonged with Zlata, but instead, he looked utterly defeated.

I felt sorry for Eeyore—or rather, Igor.

"Maybe the odd combination is explained on Zlata's Facebook," I said to no one and then turned my search to her.

Zlata's Facebook page stated she was thirty-five and born in Sofia. She left at eighteen and studied in many foreign countries before returning home, prior to marrying Igor. She could speak Bulgarian, English, Russian, French, and Italian—not all that unusual in Eastern Europe—and claimed to be a part-time model and housewife. It appeared that she and her husband had no children. She loved to work out and go to the spa. There was nothing all that unusual in her profile.

On the other hand, her posts were startling.

There were glitzy pictures of her with important-looking people everywhere. Endless beach shots and fine homes in Cyprus and Sofia spilled from the screen. Several photos showed her lounging in a living room decorated stylishly in blue and gold velvet, with mirrors and gilded furniture. It was shocking in its opulence—like multimillionaires in *Architectural Digest*, not a midlevel politician. The sofa captured my eye the most. It was like nothing I had ever seen—oversized, with deep, inviting cushions made from yards of pale-blue fabric the camera caught shimmering in a beam of sunlight, like only true silk will do. Thick, braided gold tassels fell off every edge of the sofa. If the sofa was Zlata's, then she had money. Real money. Or, at a minimum, her friends did.

I couldn't understand it. Nothing about Igor screamed money or taste—most definitely not his government job. Maybe she was rich when she married him.

"Nah," I told myself. "Rich women don't marry someone like Igor."

I even wondered whether it was due to her theft of the funds from the charity account, but AIC's money couldn't have paid for one picture on the wall in the room. Speculating was doing me no good, so I went to check out local news stories on Zlata.

Predictably, she was all over the media in short, poorly edited modeling videos and in one or two pictures of her at the beach. There were several of an apartment in Sofia that looked very similar to mine, with standard-issue furniture and few personal belongings. I imagined it was one her husband secured as a government employee, and the mansions belonged to family or friends.

There were many more posts of Zlata hobnobbing with the rich and famous at exclusive social events. In most of them, she stood straight and tall, looking at the camera, while men who wore clothes that screamed money wrapped their arms around her shoulders or waist and gazed at her beauty. There were also some of Zlata and Volkov, the Wolf, at government events. In some of those, his hand draped across her lower backside—way more intimate—and in one, they smiled directly into each other's eyes. But he was her husband's boss, after all. Perhaps she was too polite to complain.

In the end, when I turned off the computer and sat back in my chair, all the research had led to an incomplete read on Zlata. Was she rich and smart or just climbing the social ladder of Sofia?

I didn't have much time to think about it. About that time, the kitten woke from its nap, stretched its back, and walked toward me, rubbing against my ankle.

It made me aware of its need for some attention.

"How could it hurt to pick up the kitten for a while?" I asked myself. Bending over, I put the palm of my hand under it and carefully tucked it against my chest for warmth.

It showed its appreciation by loudly and continuously purring. It was a good time to leave the computer table for a while and take my tiny guest on a tour of the apartment as I did small, one-handed chores. When I got to my room, I put the kitten on the bed and pulled out the chart.

"I'm going to add the Wolf's name above Igor's name," I told the kitten, who looked at me and gave a short meow, as if in agreement. "And the name of Igor and Volkov's government agency on the bottom of the chart, along with the psychic. When I get colored ink for the printer, I'll add Zlata's and Igor's pictures, plus the Wolf."

Unsurprisingly, the kitten said nothing back. It was suddenly bored and walked precariously close to the edge of the bed. I picked it up before it could fall and carried it back to the rug in the sun. Once again, without so much as a cry, it curled into a ball and went fast asleep.

I watched it for a few minutes and then turned my attention back to the computer and Zlata.

Having nothing better to do, I decided to waste time by reading the comments below the news stories. They usually were entertaining and enlightening, no matter what country you lived in. Everyone knew that most of the people who commented weren't nice.

There were several pages of them, and they all brutally attacked Zlata in some way. Many comments sowed seeds of doubt on her marriage to Igor, even though poor Igor was rarely in a picture.

Zlata "stole" Igor from his childhood sweetheart.

No one knows why Zlata married Igor, unless she had some visa problem.

Igor is an idiot, and no one knows how he works for the government.

Then, there were just nasty, mean, personal attacks toward Zlata. For example, they said that Zlata had a nose job, breast implants, cheek filler, and pretty much any other surgery one might envision. There were dozens of comments about her supposedly altered appearance. I doubted all the claimed surgeries were true, but it caused me to carefully study her Facebook page and look for obvious improvements in her appearance, kind of like the game where you circle the image that doesn't fit the picture. I definitely found a few.

Some also commented that Zlata thought she was prettier, smarter, better, etc., than anyone else in Sofia. I attributed those to jealousy.

In the end, I was beginning to feel sorry for Zlata—the trolls were out for her, and I felt guilty in reading what they had said. Nothing was really bad about her—just mean. But then, at the very end of the comment section and right as I was ready to give up on the whole search, my opinion changed. There, standing alone in bold print, was the following:

Zlata is a thief. Follow the money.

CHAPTER
TWENTY
ONE

THE INTERNET COMMENT REGARDING THE THIEF WAS DATED A FEW WEEKS before I learned that the money was stolen from the charity's bank account, and the comment was sent from an anonymous source. Some newspapers had a section dedicated to anonymous contributors. They typically wrote hateful things, but the "follow the money" comment sounded instructional.

I leaned back in the desk chair and began to consider the bold assertion. Zlata was our charity's treasurer, but that didn't mean she was a real accountant. She could have made an error. Also, our finances were small; it made no sense that she would take the charity's funds and risk her husband's career.

But where was she? I really wanted to defend her, but the last social media comment clearly instilled more doubt about her plausible innocence.

Just as I was about to go back to the newspaper articles and reread them, Andy returned to the house and sat down in the living room to talk. He had something on his mind.

"We need to plan the trip to Shumen," he said. "When do you think we should go?"

"It depends. How long will you be here?"

"I don't know. I've been thinking about it." He hesitated and then said, "Truthfully, I'm in between apartments at home and can work from here just fine for now. There's no rush. My ticket to the States is open-ended. Then, there is Natasha."

The way he mentioned her name said everything to me.

It was clear that he had fallen for her.

I couldn't really blame him—she was enchanting—but I felt the need to pour as much cold water on the relationship as I could without further alienating Andy. "I know you probably like her, but you don't know much about her background, do you? Maybe it would be good to have a long-distance relationship for a while." *As in, a relationship not based upon looks.*

"I hope you're kidding about Natasha, but sure, I'll leave if you want me out of here. I understand you want your privacy."

"No, no. Zach likes you being here." I began to regret my choice of words. "*We* like you here. All I meant was for you to go slow with her, please."

"Thanks," he said, showing some signs of relief.

"By the way, what happened with your last girlfriend? She looked nice."

"I agree; she was very nice and even checked off most of the boxes on my list," Andy said. He put his hands behind his head and looked up toward the ceiling, as if to consider her once again.

"Well, then, what went wrong?" I asked.

He turned his head back toward me, so we were eye to eye for a minute or two. I could almost see the wheels turning in his mind; I was sure he wouldn't divulge more to me. It was a surprise when he went to the refrigerator, grabbed a beer, and sat back on the couch to talk.

"It's hard to explain. I guess it was that she had a lack of curiosity about anything other than the world in her immediate vicinity and was very happy in her bubble. She didn't want anything to change."

Andy told me that he knew from the beginning that she felt that way, but he admired her loyalty to friends and family. She was different from the other women he knew. He loved her calm and predictable manner and especially that she loved being pampered. Unfortunately, the façade of the perfect relationship began to crack when she wanted him to take the same cruise vacation that she took every year to the same places in Caribbean, with the same friends, and announced she intended to do it forever.

"I finally agreed to go on the cruise, but in return, I asked her to join me on my trip to Greece, but"—he stopped to take a swig of beer—"it turned out that she wasn't willing to go to Greece or even consider it."

He shook his head and added that someone told her Greece was old and the economy was bad. She didn't want to spend one of her two-week annual vacation there. "I told her that of course it was 'old,' but we weren't planning on making any investments so the economy didn't matter, but she said she didn't want to see ruins." That's when he decided to rent a countryside villa with a vineyard to woo her to join him. "Joke's on me. She wasn't enticed and went on the cruise with her friends instead."

I winced.

He took a longer swig of his beer and stared aimlessly at the wall before continuing. "I kept thinking she'd surprise me and show up on the doorstep, like they do in a Hallmark movie, but it was not to be. When it became clear that no happy ending was in sight, I spent my time in Greece lounging on the outside terrace, like a rich vintner, drinking wine and eating olives, while whining about lost love and bad grape harvests to the gardener." He smiled ruefully as he remembered the humiliating event. "That is why the villa thing didn't work out—it was a lover's hideaway with only one sad lover, who was stuck with a useless engagement ring in his suitcase."

That shocked me. In hindsight, I couldn't believe how cruel my kidding about his marital state had been.

"In any event, we eventually talked on the phone and agreed that it was an insurmountable hurdle for us to cross—she was too fearful of the unknown and wasn't willing to change. She's really a nice person. It's my fault—I shouldn't have tried to make her change."

"I'm so sorry, Andy."

"Well, sooner or later, we would have ended up hating each other. What really gets to me is that I heard that she invited her ex-boyfriend to use my ticket on the cruise." He downed the remainder of his beer.

"I'm glad you came here to visit," I said softly.

"The irony was that I intended to bring her to Sofia as a surprise to meet you." He stood to throw his empty bottle into the recycling bin.

Silently, I pledged to make full amends and salvage his trip as best I could. "You know what? Maybe it's a good thing you're seeing Natasha for now," I said, not believing the words were coming out of my mouth. "It'll take your mind off what happened." I realized that my worrying about Andy and Natasha was ruining his time in Sofia, and he deserved to have fun. I vowed to keep it light after that.

"Thanks, I need the kind of diversion she has offered." With those words, he gave me a boyish smile.

This time, I rolled my eyes and changed the topic as I walked toward the window in the kitchen and opened it for a bit of fresh air. Once again, I saw the man I presumed to be Don, hanging out in the road near my house; this time, he was leaning up against a black Audi, a few apartments down. I motioned for Andy to step next to me, and he agreed that it was the same man as in Nessebar.

"Nice car," he said.

We stood watching as Don opened his car door, lit a cigarette, reclined his seat, and began a conversation on his cell phone. He settled in the leather seat as if he was expecting a long call. It would have made sense, but it was a hot afternoon, and his car had to be a hundred degrees inside.

"OK," Andy said, "that's officially weird."

"I think so as well." I took my phone out and snapped a shot. "He's law enforcement—maybe FBI. I bet he is on a stakeout, watching someone nearby."

"If so, he needs to work on his technique," Andy said.

I just laughed. "Back to Shumen," I said as I shut the window. "Let's plan to go in a few weeks, after my bazaar. The timing should be good. I'll go online and get a hotel and some information on the area in general. In the meantime, how about finding me a Coke Zero? I'm going to start supper."

Andy had plans to meet Natasha for a movie that night at one of the new theaters with fancy reclining seats and a full bar, but he wanted to join us for dinner before he left.

Just as I turned to walk out of the living room to the kitchen, I heard Andy let out a loud *ouch!*

"What the—" he said, as we both looked down at the tiny paw that was attacking his foot from under the couch with comical feline ferocity.

I laughed and told him the story of why the kitten was there.

"What will Zach say?" Andy asked.

"Oh, we agreed no pets, so we'll find it a good home," I said.

Andy looked at me with well-deserved skepticism. He remembered my attachments to the farm animals. I ignored him; this time was different, and I was a grown woman.

When Zach arrived home and heard the kitten story, he was convinced that I had something to do with it.

"Why would I do that?" I demanded. Righteous indignation poured out of me. "All you have to do is talk to the property manager or whatever the creepy man in the basement calls himself, and you can verify that I'm telling the truth."

"Jeni, are you trying to tell me you want to keep the kitten?" Zach asked.

"No," I said, still stinging from his accusations. "No, we agreed, and it makes sense. I'm OK with it." It would have helped my case if the kitten had not just nuzzled up against my leg. "Anyone would love to have this kitten. We won't have trouble finding it a home."

Something about the kitten or the purr reminded Zach to ask Andy about Natasha. "Andy, are you sure you got her birth date and place of birth correct? It looks like one might be wrong," he said.

"No, I'm not sure. I don't always understand her English," he said with a boyish smile. "I'll ask her again."

"Thanks, I hate to harass you," Zach responded.

"I'm headed out now to see her," Andy said.

When Andy left, Zach asked me about my plans for the next day.

"Rosa and I are going to meet at the cathedral so I can have a real tour in English, as opposed to attempting to read signs and brochures written in Bulgarian."

It dawned on me then that we were alone for the evening for the first time in a long time. I went to sit on the sofa next to Zach. "I'm not sure when Andy is leaving, but I think it will be about two weeks. We have so little time alone together," I said.

"That's true, so let's enjoy tonight while he's gone," he responded as he pulled me closer toward him. "How about we have a glass of wine on the terrace and watch the city lights? It won't be all that long until we'll be missing the view."

I smiled and gave him a light kiss to signify my approval.

CHAPTER
TWENTY
TWO

THE NEXT DAY, AS PROMISED, ROSA MET ME AT THE MAIN ENTRANCE OF THE massive Alexander Nevsky Cathedral in the center of Sofia. This imposing and beautiful building, one of the largest cathedrals in the world, supposedly could hold ten thousand worshippers. I had ventured in on occasion, but knew little about it, including why it was named after a Russian prince.

"It's not all that old, in the European sense," Rosa said. "They began building in 1882 and finished it in 1912."

It was constructed to honor the Russian, Ukrainian, and Bulgarian soldiers who fought in the Russian war against the Turkish forces in 1878. It was a difficult and costly battle, but the soldiers liberated Bulgaria from the Ottoman forces. The name was to honor Alexander Nevsky, who was a sainted prince in Russia in the thirteenth century and known for his piety, humility, and intelligence. Once, after World War I, when Russia and Bulgaria were at war against each other, they changed the name of the church, but shortly thereafter, it went back to the saint's name.

"Lots of Russian ties," I mused.

"Lots. Do you see the gold leaf dome?" Rosa said as she pointed toward it.

"How can you miss it?"

"I understand that the Russians were the ones who donated the gold leaf in 1961."

"It's gorgeous," I said, acknowledging the obvious, although something about the Russian connections made me uneasy.

We admired it for a minute or two and then wandered into the cavernous interior, with its five aisles and three pulpits.

"The interior of the church is composed of the best materials from all parts of the world. Brazilian onyx and alabaster are on the columns. There's Italian marble, and look over here—those are the mosaics from Venice. They're incredible, aren't they?"

We wandered about, getting the full effect of the church's beauty as Rosa pointed out the Lord's Prayer in gold script and the impressive display of royal thrones.

There was even a case with the seven-hundred-year-old relics of Alexander Nevsky that had been donated by Russia.

In the basement, better known as the crypt, was a museum that held some of the most important icons and masterpieces in Bulgaria. This was where Rosa came alive. She was animated and in her element, using her whole body—arms in constant motion—to describe her country's art and artifacts. I had no idea how a tour with an art historian could illuminate a basement full of old icons and relics.

"That was incredible," I told her afterward, as we exited into the bright sunlight.

"I appreciate your being a good sport in listening to me. My family tells me I talk too much about art!"

"No way. I'm so appreciative; let me buy you lunch for your hard work, and you can tell me your secret news."

With that, we headed to the closest outdoor café. It was time to get back to our real mission.

While we waited for our lemonade and Bulgarian salads, Rosa smiled broadly and leaned toward me, elbows on the table and chin in hands.

"Here it is," she said, slightly lowering her voice as I instinctively leaned toward her. "Leo has been told that he is in line for a promotion next month to a better permanent position and that means—*ta-da*—we get to buy a house of our own." She couldn't help but jump back in her seat and quietly clap her hands. Her face gleamed with joy—cheeks flushed and eyes flashing. I had never seen her like this. I knew she had been saving for a home, but it made sense that a good, steady income was what they needed.

I jumped up and ran around the table to hug her. They had worked so hard, and I knew that living with Leo's mother in her Communism-era apartment was difficult.

"It also means that we can afford to have a child, once we have more room." She beamed as she talked. "But it is not all finalized yet, so *don't tell anyone*. Leo won't know about the promotion for another few weeks. Then you and I can go look at houses!"

Her excitement was infectious and made me momentarily wish that Zach and I were also putting down permanent roots.

After we exhausted talking about the type of house she wanted, Rosa suggested we return to the issue of my lost money. I told her about my research on Zlata, the lost treasurer and wannabee model. Then it was Rosa's turn.

"There is not much information anywhere about the bank manager. He was from a small village and unmarried. His lack of credentials made me wonder about Radko Volkov, the politician defending the bank manager," she said. "Do you know much about him?"

"Not much, other than that Volkov means *wolf* in Russian, and he kind of looks like one," I replied.

"The best I can determine is that he isn't married either, but he is smart and politically ambitious. He worked for a bank in Ruse for a year or two, did well, and then got the government job here a short time later." Ruse was one of the largest cities in Bulgaria and located on its border with Romania. The countries were divided by the Danube River, and to get from one side to the other, one had to drive across the scariest old bridge I'd ever crossed, with repairs often sidelined by the disputes of a common ownership.

Ruse's downtown—or city center, as they referred to it in Europe—was surprisingly beautiful, tucked away from the riverbanks, replete with neoclassical buildings and impressive parks left over from better times, many of which were being slowly restored to their former glory.

Rosa went on to confirm that both Igor Petrovic and Radko Volkov worked for the minister of a Bulgarian international finance council. Its stated mission was to foster foreign investment in the country and help with banking matters, but that was where it got weird. Bulgaria already had ministers who did that kind of thing, and they'd been around for decades.

"No one knows why Bulgaria needs another bureaucracy," she said.

The agency was created by the former leader of Bulgaria, who everyone said was corrupt. The new president wanted it disbanded, but the old-guard politicians had so far been able to force him leave it alone and fully fund it.

"Hmm," I said as I considered her news.

"Right now, they are still fighting over it. The government is struggling with balancing new European Union finance regulations with the business leaders' desire to grow the banking and business sector of a country that is known for its lax oversight," she continued. "It's a mess. Now, the minister of the new agency is slowly casting doubt about the government's cooperation with the EU on all banking issues."

"Who is the minister?" I asked.

"His name is Lasarov Panov, and his wife is Maya. He would be Igor and Radko Volkov's immediate supervisor."

"Those are really pretty names—Lasarov and Maya sound almost regal."

"Well, I'm not so sure they don't think they are regal—they act like it," Rosa said, jutting out her chin and nose up to emphasize her point. "Lasarov might have some tenuous claim." She said it was rumored that he was born to a descendant of the Russia royalty, which lost most of its money and power, but that Maya was born in a simple village outside of Sofia.

Rosa smiled at me sweetly. "You'll probably laugh at this, but Maya's vague claim to fame is that she is distantly related to Baba Vanga, although it doesn't seem to me to be historically or genetically possible."

I did indeed laugh. "What is Maya like?" I asked, thinking of the bizarre connection.

"She's really pretty but in a more Russian way—not very tall but with an hour-glass figure and long curly hair. Kind of ooh-la-la." Rosa swished her hips. "I've seen her take over a room—with her dominating presence more than her looks—and I've also heard that she can be very mean if she wants to be."

"Do people believe she is related to Baba Vanga?"

"Not really, but then again, no one really cares one way or the other. She trades off the success of her husband. She's clever and went to a good foreign-language school to help him in his work."

Apparently, Lasarov was also shrewd in local politics, although he didn't have the command of the English and Russian languages that Maya did. They were a team, and both were sought after in Bulgaria for international work, especially with contracts and finances.

"They have an extremely large villa in town," she said. She took a sip of coffee and then shrugged her shoulders. "I don't know how they afford it. Perhaps he inherited money. I'm just not sure."

I thought about what she said while we drank our coffee. Igor worked for Radko Volkov, the Wolf, who, in turn, answered to Lasarov, the head guy. Two of the men were married—Igor to Zlata and Lasarov to Maya.

"So, Volkov is the only one unmarried—a lone wolf?" I asked, pleased with my lame pun.

"Best I can tell he isn't married," Rosa said.

"I'm concerned that Igor and Zlata are long gone," I said. "I don't know who or what spooked them, but they seem to have left for Cyprus without much warning or explanation." Then I remembered that there were no Facebook pictures from Zlata for a while, so I added, "They may not even be in Cyprus."

Rosa nodded her agreement.

"Do many people go to Cyprus?" I asked.

"A lot of people from Eastern Europe, especially Bulgarians, vacation or have homes in Cyprus. Even more so with people who have Russian connections. There are convenient, cheap, quick flights, so it's a nice little weekend jaunt away."

We talked for a while about Cyprus, the banker, and where Zlata could be before we tired of the subject.

"How's the kitten?" Rosa asked.

"Cute," I said. "I just need to find it a good home."

"I'll call around and see what I can do," Rosa said. I nodded my appreciation. My Facebook posts searching for a family to adopt our little furball were going nowhere.

"I know we agreed not to talk about the charity, but how's the bazaar going?" she asked, moving to what should have been a happier topic.

"Oh, OK, I guess. Paka is helping a lot. She managed to find us a great place in which to hold it, or rather, someone she knew did …" My voice trailed off as I remembered that Paka didn't want me to mention her name in connection with the bazaar space, and I already had betrayed her confidence.

"Well, make sure she does the seating arrangements," Rosa said. "Will you be the one who invites the politicians?"

"*What* politicians?" This was new and not welcome news.

"The president, ministers, etc. They love the photo ops and expect to be invited to any international event, especially one with the embassies." She smiled at my shocked face. "They may not actually come to the bazaar, but you'd better invite them anyway."

I groaned.

She explained that if the president appeared, it might be good for the charity, and she offered to give me the names and addresses of politicians the committee should invite.

"I'd be indebted to you more than I already am! Thanks a million!"

We left soon after that so Rosa could go to an art class. It made me sad that I had no hobby I could rush off to do, and for a second, I stood still and watched her walk away, wondering what I could do to occupy my afternoon. She must have had a sense that I felt bereft because she turned back and yelled to me past the crowd of pedestrians that had already formed between us.

"They're having an Orthodox saint's festival this Saturday in the park near your apartment. I'm not sure which saint, but you might want to go and get some ideas for the festival."

"Thanks!" I called after her and waved goodbye, smiling at her thoughtfulness.

When I entered my apartment, I was pleased to find that Andy was in the living room, typing on his computer.

"Hey! I thought you were working nonstop at the coffee shop."

"Their internet is down, and I'm to a point that I'm just correcting some numbers on documents before I send them. Once I do, I'm free to leave the computer behind for a few days."

"What are you going to do then?" I asked.

"Natasha has invited me to her brother's vacation home in Cyprus. What do you think about my going there?"

"I was just talking to Rosa about Cyprus," I said. "Apparently, lots of people in Bulgaria go to the beach in Cyprus because the flights are cheap. Sounds like fun, but don't you think it could be awkward? Isn't this too early in your relationship?"

"It might be, but I'm thinking about going anyway," he said. "I really like her."

"Cyprus sounds beautiful. I'd probably go as well," I said as I checked the time on the clock. "I hate to be bad hostess, but I need to spend some time working on the bazaar. I didn't know we had to invite politicians, and I need to get the board members started on them tonight. The bazaar is coming up way too fast."

I was grateful that Rosa would help me with the list, but I knew that many of the officers had their own favorite politicians, and they could contact them without delay.

It didn't take a minute after Paka received my email before she sent me a form letter they had used in the past. Once again, a task was made easy by the mysterious Paka. But for her, no bazaar would have been likely in the first place.

CHAPTER
TWENTY
THREE

Jeni,

*We have to talk this morning. Please meet me at the McDonald's
at the new mall.*

Rosa

"McDonald's at the mall?" I said out loud when I read the text,
first thing the next morning. "Who would even think about talking at the
loudest restaurant in town, crowded with teenagers? And hamburgers and
Cokes?"

I called to see if Rosa really had texted me. "Did you text me about
meeting at the mall?" I asked.

"Yes," she said. "Can't talk. Will see you there in an hour."

That was even weirder. I had no chance to even say no to the meeting, and
I had just seen her the day before. It was all so unlike Rosa. I worried I'd done

something to offend her. No, it had to be important news about the papers I'd given her to review. Or maybe she was going to tell me about Leo's promotion.

Suddenly, I was excited to go to the mall—it had to be good news. I fed the kitten and told it to behave while I was gone, although it didn't appear to understand my instruction. Before I left the apartment, the ball of mischief was unraveling a piece of hanging fabric from under a chair seat owned by the government. I'd deal with that when I returned home.

When I arrived at the mall, I could see the back of Rosa's dark-black hair as she sat with her head down, looking down into what I presumed was a cup of tea or coffee in her hands. She had chosen a table in the center of the food court, surrounded by McDonald's patrons—the loudest possible spot—even though she had purchased tea elsewhere.

"Hi," I said and gave her a quick kiss on each side of her face.

When she turned her head and looked up at me with bloodshot eyes, dried of recent tears but ready to spill more if the opportunity offered itself, I became alarmed.

"Oh, Rosa, what's wrong?" I was shocked by her pallor. There was no quick smile or easy laugh that I had come to expect from Rosa.

"Jeni, please sit."

I obeyed and then leaned toward her to listen as she began to speak slowly. The family at the table next to us was loud and boisterous, making normal conversation impossible.

"I'm sorry, but I can't see you anymore," she said, while looking down at the table. "I'm … I'm only here to give you back your invitations and the list of politicians' names and addresses, like I promised."

"I don't understand. What do you mean you can't see me?" I diverted my eyes to the folder of papers she slid toward me on the white Formica tabletop. I took a quick glance. They weren't that important. In fact, she could have thrown them away. I could have gotten the addresses on my own, if I'd known it bothered her that much.

My mind was reeling. Rosa was my best friend. *What is this about?*

"I just can't see you anymore," she said. Her head now was raised, but her eyes were averted, alerting me to the fact that the words to follow would most likely not be her true thoughts. "You'll be leaving soon anyway. You should make new friends. I like you—I do—but you are too much for me right now."

I was in shock.

The only thing I could do was look at Rosa in disbelief. *New friends? I'm too much?*

I sank back in my seat, transfixed on Rosa's face. When she finally turned her eyes toward me and saw my anguished face, she began to lose her resolve and her voice wavered.

"Please, Jeni, don't look at me like that," she said in a barely audible whisper. "It's not my decision. I have no choice."

"How's that possible? You're a free woman. Leo would never tell you not to be my friend."

"No, Leo agrees," she said as she lowered her voice even further. "He's been told that I'm to stay away from you, or he'll suffer."

"That's insane! I haven't done anything wrong." Although I tried to keep my voice low, it was hard.

Rosa immediately raised her hand a few inches, signaling me to speak softly. "I know, Jeni. It's not that."

"Well, what is it?"

She looked toward the table and spoke earnestly and firmly. "You have to understand." Her tone was intense, commanding me to truly listen. "We are Bulgarians. We live here, not just for four months but forever. Leo cannot risk his job for something that I'm doing for a temporary friend. Surely you understand that." With those words, she sat up in her seat, pushing the papers further toward me. "Here are your AIC invitations."

I didn't know what to do, other than open the folder and take a longer look inside. I flipped through the papers while I gathered my thoughts and tried to recover from the sting of her words *temporary friend*. It was then that I saw the paper from Maria, hidden among invitations and lists of embassy addresses.

I sat quietly for a moment, trying to understand what was happening. Deep down inside, I knew that nothing I could say would change her mind.

Begging for friendship wasn't an option. Neither was apologizing. I hadn't done anything wrong.

"I'll agree to go quietly, but can you tell me one thing?" I finally asked, leaning toward her, never taking my gaze from her eyes.

"If I can," she said, once again breaking my stare and looking toward her now-cold cup of tea.

I looked around to be sure we were not overheard. "Who told Leo his job would be in danger if you continued to talk to me?"

"Oh, Jeni, I can't tell you that." She suddenly sat up tall in her seat. "In fact, I can't tell you anything else because there is nothing more to say. Leo needs to concentrate on his job, and I'm a distraction."

"Can you at least tell me if I would I know who he is?" I asked, scooting my chair to come in so close to the table that it hit my stomach. "Is it even a 'he'?"

At first, she kept her eyes cast down to the table and simply nodded no, a visible assurance that she would speak no more to anyone who might be watching. She placed her mouth at the teacup's rim, as if to take a sip.

I reached over to touch her free hand, so it was shock that made me jump back in my seat when Rosa lifted her head, jerked her hand away, and glared at me like a rabid dog, suddenly enraged.

"You have to stop this!" she said forcefully, no longer caring who heard her. "You keep badgering me. I don't want to be your friend. You always act like you're royalty—that's it. You like telling everyone what to do. You think you are royalty and give orders, but you're not." She almost spit the words out, deliberately emphasizing the word *royalty* each time she used it, so much so that she attracted attention from the other tables.

I glared back in response.

"You know what? You're right. We have *nothing* in common," I said, pushing my chair back after parroting her loud voice. With no more left to say, I gathered my belongings to leave. By the time I finished, Rosa had stood and her back was toward me.

I watched as she walked briskly away. She crumpled the plastic teacup in her right hand, with remnants of tea spilling to the floor, and slammed it into the nearby garbage can.

Looks of pity from hamburger patrons did little to comfort me as I tried to hold in the tears. It was humiliating. I had to talk to someone before I burst out wailing, and that someone was Zach. He would have to fix this. It was so unfair.

In less than ten minutes, the taxi dropped me off at the front of the embassy, and I hurriedly passed through the gates, doors, and metal detectors. Zach was waiting for me in the small cafeteria with a pastry and coffee.

I started talking before I fully sat down in my chair, my arms flailing and face flushed. "Zach, this is awful. You have to *do* something!" Then, I proceeded to tell him all about my meeting with Rosa, including her final comment that I was acting like I was some kind of imperious queen or other royalty.

"This is all news to me," he said, as he bit his bottom lip. It took a second before he spoke again. "Jeni, Leo works for Bulgaria, not the US. I know you don't want to hear this, but I can't help him with his own politics and job. He's right to do what they tell him to do, if that means he can buy a house and put food on the table." Then he reached over and touched my hand, as I had done to Rosa's. "You have to think like them. It's not like they are telling him to commit a crime—just to not have his wife running about with an American who's asking all kinds of questions. I can kind of understand the situation."

"You've got to be kidding. You're not going to do *anything*?" I tried to remove my hand from his grasp, but he wouldn't release it.

"Please, Jeni, let it go. I have to work with Leo, although we aren't left alone anymore," he said slowly. "I didn't think much about that until you came today. But we have to respect their decision."

My eyes began to once again well with tears, but I held back the floodgates.

Feeling sorry for me, Zach offered to mention the situation to Frank. "He works with the law enforcement side of the office and interacts more with Leo. I'm in law enforcement, but mostly policy-making in Sofia. Our jobs coincide, but I don't know anything about this matter. Be positive. Maybe it's something that will all blow over soon."

"It just isn't right!"

"No, it's not. It's high politics." He took a sip of coffee while looking at the artwork on the wall. One of the paintings of a Bulgarian castle must have reminded him of something I'd said. "Why do you think she called you royalty?" Zach asked. "Do you know what brought that on?"

"She did it two times—used the word *royalty* twice when I pressed her to tell me who was threatening Leo."

"Jeni, that doesn't make sense. Why would she call you, of all people, *royalty?*"

I bit my bottom lip, worried that I might be wrong, but Zach's intense gaze told me he wasn't going to take an evasive answer.

"I think she means Lasarov Panov—we had joked that his first name sounded like royalty. He's not Leo's boss, but he's powerful and connected to the missing treasurer's husband."

Zach grew silent. His jaw tightened, and he rubbed his temples. "*Lasarov Panov?* Jeni, how do you know him?"

"I don't," I said. "Like I was explaining, he's the boss of AIC's treasurer's husband, and—oh yeah—he's the boss of the man who was on the TV defending the Vorbank manager who was arrested for stealing money. I've been wondering about all of them."

"Well, don't wonder too much, and, please, for a little while, just be a wife who stays at home," he said, finally releasing my hand. "Actually, spend more time sight-seeing with Andy. That would be better for both of you."

It was a strange comment for Zach to make. Me, stay at home and just be a wife? But instead of asking why he would say such a thing, I remembered Andy's news.

"Oh, I forgot to mention—Andy is going to Cyprus to stay with Natasha at her condominium there."

"*Cyprus?*" he said, almost like it was more than he could take.

"I'm sure it'll be fine," I said. "He's sharper than you think."

Zach slowly reached into his backpack, took out a bottle of aspirin, and popped two into his mouth.

It is more shameful to distrust our friends than to be deceived by them.

✗

—Confucius

CHAPTER
TWENTY
FOUR

That night, Zach, Andy, and I were mostly lost in our thoughts as we ate a simple supper of chicken salad and fresh bread.

"So you're going to Cyprus with Natasha," Zach said to Andy, breaking the silence.

"I'm looking forward to it," Andy said.

"Do you already have your ticket?"

"Yeah. I got it a few hours ago."

"Nonrefundable, I take it?" Zach asked.

"Yep," Andy answered as he quickly glanced sideways at Zach.

"Well, it must be a good deal. I know this sounds weird, but would you mind if Jeni and I tagged along on the plane ride?" Zach said.

I looked at him in shock. Two minitrips in one month? I recalled that Zach had turned down a scheduled conference in Cyprus, but apparently, now he wanted to go.

Andy hesitated for a moment but then smiled at Zach. "Sounds great to me. I'll forward my ticket details to Jeni in a few minutes. I think Natasha has my visit all planned, so I'm not sure about spending any time with you both, but I'll try."

This turn of events was amazing, releasing me from my prison of self-pity over losing Rosa's friendship. Going to Cyprus sounded like a great diversion, even if I could sense a lack of enthusiasm from Andy.

"Will we be near the beach?" I asked. The recent trip to Sunny Beach had only whet my appetite for sun and swimming.

"No, the conference is in the capital of Nicosia," Zach said. "But maybe you can take a bus to the beach from the hotel with another spouse. The island isn't all that large." He added he would only be attending the part of the conference that coincided with Andy's planned trip so he wouldn't feel free to miss a minute of it.

"No problem. In the meantime, I'll call the embassy and see if they know someone who will feed the kitten while we're gone." I knew that would be an easy task; everyone there loved cats.

Getting last-minute cheap tickets was a breeze, as Cyprus was hot and off-season. Andy told us Natasha was already in Cyprus, so the next morning, we piled into a tiny taxi en route to the airport.

As we flew through the clear summer skies over Turkey, we enjoyed unobstructed views of Istanbul and the Bosphorus Strait, magnificent harbors, and what looked like tiny toy ships crisscrossing the deep blue waters under our wings. It made the flight to Cyprus seem like minutes, not hours, and we were all expectant and happy when we landed. Andy grabbed some flowers from a vendor to present to Natasha.

It was unnerving when, instead of his new love waiting with outstretched arms, there was a beefy man in an ill-fitting black suit, holding a crudely written sign for "Andy," waiting for us at the terminal exit. I could see Andy considering what to do about the slight and then quickly reconciling it after only a minute or two. While he waited to see if Natasha might appear, he smiled at us and shrugged his shoulders to show us he was OK.

He probably assumed she had a very good reason for not being there. I wasn't so sure. But before I could say anything, Andy slung his backpack and flowers on the rear seat of the Mercedes, slid in, and waved a cheery goodbye.

"I guess we're on our own now," Zach said, attempting to be upbeat as well, but I could tell he was concerned about the driver. Neither of us said what was on our minds—what had Andy gotten himself into?

It was stifling hot in the parking lot, without a breath of wind. I had heard the heat in Cyprus could be oppressive at this time of the year, but I didn't expect to melt on an island surrounded by cool waters.

"Why would they choose this time of the year for your meeting?" I asked.

"It's my understanding that Cyprus was originally chosen as the site for this conference in order to give a boost to the struggling economy after the banking collapse in 2013. Plus, it's cheaper at this time of the year."

"Why Cyprus and not one of the other hundred countries that were hit hard by the recession? You know, somewhere where it's not so hot in the summer?"

"Cyprus had other important global issues they were tackling." During the long ride to the hotel, Zach explained the situation.

Prior to 2012, Cyprus wasn't just known for its Turkish occupation but for its money-laundering business, primarily with the Russians. Cyprus's leaders were OK with the illegal industry—until the country wanted to join the EU, and money laundering was frowned upon. Therefore, in accordance with the norms of progressive Western countries, Cyprus adopted and enforced a series of anti-money–laundering laws, cleverly called the Know Your Customer (KYC) laws. It attached stiff penalties and fines for bankers who might be tempted to look the other way when large sums of money were deposited.

Almost overnight, worried bankers began to require their foreign depositors (almost a third being Russian) to show definitive proof of the source of the money within their bank accounts or risk loss of funds. Predictably, many foreign depositors chose not to provide that proof and acted rather swiftly to withdraw their funds and seek other tax havens, which left Cyprus not only hot but without rich people spending lots of money. By 2013, life in Cyprus was difficult; the economy had collapsed.

"The new KYC laws, bad global economy, and war brewing in Syria, one hundred miles away, caused Cypriots to be understandably depressed," Zach said. "But I've been told that now it's different—the economy has recovered to some degree. The bad news is that the law didn't change—bankers must still know their customers—but it's easier to launder money because the depositors are no longer foreigners. Rich Russians are simply becoming Cypriots, due to a change in the law that allows them to become citizens in Cyprus in less than six months, in exchange for investing millions of euros into property, government funds, or companies."

"You've got to be kidding," I said. "How does that work?"

Zach explained it like this: "A wealthy man—let's say Russian, for this example—is sitting before the fireplace in his palatial Moscow home on a cold evening, drinking vodka and eating caviar, and he begins to worry. He's not all that popular in his hometown, and the main politician is jealous of him. Perhaps one day, the government might find a reason to seize his ill-gotten money, ending his cherished and decadent lifestyle. Or maybe, he thinks, the Russian banks might fail. He worries that he'll be jailed and his assets frozen—or worse, stolen.

"In any event, the oligarch knows that life is not so predictable in Russia and decides that it's time to take action and hide his money. While he's at it, he thinks another passport might be nice, just in case he needs to flee the country one day with his family. It takes only minutes of research for him to find the way.

"All he has to do is move his money into a shell corporation in a country like the Seychelles or the Netherlands and use it to buy at least two million dollars of real estate in Cyprus. There's no need for a bank account. Bingo— in two easy steps and in less than six months, he will have his villa on the beach, passport, *and* clean money. And not only does he have a passport, but he has an EU passport, enabling him unfettered access to over 140 countries, including the United States, without a visa and, for sure, no extreme vetting.

"Why wouldn't he do this, and do it sooner rather than later?" Zach asked me as I sat beside him, dumbfounded by the news. "Understandably, the rest of Europe is not so keen on Cyprus selling EU passports in such a tawdry way."

Neither of us needed to mention that the US did it as well—visas that led to green cards for wealthy foreign investors.

The worst thing was that even if Cyprus suddenly stopped helping the money launderers, another struggling country would be willing to pick up the slack.

Our taxi arrived at the hotel right before I became so totally depressed about the state of international finances and from the oppressive heat that I wanted to run back to the airport and take the next flight back to Sofia.

The hotel was an older high-rise, situated in the middle of town, with a large pool, amazing landscaping, and lots of conference rooms. Zach would be stuck in a windowless room, wishing he was in the pool, for most of the two days we were there, which is why he hadn't wanted to attend in the first place. At least we had time for a delicious Cypriot lunch and a bottle of cool sparkling water at a nearby restaurant before his attendance was required.

After lunch, I checked with the front desk clerk to inquire whether there was a city bus I might take to the beach near Limassol the next day. I was interested not just in the beach but in the town as well, which was famous for money laundering.

"There is, but we also have a small group headed to Limassol in the morning and then to Northern Cyprus in the afternoon. Perhaps you can join them. It'll be a faster trip than the city bus," she said.

"If I go with them to Limassol, can I skip the Northern Cyprus part and stay at the beach longer?"

"I'm sure they won't care. The tour director can show you the bus stop for the return trip back here. It's reliable and safe—you'll be fine alone."

As I finished with the desk clerk, I was surprised to see Frank, the very same man who had interrogated me at the embassy, appear at the entrance to the hotel, bag in hand. Then I realized I shouldn't have been surprised. His job and Zach's, although not the same, were connected through law enforcement.

I had noticed, over the past year or so, that most of the Americans in the office attended the same conferences.

Frank nodded hello and proceeded directly to the elevator. He was wearing the same crumpled suit from the first time we'd met at the embassy. I was glad he didn't stop to talk. I wasn't sure about him. I looked around the lobby to see if Don, the stalker, was there as well and was relieved to see he had missed the memo to fly to Cyprus.

I stayed inside the air-conditioned hotel for the rest of the afternoon and researched my options at the beach, hoping there would be a sea breeze when I arrived there. I thought for a second about going with the tour group to Northern Cyprus, where it might be cooler, but ultimately decided against it.

Northern Cyprus was totally occupied by Turkey. Taking advantage of an internal struggle between the ethnic majority Greek Cypriots and the minority Turkish residents in 1974, Turkey had sent in its powerful military, ostensibly to protect ethnic Turks living in the northern region of Cyprus, escalating the intensity of the bloody civil war. When the world complained, Turkey said it was in town merely to help its people when they needed it.

The rationalization was a lot like Ukraine and the Russians because in the end, instead of leaving when the conflict died down, the Turkish military decided to stay forever. In 1983, they built an impenetrable border wall between Northern Cyprus and southern Cyprus, separating friends and families, and declared the region to be sovereign.

For the last thirtysomething years, all Western countries had sanctioned Northern Cyprus by banning international companies from doing business there. Sadly, other than wringing hands and banning the likes of Coke products, the EU and UN had accomplished little else to solve the problem. Northern Cyprus remained isolated from the rest of the country and much of the world. And the same was true in Ukraine, and Turkey was encroaching into Syria.

I would've loved to see its ancient harbor, quaint cafés, and the amazing fort, but in the end, I decided that touring Northern Cyprus for fun didn't make sense. I preferred to be part of the boycott.

Soon enough, I became tired of guidebooks. Boredom set in, and I began to think about Rosa, which made me think of Zlata. Just that quickly, a plan began to take shape in my mind. I pulled out my laptop and went back to Zlata's biography and Facebook page to search for an address in Cyprus. The island was not so big—maybe I could find her second home, if she had one, get access to AIC's money, and return to Bulgaria a hero. And even better, no need for a bazaar.

I smiled to myself. The stars were suddenly aligned. I was in Cyprus and had a full day alone to follow my nose. It was meant to be.

CHAPTER
TWENTY
FIVE

It took a while of searching on the computer, but I finally found an address for Igor Petrovia, situated on a remote road about twenty kilometers outside Limassol. Blurry satellite images exposed the roof of a midsize villa, hidden behind a gated entrance with a slight view of the water in the distance.

Based upon my research, even if I spent the morning at the beach with the tour group, there would be ample time to take a taxi to Zlata's address, look around, and be back at the hotel before Zach was finished. In fact, it made perfect sense.

I didn't have the opportunity to discuss my plan with Zach until late that night. It wasn't like I intended to keep it a secret, but he asked Frank to join us for dinner, and I worried that Frank might throw a wet blanket on the idea.

As it turned out, they weren't interested in me or my daily activities at all. Instead, the dinner discussion was about their careers, which left me to listen and periodically drift off into my own world. Frank was on one end of the spectrum—retirement age—and Zach was nearer to the beginning of his career.

Working for the government could be tough and sometimes demoralizing. Political appointments always shaped careers, and ideological changes in the law every four or eight years could shake one's faith in the system. On top of that, the lure of much better pay in the private sector always was a tempting prospect for a government worker, especially those with specialized knowledge.

In the end, Frank gave Zach some seasoned advice that he needed, encouraging him to keep on course, despite the political headwinds that gusted in November every four years.

"The pendulum always swings back," he said. I thought it was good advice for anyone.

Still, it wasn't like the advice helped me. My career as a lawyer seemed light-years away. I thought about all the continuing education I had missed while overseas, not to mention the changes in the law and electronic filing. I thought about the legal organizations I had abandoned without so much as a warm goodbye. I had quit. My career was likely toast.

It often gnawed at my insides; I had guilt over the cost of an education now wasted. But I carefully watched lawyers like me try to do it overseas—overly qualified lawyers working in English-speaking firms, usually British, in low-level positions. I came to the conclusion that they were often unhappy and might as well have been back in the States, making real money. That discovery sealed my fate. I chose happiness and decided to use my legal education in helping nonprofits—like AIC in Sofia.

"I'm taking a group trip to the beach in Limassol tomorrow and then coming back on the bus in the afternoon," I told Zach as we were getting into bed.

"Sounds fun. Just fully charge your phone in case you need a ride or have trouble. Do you know anyone else on the tour?"

"No, I assume that they're tourists like me." Then I threw out my other plan. "I might also try to find Zlata—you know, the AIC treasurer? Anyway, find her house and see if she is still here." I wasn't sure what I would do if I actually found her, but I didn't see any reason to formulate a plan too early.

Zach looked up at me from his files, pulled off his reading glasses, and carefully considered his response. I had not asked his permission, as I knew he would have reservations and he knew I would make my own decisions. He shook his head in mild exacerbation and finally answered.

"I don't think you'll find her house, *but* if you do, don't get into a confrontation, and don't go into her house. Please stay on the beaten track and take a phone charger. And write down the address so I know where you're headed, in case you get lost." He pulled the charger from the hotel-room desk and put it in my hand. "If you go, keep in touch."

The six women, covered from head to toe in black scarves and full-cover dresses, were not, in the least, like me. They were all friends or family, gleefully talking to each other, excited about the day.

I stood out in the lobby like an American stick figure, all alone and quiet. The white shorts, striped T-shirt, and skimpy sandals I wore only made me more out of place. I reconsidered the money I'd prepaid for the trip, dreading the ensuing awkwardness. Had I not lived in Eastern Europe, I never would have considered hopping alone on a bus and heading to an unknown location, but I was so accustomed to traveling about the continent, generally on busses or trains, that it was as natural as taking a subway at home. Of course, this time was different—I had imposed myself on the good will of strangers.

"Are you Jeni?" a handsome young man asked before I could bolt. His shirt was embroidered with the tour company name.

I nodded yes.

"OK, we're all here! Let's head to the beaches. The van is just over here." Then he turned and repeated his words in Arabic to the ladies. We all followed him out the door, with me almost stepping on his heels, trying to get more information about the tour.

"These women are from Saudi Arabia and are here to visit family they have not seen in many years. Today, they asked me to take them to the beach," he said and smiled broadly. I could tell he was as happy for them as they were for themselves.

"They'll go swimming?" I asked.

"Of course," he replied. "Why not? They have dresses made for swimming. It is not so different from you Americans, with long-sleeve swimming shirts to cover up from the sun."

"Won't they be hot?"

"Perhaps if they were lying out in the sun on the beach, but, you see, they brought umbrellas. You are more likely to get hot because you'll burn your skin."

I scoffed at that. He clearly didn't know the amount of sunscreen I had in my bag.

As weird as it seemed, the trip to the beach made me as lonely as any trip I'd ever taken. Everyone else was chatting, taking selfies, and, in general, having a ball. I was a dour American by myself, missing Rosa.

It didn't help that when we hit the outskirts of Limassol, with its new, sprawling suburbs, I was disappointed by what I saw outside my window. The "city" was primarily a line of tall, high-rise, concrete condominiums that snaked along the flat beach edge, interspersed with random restaurants and bars. Many of the buildings had been recently constructed in a hurry—and cheaply—for Europeans who desired a package-price vacation. It showed. Limassol lacked planning and charm.

Before I could become even more maudlin, the minibus hit the public beach where we would spend the morning. Our affable tour director left us at a set of dressing rooms, suggested a place for lunch, and told us he would return in two hours; he reminded us to stay hydrated.

I reluctantly changed into my suit. Most beachgoers on the beach were scantily clad, while everyone in my group was covered head to toe in black. I found myself a one-piece oddity, covered in sunblock, without proper shoes in the hot sand.

"Please take." I heard halting words from one of the women from my group after I left the changing room. She smiled and handed me a pair of water shoes from her bag. Then she held up two fingers, showing she had not one but two pairs, and pointed to her feet to show they were properly protected. "OK?"

"OK! Thank you so much," I said, almost tearfully. I was so grateful.

Then, just as surprisingly, the woman grabbed my hand and pulled me with her as they all ran, en masse, into the water—joyfully, like children. The refreshing water cooled us down.

After about an hour of floating and enjoying the water, we retreated to get some shade. They changed out of their wet dresses into exact replicas that were dry and reapplied their eye makeup. Several put up their umbrellas, some walked along the beach, and others sat in chairs under the trees. It was civilized and social, although I had a hard time shaking the fact that many of them had no choice in the attire they could wear to a beach. Surely, they had to be hot, and some, even if just a few, would choose to dress differently, if given the freedom to do so. Under any other circumstances, I might have asked, but not this day, not while they were having fun.

In any event, it was lunchtime and almost one hundred degrees.

I was ready to leave the sun and the beach. I was on a mission to find Zlata.

CHAPTER
TWENTY
SIX

"Will you be going close to this address?" I asked the tour guide; I showed him the address and what little information I had on the villa while we ate lunch. I knew that his current route had him returning to the hotel to drop me off and then proceeding to Northern Cyprus for the remainder of the day.

"It's not too far out of the way. I don't mind taking a detour and dropping you near there, if they don't mind," he said. Then he asked the group in Arabic if that was OK. "I'll just skip going back to the hotel."

They all nodded. By then, their curiosity of me was equal to mine of them.

It was a meandering drive to the villa, and I worried that it was taking the tour bus farther out of its way than the driver had intended. Just as I decided to tell the guide to call off the search, the van stopped before a gate on a quiet road with a smattering of homes. It was not what I expected.

"Surely this isn't it," I said, eyes frozen upon the scene in front of me.

"Yes, madam, it is. See—here is the house number on the gate, and the street name is over there." He pointed to an unpolished bronze plaque on the gate with the address etched inside it.

Everyone looked. He was right. My companions were sad for me. Whoever I was visiting had fallen on very hard times. The rusted gate was locked by an industrial-looking padlock, and the equivalent of *no trespassing* was written on a sign at the entrance. Vegetation was beginning to grow in the cracks of the driveway, emphasizing that this home had been abandoned for several months, if not more.

I checked my phone. It was the right address.

Confusion reigned. The women talked to each other in hushed tones, and the driver seemed to contemplate what to do as he looked at his map and watched me intently. I knew what was coming before he spoke.

"I cannot take you back to the city," he said, pointing in that direction. "It is the wrong direction. You can go with us to Northern Cyprus, or there is a bus stop near here—a block or two up the road, according to the map." He paused as I considered that information. "Are you OK if I leave you here? I hate to do it, but I am already late, and perhaps you can ask around about your friend. It is a safe area so you don't need to be afraid."

I gulped and thought hard. He was correct. I had no right to deprive the women of their time in Northern Cyprus, where they were meeting family.

"No problem," I said as I tucked my phone back into a zippered pocket in my small shoulder purse. I forced a smile to emphasize it was truly OK.

That was all he needed to hear, and he hurriedly opened the door for me to exit. The van took off before I could change my mind and ruin the rest of his day. I watched as the women waved goodbye to me out the bus windows, looking much like an aviary apparition of flowing black wings encased in a white box in motion.

It was only as I saw the van pull out of sight that I realized I had forgotten my beach bag with water and sunblock.

By then, it was well over one hundred degrees. The road had little shade and not a breath of wind. I decided I had to move fast or fry, so once I decided the gate was impenetrable, I began to walk in the direction of the bus stop.

Before I could get far, I saw a man working in the yard next door. His shirt was unbuttoned, exposing a large tan belly, glistening with sweat.

"Excuse me," I said. "Do you speak English?"

"Are you lost?" he responded, not looking up or stopping his digging with a shovel.

"No, I think I have the right place, but I'm confused. Do you know where the people are who own this house?" I asked, pointing to the abandoned home.

"Bank owns it."

"Did you know the previous owners?"

"Yeah. From Bulgaria, I think. Been gone a while." This time, he stopped shoveling, put his elbow on the handle to keep it upright, wiped sweat from his brow, and glared at me.

"Do you know anything about them?"

"No."

He was a man of few words, but the fact that he kept his eyes averted when he spoke told me that he knew more.

I pressed on. "How did the bank get the house?"

"I know *nothing*," he said, throwing the shovel to the ground so hard that it smacked on a concrete ledge, and I could hear the handle crack. Angry over either a cracked shovel or my questions, he began to shake his fist, full of mud and sweat, in my face, as if I were a bad child. "You are the second person to ask where they are today. Who are you to bother me and ask these questions?"

"I'm sorry. I didn't mean to bother you," I said, jumping back and trying my best to calm him down. "I'm looking for an old friend and worried about what might have happened to her."

"Humph," he grunted and turned away. "If you are her friend, you would know everything."

Conversation over. He turned, picked up the broken shovel, and walked to his truck.

He was right. I shouldn't have stopped him while he worked. But as a yardman, he probably knew lots of secrets. Unfortunately, I appeared to be the last person he would ever tell anything. That is why I didn't bother to waste more time and ask who the other inquisitor was.

During our entire conversation, not a car passed by and not another soul appeared to exist in another house. In fact, many windows were shuttered as their owners likely had escaped to cooler locations. There were no visible water hoses or spigots for water. I knew I had to get moving.

Reluctantly, I began the almost vertical uphill trudge to the bus stop, without any indication of how far it was. I could tell why Zlata's villa had no buyers—it was too far from everything. If anything, it was more like a looter's or lover's retreat.

When I finally arrived at the bus stop, I was dismayed to find that it was simply a tiny bench under a canopy, about the size of a bath towel, with rocky terrain surrounding it. I could shade my face under the canopy, but the remainder of my body remained exposed. Those areas of flesh on my arms and legs where the sunblock had washed away in the water were turning a brighter shade of red with every passing minute.

I knew my face was faring no better, as beads of sweat poured down my cheeks, and the sun reflected off the white stones and through the thin plastic above me. It wasn't long until I began to wonder if the bus was delayed or even canceled.

Finally, I caved in and decided that it was time to ask for help. I pulled out my phone to call Zach—conference or no conference. It was then that I found my phone had become too hot in my pocket. The screen was totally fogged over, and now it wouldn't work, something that had never happened to me before.

"What a mess," I said out loud as I tried drying the screen with my breath, which only made it worse.

By then, I was very worried and seriously wondered how long I could last on the tiny bench. I bent my head down to keep my face out of the sun and looked at the worthless screen on my phone. My legs were curled up under the bench, and I had stretched my T-shirt sleeves down as far as they could go to protect my arms. The sun's position told me that it was close to three in the afternoon, and it was only getting hotter.

When a car finally appeared on the hazy horizon, it looked like a mirage—the heat of the pavement steamed up and blurred the lower half of its body. But it was a real car, and the sound of the tires as they echoed loudly in the distance heightened my expectation. I stood up, ran to the middle of the road, and began to wave my arms to flag it down. I decided that being killed as a hitchhiker was preferable to death by sunstroke. I only stopped when I recognized the driver of the car, at which time I groaned and retreated back to the bench.

It was Frank. *Well*, I told myself, *that may answer the question as to the identity of the other person who questioned the yardman*—even though, for the life of me, I didn't know why.

"Need a ride?" he asked as he stopped beside me and lowered his window; his face was expressionless, as if this was an everyday occurrence.

Pride has a way of making people do stupid things.

"No, I'm just waiting for the bus." I sat up straight and looked past him, as if to show that everything was under control, and it was just a matter of time before I left.

"Really? Do you know when it will arrive?" he asked.

"Soon." Even when I felt the cool breeze from his air conditioning waft out his window, I sat stiff and unmoving.

"Jeni, I don't think you can read the sign; it says the next bus won't arrive until six—about three more hours. Are you sure you don't want a ride?"

He had me there. I looked at the bus sign in earnest for the first time. The words were undecipherable, but the number 1800 was not. I had misread the sign. Without responding, I walked around the front of his car, opened the passenger door, and slid my white shorts onto the cold leather seat.

"I have some bottled water in the back seat, if you want one," Frank offered, swinging his arm to point out the bottles.

Without a word, I grabbed one, unscrewed the bottle cap, took a long swig, and slunk back against the cold leather seat.

CHAPTER

TWENTY
SEVEN

"Well, Jeni, do you want to tell me what you were doing out on that bench?"

"I was trying to find the woman who used to be the treasurer of the charity I work with, and, of course, she wasn't there. I'm not sure she ever was there, and now look at me." I pointed to my red, blotchy face. "I think I would have died and been eaten by vultures if you hadn't just miraculously driven by—which is a little odd, your driving down this particular road when I am here at the same time. Doncha think?"

He smiled for the first time that I could remember. "Fair enough. I wanted to get out of Nicosia for the afternoon and just happened to be here."

"Why?"

He hesitated for a second, and his demeanor suddenly changed. He glanced at me but then turned his attention back to driving and began to talk slowly, sounding wistful. "I don't know what Zach has told you, but my wife died of breast cancer three years ago."

I involuntarily shut my eyes to let it sink in—what a horrific thing.

Frank continued. He said he'd retired from the government to be with her and got her the best care he could find, but it wasn't enough. "She fought hard, but she didn't make it."

He told me that his wife's mother was from Cyprus, and they visited often while she was alive. It was only a last-minute decision that caused him to join the conference, and once in Cyprus, he found that sitting in the conference was too depressing.

"I'm so sorry about your wife," I said and meant it deeply. I couldn't get his sad revelation out of my mind.

"Thank you," he said. "Anyway, I didn't expect to come back here to Cyprus when I took this posting. I thought my work would be in Bulgaria, somewhere we never went with the kids."

"You have children?"

"Yes, I have two adult married children, but they are happy and busy with their lives." I saw him perk up at the mention of them. "They told me I had to 'move on' with life, and my only option was to go back to work. I don't golf or build things—I work."

"How long will you stay in Europe?"

"Until my kids have kids, and then I'll go home to be with them. I'm a great cook. It'll give me some purpose," he said. "Anyway, that's my plan. You and Zach don't have children yet, do you?"

I winced. That was a subject that stung more than the loss of a career. "It hasn't happened yet."

"You still have time."

For a while, we were both quiet as I cooled down, gulping not one but two bottles of water, and watched the landscape as Frank cut through it—full of olive trees and masses of brightly colored flowers.

"Well, I'm really glad you came by, even if I still think it was awfully coincidental."

"But I still don't understand why you were on that park bench," he said.

I took a sip of water as I vacillated between not trusting Frank and the belief that if I told him everything, he might help me.

In the end, I told him the entire long story, beginning with Zlata's disappearance, which he listened to without comment. I even told him about the death of the banker and Maria. In fact, I spilled the beans about everything. My story was disjointed and often illogical, but he got the facts as I saw them.

"What I don't understand is the villa. I saw pictures of it on the internet. It looked beautiful from above." I shook my head in confusion.

"The photos obviously were taken a while ago or maybe taken somewhere else entirely. Or it may belong to the bank, and her husband claimed it was his, or he was a squatter. Who knows? People do that all the time—you know, post fake pictures to make themselves look special."

He stopped the car to let a farmer with some cows cross the road to a grassy field, interspersed with red and yellow flowers on a rocky base. It was as idyllic a scene as anything I had seen all day.

Then he confessed.

He told me that Zach had indeed asked him to check on me and that he had also tried to talk to the yardman next door, but he got nowhere. It wasn't an accident that he saw me on the bench, just really good timing.

"Do you know anything else about Zlata or any of the people I mentioned?" I asked.

"I couldn't say if I did," he said.

"Wow. That's infuriating," I said, even though I know Zach would have said the same thing. Law enforcement was like that. But it made me want to throw out a final comment as we drove up to the hotel entry and the ride was over. "I just want you to know now that you sound just like the psychic."

He looked at me curiously, but the bellman opened my door before he could get out more than "What psychic?" After that, we were in the lobby, surrounded by the participants leaving the conference, one of whom called out to Frank. It was his loss that he left without hearing about the day I spent at Baba Vanga's.

The afternoon chaos in the lobby almost caused me to miss seeing Andy at the front desk. Something was wrong. He was brushing his hair from his forehead in frustration. I walked up just as he said, "Are you sure that's the cheapest room rate?"

I could see the clerk wanted to help him, but it was a full house. "Yes, sir. I am so sorry. It is our last room."

"And my last dime," Andy said, pulling his wallet out and almost slamming it on the counter. "I have no choice. I have to take it." He was signing papers before he noticed me standing next to him.

"What's going on?" I said.

"I thought it would be better for me to spend the night here," he said. "We can ride to the airport together. I'm just frustrated because my pay from the States is 'pending' in my account until tomorrow."

"Did you have fun?" I asked.

"Not sure how to answer that one—let's go with yes and no."

So, he and Natasha had some lover's spat. *Good*, I thought, *it's over.*

"We'll take you to dinner—our treat for getting us out of town for a day or two," I said.

"Thanks," he said, but just then, I saw his eyes look past me to the lobby entrance. I turned to see what had captured his attention.

There she was, like in the Hallmark movie he'd dreamed about with the ending that he always wanted. Natasha stood there, dressed in skin-tight white capris, a blue midriff top, silver dangling earrings, and stiletto sandals. All the male eyes in the room were fixed on her, no doubt wondering why this goddess had blessed them with her presence.

Natasha slowly walked toward Andy, and when she was close, I saw her dark eyes were misty in that way that only a true pro can pull off—both vulnerable and desirable. Either she was a great actress, or the relationship was real. When she finally reached him, she tenderly took Andy's hand and led him away from me toward a nearby couch. Andy was mesmerized or mute—he never spoke as they sat next to each other. It was Natasha, seeking forgiveness with an intensity that only a heartless fool could resist. It was certainly more than Andy could handle. He relented. He smiled. Whatever had happened, now it was all OK.

I watched from the sidelines, like a voyeur, as they gently kissed goodbye, and I heard Andy say he loved her.

I groaned. He was hooked even more than before.

CHAPTER
TWENTY EIGHT

"Jeni, what happened to you?" Andy asked after Natasha had left the lobby and he had returned to my side.

I was confused for a second, and then I looked in a nearby mirror. "Oh no, this is awful!" My T-shirt was pulled out of shape, my hair was matted from the swim, my previously white shorts were now filthy from the bus stop bench, and I had red welts all over my body where the sunblock had failed, including my face. "I have to get washed up and changed. Just keep Zach here and have a drink. I'll be back as soon as possible for dinner."

While I resisted wearing linen because it wrinkled, this was one of those occasions where the soft and light fabric was required. A lobby store had just what I needed in the shop window—a white dress with flowing long sleeves, made for tourists. I hurriedly paid for it and took it to my room.

Make-up helped reduce the angry appearance of the red welts on my face but not the pain of the burn that accompanied them. I began to hate Zlata, and I still hadn't met her.

Zach and Andy were finishing a beer at the lobby bar when I joined them. They had picked out a modern restaurant for dinner on the edge of the city's beautiful Nicosia Park.

"Well, Andy, I've been waiting to hear the story. What exactly happened with Natasha?" Zach asked once we sat down to eat. I was relieved that he asked first because I was also dying to know.

"It all started out great. They have an amazing condominium on the top floor of a high-rise. It's probably worth more than a million dollars," he said, as Zach let out a breath. "Her brother was there, and a few of his business friends drifted in and out. They offered me Russian appetizers and vodka when I arrived—that was cool—but then things got strange."

Andy said the Russians were curious about Zach and me—very curious. At the same time, Andy was interested in how Natasha's brother, who didn't seem all that sharp, had so much money. At first, it was fine, each asking questions of the other. Natasha's family owned grocery stores in Russia. He told them he was in the tech business, which was true.

"But they wouldn't stop asking me questions, mostly about my job and you guys, and they kept drinking and drinking. Then the questions got really personal, like how you two get along, when you're leaving, how much money you have—all kinds of crazy things like that. Finally, I had enough and told Natasha I didn't feel so well and went to bed."

"Did she believe you?" I asked.

"I don't know," Andy said, shrugging his shoulders. "Later, I could hear Natasha and her brother having an argument in Russian—maybe it was about me."

The next morning Natasha awakened Andy with coffee and some aspirin and asked how he felt. He figured she knew why he'd left the party, and there was no need to dredge it up. So they went downstairs, and her brother fixed breakfast and made drinks for everyone.

The drinking began in earnest all over again, and the brother's friends were talking about working in their grocery business, which all of a sudden didn't sound like real groceries.

"Natasha was taking a lot of pictures of me for her Facebook page, which I hate, so I told her I wanted to get out and go to the beach for a walk. The walk was the best part of the weekend."

"In that heat?" I asked.

"We wore hats—unlike you," he said, pointing to my face. "It was bad when we returned to the condominium. Not only did they have vodka and caviar but a boatload of drugs. I panicked, while they were trying to tell me to relax. I'm no fool; I got outta there fast."

"Good move," Zach said. I could tell he was distressed over this latest revelation.

"So Natasha came to the hotel to tell me she was sorry and that she didn't know about the drugs until she saw them," Andy said. "Basically, Natasha said her brother was stupid, and it wouldn't happen again."

Neither Zach nor I knew how to respond to that information.

"Something tells me she is being truthful with me; you can't help who your relatives are," Andy said. I wasn't so sure he didn't mean me as well. "She begged me to give her another chance, and I said yes, but for good measure, I decided to stay here at the hotel and head out tomorrow on my own—just to keep the brother at bay. That's why she isn't here."

"Ugh," I said. I couldn't believe he intended to keep seeing her.

"You don't know her, Jeni," Andy replied with such force that he almost came out of his chair. "Natasha wants to be with me wherever I go. She's genuine. She's not like her brother."

"What's her brother's name? I probably need to know that," Zach said, providing a much-needed change in the discussion. "And his business?"

"I'll try to get the info tomorrow, but I do know that her brother's first name is Boris," Andy said, turning his full attention to Zach. "I know I owe you her birth date as well. I keep forgetting to follow up on that. Sorry."

"Nah, it's OK," Zach said.

That night, I told Zach about my day. I wondered if he thought Frank might be following me.

"I doubt it," he said. "You're just lucky I mentioned that you were going to check out Zlata's house, and he offered to drive by it himself, in case you didn't find it. He got her full name from the AIC website."

"Smart."

"Yeah, it's nice to have Frank around."

"How about that Don guy?" I asked. "Why isn't he here? Isn't he in your office? He always seems to be around."

"He's not here because I asked him to stay in Sofia in case we had any calls while I was gone. But, for sure, he's not someone I would ask to help you out. He probably needs someone to help him." He winced as he bit his lower lip. "I shouldn't have said that. Forget it. He's just new to the job."

Before I could ask more questions, Zach suggested we stop talking about his work and take an evening walk around the hotel garden.

I was left to wonder what he wasn't telling me about his two colleagues.

On the flight home, Zach asked me about my plans for the week.

"I don't know. We'll probably have a meeting to discuss the charity bazaar. Rosa suggested I go to the Orthodox festival they're having on Saturday for a saint's day to get some ideas for the bazaar. Other than that, nothing much."

"I'll be very busy this week and want to make sure you are OK. Keep an eye on Andy, if you don't mind."

"Sure," I said. That went without saying. "Zach, did you give Maria's paper to anyone?"

"Yes, but I haven't heard back," he said. "It's probably just a scholarly paper, but you know I can't tell you anything."

"At least tell me if you gave it to Frank."

"Can't say if I did," he replied.

I looked at him in disbelief. "What kind of response is *that*? Like I'm supposed to think that means something?"

Zach reached into the seat pocket, pulled out the airplane magazine, and began to read, ignoring my outburst.

I turned my face to the window and yanked the summer scarf from my neck, suddenly hot under the collar. I wanted to scream. Nothing was making sense anymore.

CHAPTER
TWENTY
NINE

"Maybe it's time for us to return to the States," Zach said as he poured coffee the next morning, back in our apartment.

"No," I said. "I crossed the line in Cyprus and know it. The argument was all my fault. This is what you were trained to do, and you love it. Leaving isn't the answer."

"Jeni, face the facts. We've never argued with each other like this before," he said solemnly. "It's different. You're not as happy, and I work too much. We don't have to make a decision now, but think about it. Something has to change."

I knew he was right. It wasn't the same. After over a decade of marriage, we seemed to be living parallel lives, and mine clearly lacked any income or enough real meaning.

"I'll think about it, but not because I want to leave or don't love you. Just because you asked me to."

With that, we said our goodbyes, and Zach left for work—this time with a tight hug included.

Andy was working on his computer when I knocked on his door, later in the morning.

"Come in," he said.

"I was wondering if you had any luck finding out where Uncle Bob's POW camp was in Shumen," I asked.

"No, but we probably should plan to go next week. I get the sense that I need to be back in the States to make a personal appearance at work before long," he said. "They like to have one-on-one contact periodically, and since they finally deposited my paycheck, I'm willing to do as they ask."

"What about Natasha?"

"She's looking at traveling there with me."

"Oh."

"It's nothing serious—she has friends in the US. Don't worry. By the way, she wanted to talk to you about something. Here's her number, if you don't have it handy."

"Sure," I said, assuming it was about the bazaar.

It wasn't.

"Jeni, I have a great surprise. I'm going to Amsterdam for business this weekend and want you to be my guest on a girls' trip." She waited for me to squeal with joy at her invitation. Instead, I was quiet. Undaunted, she continued. She had extra frequent-flyer miles and a place where we could stay. Now that she and Andy were close, she thought we needed to spend more time together and go shopping. "What do you think? It'll be so much fun!"

I was surprised but not for the reasons she might have thought. Ex-pat women often got together and took advantage of cheap flights to make short trips to other major cities to shop or sight-see. I had done it once before—a spontaneous girls' trip to Prague. It was just that *this* time, it was Natasha, and it was where she wanted to go and that she wanted to pay.

"Thanks so much for the offer, but I can't," I said, trying to make my voice sound as disappointed as possible. "I'm so sorry,"

"Perhaps another weekend?" she said, dripping with sweetness.

"No, probably not," I said.

"I don't understand," she said. "Is it because of the drugs? Did Andy say something? I don't use drugs; my brother never does either. That's why he was such a klutz. He just thought because Andy was an American—"

"It has nothing to do with you personally," I said, although some of it did have to do with her. "It's just not allowed."

No extra plane tickets, free apartments, free shopping trips, not even a free cup of expensive coffee—none was allowed for US government employees and their spouses.

"OK, but let me know if you change your mind," she said, sounding as cheerful as if I had accepted her invitation. "Andy told me you wanted to go there someday. You need to treat yourself, and it's not like I'm a stranger anymore. We're almost family!"

The last line took my breath away. *Family?*

When I regained my composure, I couldn't help but ask what business she had in Amsterdam, a city in the Netherlands known for its tulips and obscure corporate and banking industry.

"Oh, I'll tell you all about it later," she said, brushing off the question. "Will you be at the meeting to discuss the bazaar this afternoon?"

"Yes. I'll see you then."

I hung up, not knowing if she was really that naïve or trying to set me up. She seemed smart enough to know that an American diplomat couldn't accept valuable gifts from any foreigner, much less a Russian, no matter who the Russian was or how cleverly disguised the gift might be. I might not be the actual diplomat, but I was on the government's dime and played by the same rules. It irritated me that she would even ask.

Ordinarily, I'd have sent an email to Zach, outlining the conversation, but he and Frank had told me not to worry about Natasha. So I did like they asked and tried to dismiss the tempting offer from my mind, but it was hard. I couldn't help but wonder what *business* she would be doing in the Netherlands. In fact, I didn't even know she had a job.

To my delight, that afternoon, once again, Paka stepped up to the plate on the fundraiser, not only secretly securing the warehouse location but sending contracts to the embassies for booths and even confirming letters to the politicians. It left me in a very comfortable position as the chairperson.

"I have great news," Paka said. "The president and his wife will make an appearance. It's even on their calendar so the press will know. We are free to tell potential funders about that."

We all applauded the news.

"Anyone else?" I asked.

She rattled off a few more names that I didn't know. But the last two caused me to grab my cup of coffee tightly. "I also heard from Lasarov and Maya Panov," she said. "They are coming as well."

"You're kidding, aren't you?" I asked, irritated at myself when my voice rose and almost squeaked. "*They're* invited? I thought they hated the president, and the president hated them."

"That's true, and it's probably the only reason they are attending. But they were on your list. Didn't you want them?"

What could I say? What a surprise Rosa had left me—the president and the pseudo-royalty, Lasarov and Maya Panov, in the same place, at my event, and I would be introducing them. So much for my following Zach's advice and staying clear of controversy.

Natasha was strangely quiet, saying nothing about the invitees and playing on her phone.

The rest of us reviewed the bank statement and the finances for the bazaar. Some corporate sponsors had paid their funds in advance, and the money had been deposited in a bank more reputable than Vorbank.

"Still no news on Zlata?" I asked.

The members shook their heads no.

"I'm sure she is just visiting family somewhere. We need to forget about her," Natasha said, flipping her slim, bejeweled hand dismissively and setting her phone aside.

Forget about a missing 100,000 in euros? Something about her attitude gave me a thought. "Natasha, you and Zlata both have homes in Cyprus. Have you ever visited her home?"

The other members seemed curious to hear the answer as well.

"No … no, I barely know her," she said, furrowing her brow, apparently to show she was thinking hard.

"What about her visiting you? Did she ever go to your condo?"

"No," she said, cocking her pretty little head to one side. "I might have seen her here a few times, but that is it. No, I really don't know her."

"Oh well, if you hear anything, please let me know," I said, disappointed. "Let's move on and discuss the booths and the volunteer list."

Paka was outlining the agenda for the day when I heard my cell phone ding, indicating a Facebook post had been made, "tagging" me. No one ever tagged me.

That's odd, I thought as I took a sip of my coffee. I ignored the notification and kept my attention on Paka. A minute later, my curiosity got the better of me when my phone dinged again to remind me of the post. I moved the phone to my lap so no one could witness my rude behavior and clicked on the image, which immediately caused me to choke on my coffee.

"Jeni, are you OK?" Paka asked.

My involuntary noises had startled the group.

"Yes, I'm sorry," I said as I tried to get my voice back to normal. "The coffee … went down wrong."

She nodded sympathetically as I sipped on water in order to recover and gazed in disbelief at a photo of Andy and Natasha. They were curled up on the very same large, lush, deep-blue silk sofa that was in Zlata's Facebook photo that I'd uncovered during my research. Not only was it the same very expensive sofa, but it was located in the same room—the pictures on the wall and items on the coffee table were identical to those in the other photo. That meant that both Natasha and Zlata had been in the very same condo in Cyprus, which now, according to what Natasha had told Andy, belonged to Natasha's family.

I eventually looked up toward Natasha. She flashed a subtle smile at me and gave me a sheepish wave. I didn't know how to respond. Was it a knowing, calculated, and cunning smile to see how I would react or simply a vacuous "Facebook-y" kind of smile, to let me know she was pleased about sharing a picture of her new love?

In either event, I realized one thing: Natasha and Zlata were entwined in ways I didn't yet know but intended to discover before Andy went in too far.

CHAPTER
THIRTY

After the meeting, the rest of which went by in a blur, I ran to a computer store to buy a color printer cartridge, rushed home, went to my closet, retrieved the crumpled chart, and sat down at my computer.

Color images of Zlata's Facebook page spit out of my printer, along with the photos of her sitting on the couch. Then the smiling faces of Natasha and Andy that I had downloaded from the Facebook post emerged from the printer. No doubt about it—both pictures were taken in the same room.

I pasted them to the chart. Next, I took a red Sharpie and drew a line directly from Zlata to Natasha. Not only were they connected by Vorbank, but now there was something else that tied them together—the blue sofa in the condo in Cyprus. It was almost like a game of Clue. There had to be more to it, if I just looked hard enough.

Eventually, I leaned back, totally frustrated. This was a job for someone with real skills and resources.

Ordinarily, I would have called Zach, but for the first time ever, I decided not to call my husband. Instead, I called Frank. If Zach trusted him, so should I, despite my initial reservations. "Can we meet, please?"

He hesitated, and I thought perhaps he would decline. "Sure," he said. "How about lunch at the café near your place. I can get a sandwich."

"Perfect. See you at one," I said. As soon as I hung up, another call came through. This one was from the States and my bank.

"Mrs. Turner?"

I hadn't been called Mrs. Turner in so long it that almost threw me. "Yes?"

"This is Mr. Swetman, your bank officer."

"Oh, hi," I said, assuming this couldn't be good.

"Sorry to bother you, but I had a request yesterday to open a second account for you and to transfer your savings account into it." He stopped to let the words sink in. "It seemed suspicious so I wanted to verify it."

"Oh my gosh! Thanks for calling me!" I said, my words gushing like a geyser from my mouth. After the Vorbank incident, I had called the home bank to see about my checking accounts but not my savings account. "No, I didn't make the request. Where did it come from?"

"I'm not sure, but the fraud division will track it down. For now, I'll put a freeze on the account, and you'll need to change the password."

That also meant my ATM cards wouldn't work.

"Until your cards arrive, you can still write checks at the embassy if you need money," he said.

"I'm so thankful—you have no idea," I said. If our savings account, as little as it was, had been stolen, I would have had to return home and go back to work. Not only did the account hold what was remaining of my money from Uncle Bob, but it held all our emergency money, if we ever needed it while we were overseas.

It was all very upsetting. No one had ever attempted to steal my identity while I was in Bulgaria until now. Not once in Romania, the country known throughout the world for producing expert hackers. What was happening?

"This has to be connected to someone in the bank here," I said to myself.

Worrying made everything worse, so I tried to move forward with my day. I sent a quick text to Zach to warn him about the account freeze in case he attempted to use the bank card, and then I rushed to get ready for lunch. I hoped I could find some cash somewhere. Now, neither my Bulgarian nor American bank cards worked.

Frank was already drinking a warm Coke Zero when I arrived. "How are you doing?" he asked, looking at the big wad of paper under my arm.

"Awful," I said and began by telling him about the banker's call.

He wrote the bank's phone number on his little notepad and scratched something beside it that I couldn't read upside down. He had terrible handwriting.

"But that's not why I'm here. I know you told me not to worry about Natasha, but I can't help it." I proceeded to tell him everything that had happened to Andy in Cyprus and at the bazaar meeting.

We laid my chart out on the table the best we could, and I showed him the pictures that proved that Natasha had lied.

"Are you sure she really lied?" he said. "Maybe Zlata went to the condo when Natasha wasn't there to visit someone else. There could be many reasons how this occurred."

"That might be true, but you have to remember that both of them just happened to be on the AIC board at the same time. It's a small board for a local charity," I said. "I doubt they also happened to sit on the same couch in a condo in Cyprus and not know about each other."

"That's true; it's unlikely," Frank said, suddenly emitting a small smile. "Nothing gets past you—except perhaps the bus. You're a lot like my wife was. Always curious, like a cat, but you do know—"

"Curiosity killed the cat," I said with a smirk. "Not really funny, Frank."

He continued to study my now-messy chart while he munched on a sandwich. When he finished his sandwich, he folded up the chart and handed it back to me. He sat silently for a few minutes, I assumed considering what I had told him.

"Would you please tell me one thing?" I asked. "Did Zach give you Maria's paper?"

He took a deep breath. "I figure I owe you an answer about that since you were the one to find it. The answer is yes," he said, returning to his sandwich and not inviting follow-up questions about the paper's contents.

I knew he wouldn't answer if I wasted the breath to ask. Instead, I asked, "Did you try to speak to Maria?"

"So far, no one has been able to find this Maria girl. She's vanished—if she ever existed."

I offered a quick prayer under my breath in the hope that she was still alive.

"Now it's your turn to answer questions. Last time we talked, you started to tell me about a psychic."

"Oh, yeah," I said.

"Well, what happened?"

As I spoke, even I knew that the story seemed crazy. I began to wonder if I had just imagined most of it but was relieved when Frank listened and made no snide comments. Fortunately, he was well versed in the lore of Baba Vanga and the village of Rupite, so he was able to put it all into context. He asked me to describe in detail the man I'd seen outside the psychic's home. Other than the flash of a gold cufflink, fancy clothes, and expensive black car I didn't have much to serve up to him.

When I finished, he thought long and hard about the next step to take.

"Jeni, I don't know what is going on, but this is the plan for the immediate future." He leaned forward and put both hands flat on the table to ensure I was listening. "Just like I told you last time, you are to *do nothing* proactive on Zlata. Nothing *at all*. No following anyone, no more investigating—do nothing. If you do, I won't tell you another thing, and I'll recommend that the State Department send you home. Understand?"

"Just like Rosa! You're threatening me? You would send me home, after I told you everything?" My face and neck were blood-red with anger. It was a struggle to keep my voice low.

"Yes. I will have you sent home in a second."

If I had any doubt in my mind, all I had to do was look at his face—a stony glare, eyes boring into me. "That's so—I don't know—so ..." I tightened my fists and shook them in my lap, forcing myself to keep in control and not lunge at the man.

"Deal?" he asked and thrust out his hand to shake, his hardened face signaling that he wasn't playing games.

I could only make a small, unbecoming snort in return. I knew there were no arrows in my quiver. "What do I get out of it?" I asked between clenched teeth, not ready to loosen my fists and extend my hand in peace. I wasn't going to surrender that easily.

"I'll give you instructions when I can," he said as he calmly finished his sandwich.

"That may be nothing."

"Yep, it might be nothing. But you have to remember that I'm not the enemy. We're on the same team."

I sat and fumed, but in the end, I knew there was no option but to take the "deal," as bad as it was. Without a word, I stuck my hand out, and we shook.

"So what do I do now?" I asked, not really expecting an answer.

"Only one thing. My gut instinct tells me that Natasha will approach you again. You're her only hope for an expedited visa process. When she comes to see you, I want you to get this information from her." He scratched some questions on a piece of paper in his notepad and tore it out. "Now, she may go first to the embassy, but most likely, she will want you and Zach to use your State Department privilege to move her up in the line for a visa." He slid the napkin of questions to me. "Be ready. Memorize these questions."

"OK."

"Also, don't say a word to Andy, and don't get involved in his relationship with Natasha."

I nodded yes.

"And none of this means she's a bad person. Don't jump to conclusions."

"OK."

"And, finally, keep me informed about any other contacts you have with foreigners."

What kind of instruction is that? I wondered. Virtually all my contacts, other than with Zach and Andy, were foreign. "Should I tell Zach about today?" I asked, very sorry now that I hadn't told Zach that I was meeting Frank in the first place.

"Of course. Give him a call and tell him we had lunch together, but don't say anything else on the phone. I'll talk to him at the office today. Then, go about your everyday business." Frank paid his check and stood up to leave but then stopped on the way out. "One other thing, Jeni," he said, touching his forehead, as if the thought had just struck him. "Stay off the computer unless you run it by me. Just text your friends if you need to contact them. Tell them your email has been hacked."

"OK," I said, my shoulders further drooping. I wanted to say no, but I knew I no longer had the power to argue. The game had changed, and right now, Frank held all the cards and made all the rules.

But, I told myself, *he said we were a team*. For now, I was willing to have him serve as the captain, especially when I'd been given a secret mission to perform.

CHAPTER
THIRTY
ONE

WHEN YOU HAVE NO FRIENDS, MONEY, OR INTERNET, IT'S AN EASY CHOICE TO attend an Orthodox festival, even on a gloomy day after a rare rainstorm. I asked Andy to join me, but he had plans with Natasha to go to the movies.

Most Eastern European festivals, especially Romanian, were elaborate deals, with food vendors in little log cabin–type buildings, children dancing, and bands playing lively music. It surprised me to see that this one was more religious and less festive. The vendors were subdued, and there was no music of any type. In fact, the only items that I found universally appealing to purchase were intricate, hand-embroidered, Bulgarian red napkins that I thought my mother-in-law would appreciate.

Once I decided how many napkins I wanted, I carefully counted out the money in my purse, hoping I would have the correct amount. Just as I finished, a young Bulgarian—most likely a college student, given his casual attire—tapped me on my shoulder, causing me to jump a foot high. Frank's comments had unnerved me.

"I'm sorry to bother you," he said haltingly, "but I've been asked to give you a message from someone. I think she doesn't speak English."

"Oh, thanks. What is it?" I smiled broadly, happy to have a live human being talking to me.

"It's totally weird, but here it is," he said, shifting from one foot to the other. "She said … I think this is it, exactly … 'I've seen the future and the damage your questions can cause.' Then she said something like, 'You should go home.' I think that is right." With that, he lifted his hands and looked at the sky, as if to receive absolution for delivering the message and wondering why he, of all people, was chosen for this bizarre middleman role.

"Who … who told you that?" I asked, turning on my heels quickly to look around me.

Before the student could respond, I recognized the culprit, standing in the shadows several hundred feet away. *It's the crazy psychic.*

"Never mind," I said.

There—in her long skirt and heavy shoes; her unkempt hair now covered in a scarf that was tied in a large knot under her chin; and eyes boring into me from a distance—was my nemesis from Rupite. Once she knew that I had seen her, she turned and ambled out of sight in between two buildings.

"That's all she said?" I asked as I turned back to the boy, who was by then pointing toward her.

"Yes, that's it," he said, almost compassionately. He could tell I was very disturbed. "Please don't worry. She looks a little insane to me. I didn't want to tell you, but she insisted so I thought you might know her."

"Thanks," I said. There was nothing else to say. I watched as he fitted his earbuds back in and began moving to whatever rhythm was being injected into his head. At least he was happy. I left the not-so-festive festival in a not-so-happy mood and began a long walk back to the apartment. There was a lot to think about.

What was up with the woman? How had I made her that mad?

I was aggravated even more to see the door to the underground garage was open when I arrived at home, meaning someone forgot to hit the button to close it. I knew it was faster to go to the elevator through the garage and shut it, so that is what I did.

However, as soon as I descended a few feet on the downward-sloped garage driveway, I realized why the door was open—a barrel of oily substance near the entrance had been tipped over and spilled down to the bottom level. By then, it was too late to retreat. I had stepped into it with both feet. Immediately, I lost my balance, fell, and slid to the bottom, legs curled up under me and head on the ground when I landed.

It was only when I hit the floor that I heard the sound behind me of the garage door beginning to close. Startled, I turned my head to look back. There, illuminated in the sunlight outside the garage door, was the psychic. She was once again pointing and shaking her arms back and forth at me. When she knew she had my complete attention, she erupted.

"*Go home! Go home!*" she yelled in English, along with a slew of Bulgarian words I didn't understand, all the while pumping her clenched right fist, as the automatic door eerily closed on the silhouette of her enraged body.

I tried to stand up, but my feet and clothes were coated in a thick, tarry substance, and a sickening smell began to fill my nostrils. Not only was I in the dark garage, unable to locate a light switch, but my eyes watered and my stomach churned. I knew the smell—it was a mixture of used oil and other toxins that a maintenance company once applied on our wooden balcony to "protect" it. Unfortunately, the tenants all became seriously ill from the fumes, and the owners fired the company. They must have left the barrel in the garage, and this time it wasn't merely on our outside deck. I was literally bathed in it, and I knew I needed to get it off me soon.

When my eyes adjusted to the dark, I advanced on all fours and then stood and gingerly tiptoed past the edges of the spilled substance toward the only semblance of light in the garage—an illuminated elevator button. I repeatedly punched the button with my black fingers until it was obvious that no sound of movement was coming from the elevator shaft.

The elevator was being held in place above me. No matter how many times I jabbed at the button and willed it to move, nothing happened. Determined not to panic, I turned toward the faint red exit sign at the other end of the garage, where the stairwell was located.

Once I was past the oil slick, I discarded my shoes to avoid sliding more but discovered that I could open the heavy-steel, staircase fire door less than an inch—it had been jammed by someone's packing box on the other side, a not-so-uncommon occurrence in this little-used space. But this time I doubted it was an innocent mistake. I pulled off my oil-soaked sundress so I could gain traction against the door. I tried harder, but merely pushing the door with my hands and body did nothing. The only result for my effort was my feet sliding in the opposite direction as the oil dripped from the back of my head and onto the floor near my feet.

All the while, my eyes watered like a faucet from the fumes. Wiping them repeatedly with the inside of my camisole made every maneuver more difficult. Desperate for an escape, I summoned up enough energy to turn my upper body into the door like a linebacker and rammed it, sending sharp pains knifing through my shoulder. Nothing happened, so I tried it again—this time with my other shoulder—and for good measure, I lodged my feet against a concrete column for leverage.

This time, I felt the door shift a little. I grabbed the handle of a broom propped near the door and wedged it into the space. Once in place, I threw my entire body weight on the opposite end of the broomstick and pried open the door, just enough to squeeze through.

I stumbled and fell into the bottom space of the stairwell, almost landing on my knees, just as the automatic bright white lights of the hallway came on. It gave me hope for fresh air, but none seemed to come. Even in the stairs, the strange fumes surrounded me.

Still, I sighed with relief. The back of my head throbbed, as did much of my body, but I saw no blood dripping—just spots of black gook. My anger over the situation gave me the will to climb the flights of stairs to our apartment, using my hands on the handrailing to propel me.

Once at the apartment door, I leaned against the wall and fished my keys from my purse. The room was swimming. *There are so many keys. Which one?*

"Think, Jeni, think!" I said aloud, suddenly very tired.

It worked for the moment. My fumbling hands finally found the brass apartment key, and the door lock released.

But by then, although my mind was willing to sprint to safety, my energy source was depleted, and my coordination was too impaired. I staggered to the living room couch, just a few feet away, and fell facedown into the cushions.

"Jeni? Jeni?"

I wanted to respond to Zach—it was clear he was worried—but nothing came out of my mouth. His face, down at my level as he kneeled on the floor beside me, was fuzzy. Was it even him?

I shook my head to bring Zach into focus, and once I did, I took a deep breath of relief. I wanted to laugh because the kitten also was looking down at me from the couch, as if it was worried, but my laughter was too much of an effort.

"Did you just fall asleep here?" he asked tenderly, brushing my hair from my eyes and placing a sofa blanket to cover my body. When he removed his hand from my hair, he held it up and looked at it as if his was an alien hand; black goo dripped from it. Fortunately, most of the tarry substance remaining on my arms and my head were on a throw and not the upholstery.

I shook my head no and mouthed the word *sick*.

Suddenly alarmed, he stood up and ran to the kitchen. "Here," he said as he hurriedly opened a Coke. "Drink this—maybe it will help. What's wrong? I'm sorry I didn't get home sooner after you called."

"Huh?" I was confused.

"You called my office and asked me to come home."

I shook my head no once again, but truthfully, I couldn't think clearly.

The Coke worked some; the nausea was receding. I was able to say that I'd slipped in the garage but little else. I knew I needed fresh air, and I pointed in the direction of the balcony.

"How about a shower first?" he asked tenderly.

I had to agree. The smell was coming from me, not the living room. Zach helped me to the bathroom, where I took a long, hot shower, gradually recovering my strength.

He was anxious to hear my story when I finished in the bathroom, which I told him as best I could, including the psychic's appearance.

"I smelled that tar mixture when I got here and saw the black smears and droplets on the steps and hallway, but I figured they were at it again on the balconies," he said. "I'm going to call security right now and see what is going on."

In just a minute, he had his answer—someone had removed the top on the barrel of used oil and chemicals they had been storing at the street entrance to the garage, and it had fallen and poured down the slope into the garage. Maintenance was cleaning it up. They told Zach we couldn't use the garage for another few days.

"What about the crazy psychic lady? I bet she pushed the can over," I said. "But why would she do that? I haven't hurt her."

"I don't know what to think of the lady," he said, as he refilled my glass of Coke. "It would be awfully heavy for her to push. Maybe you imagined her due to the fall. But, first, do you want me to take you to the embassy doctor?"

I had walked enough to know I might be bruised but had suffered little other lasting damage. "No to doctor, and no to imagining," I said, vigorously shaking my head no. "I'm better now, but that reminds me—have you found out anything about her?"

He had asked a receptionist at the office from Rupite if she knew anything about the psychic. She said the woman's house was now vacant and boarded up.

"She thinks the woman was having trouble, and her daughter moved her to an apartment in Sofia," he said. "She's probably has dementia or is mentally ill, like the boy said. I didn't want to pry too much."

"It's possible," I said, not sure I bought the idea. "I know she followed me home from the festival, but how then did the barrel tip over?"

"A car accidentally hit it?" Zach proposed.

I hoped the garage cameras were working, although in the past, they always conveniently didn't work when a fender-bender occurred.

A few seconds later, Zach pulled the phone out of his pocket as if he'd remembered something important. "Are you sure you didn't call me at the office?" he asked again, looking at the messages on his phone.

"No, check my phone."

Zach pulled the cheap piece of electronics from my purse and handed it to me to operate. I opened it for him to see for himself.

A puzzled look emerged on his face. I definitely had not called. So who did call? "I guess it doesn't matter. I'm glad for whoever called so I could come home and check on you. Where's Andy?" he asked, eyes still riveted to the phone.

"With Natasha at a movie. I don't know when to expect them home."

"So, he wouldn't have called me?"

"No," I said, shaking my head slowly from side to side.

I could see the wheels turning in Zach's mind; he was worried. For now, there was not much else to say. Zach suggested I get more rest and that we could talk some more when I felt better.

It was a great idea. I crawled into bed and fell into a deep sleep for ten hours. *Maybe*, I thought, *the crazy psychic ought to market herself to insomniacs.*

CHAPTER
THIRTY
TWO

THE NEXT MORNING, I WOKE REFRESHED AND COHERENT, WONDERING IF the day before had even happened. The kitten had managed to crawl under my bedspread and was snuggled against my feet. It was comforting and enticed me to stay in bed, but I was ready to get up and out.

"You need to stay in the apartment and recover," Zach said as he brought me a cup of coffee and saw me beginning to stir. He was already dressed and putting on his tie. In the room next door, I could hear Andy shutting closet doors and preparing for his day. The sound of cars and voices below drifted up through the open windows. The world was moving, and I wanted to be a part of it.

"That's all I do already," I said, more peevish than I meant it to be. "No, that's really not true. But I feel fine now."

"If so, what plans do you have for today?" he asked, adjusting the knot in his tie in the mirror, apparently preparing for an important meeting.

"I'm supposed to be at a lunch meeting to finish up plans for the bazaar next week," I said.

"That sounds like something you need to do. Just call if you start feeling nauseated again. Stay in touch."

I knew he was worried that I might have a concussion, but I really did feel like a new person.

Andy met me downstairs a few minutes after Zach left. He grabbed a glass of orange juice and sat down beside me. "I talked to the office at home this morning, and they want me back before the end of the quarter. I still have a couple of weeks to hang around, but that means you'll be rid of me soon," he said, looking at me to see how I was taking the news. "I'm searching for plane tickets now but waiting to hear from Natasha to make sure we fly together."

"I'll miss you," I said. "I mean it. It can be boring here when I'm all alone."

"Based upon my time here, I find it hard to believe Sofia is ever boring."

He was right—it was as fun and exciting as it was intense and intriguing, even on the worst of weather days.

"That's probably true, but it doesn't mean I won't miss you." Then I changed the subject before I became maudlin about his departure. "How did your bosses like your report?"

"They liked it a lot. Maybe I can land a better position with them when I get back to the States," he said. "I still have more work to do on it, and I'll be busy for the next week or so. Let's plan to go to Shuman right before I leave."

"Perfect," I said, wondering if a long-distance job might work for me one day.

Before I could talk to Andy about the pros and cons of his employment, he already had his computer and files packed so he could work at the coffee shop. "I get the booth in the very back of the coffee shop," he said. "They never bother me. It's like home now."

I took my time getting ready for the meeting at noon, periodically watching the news. It only depressed me more. Although I had no idea why they were at odds, it was clear that our esteemed bazaar guests, the president and Lasarov Panov, were in a dispute over something political. It was the first time I had a glimpse of Lasarov's wife, Maya, on TV. At least, I thought it was her; she stood behind Lasarov and occasionally whispered into his ear.

She was as short and voluptuous as Rosa had described her, but on camera, she managed to possess a confident posture, with shoulders back and head held high, making her, with the help of four-inch heels, appear much taller than she probably was. I wasn't sure if it was her imperious attitude or the heavy gold-and-diamond necklace, but there was something about her that warned me—and anyone else outside of her inner circle—to give her a wide berth. How could her lack of warmth be felt even from a television screen?

"I think all the final arrangements have been made," Paka said, once we sat down at the table in the NGO. Once again, she was dressed to kill but this time with a small cluster-of-diamonds earring in each ear. "Here's the agenda for the day and where everyone will be located." She passed out a stack of papers. "Here's what you'll say, Jeni,"

Before she could finish her instructions to me, she was interrupted. "Where's Spain's booth?" asked the embassy representative from Spain, who had volunteered to help with setup. Dismay was written all over her face. She held up one of the papers that Paka had just given her—the carefully drawn floor plan.

"It's right here," Paka said, pointing near the Italian booth, oblivious to the trouble brewing.

"Well, that's not acceptable," the woman said. "Kenya and the US are near the front stage. Spain wants to be there as well."

"OK," Paka said, her soft voice slightly pained. No one wanted to get into an argument, so Paka swapped out Spain's location with that of Macedonia, which moved Spain closer to the stage.

But then, Paka noticed that change put Greece and Macedonia next to each other. We weren't sure that, even after Macedonia's name change, they weren't still were angry with one another, so Greece had to be moved and was swapped with Israel—but that meant the booths of Israel and Palestine were getting too close, so one of them had to be moved, and so it went on for two hours. Countries were moved around like chess pieces until we came up with a final floor plan that provided the required degree of diplomatic separation between feuding countries—at least the ones we knew about. Diplomatic social distancing.

My head was swimming by the time the meeting adjourned. That's why I was so unprepared for Natasha.

"Jeni," she said as she grabbed my arm before we entered the elevator, pulling me back toward her.

"Yes?" I responded as I watched the elevator doors close.

Her eyes began that Hollywood-teary thing.

"What's up?" I asked. "Do you want to talk here?"

"I need your help. I have a terrible problem. Andy is going back the US, and he wants me to join him. I … I lied and told him I already had a visa to go see friends, but I don't. I thought it would be easy to get one, but it's not."

She paused to wipe a large tear with her index finger, very careful not to touch her mascara. Only after she confirmed there were no smudges by looking in the mirror on the wall beside us did she speak further. "I know that you can request that I be moved to the head of the line to get a visa. Can you do that for me?" She waited for my response. It didn't come fast enough for her. "I know there are no guarantees or anything. I just need help to make the process move faster. So would you do it for me? *Please?*"

I tried to recall exactly what Frank had told me to say if this situation occurred. Natasha took it as reluctance to help on my part.

"You don't believe it, but I really love Andy!" That declaration both surprised me and also let me know how desperate she was. "I want to start a new life with him."

"I'm sorry. I didn't mean no. I was thinking about how to help you. I'll try to do it, but I need some information."

She reached over and gave me a quick hug in appreciation.

I retrieved a pen and paper from the bottom of my purse and asked her all the questions I could recall that Frank would want me to ask—her birth date and place, addresses, schooling, family business, etc.—and I scratched her responses on the paper I held against the foyer wall.

At first, she was so relieved that I'd said yes that she answered without hesitation, but after the fourth or fifth question, she abruptly stopped. "I'm confused," she said. "What do these questions have to do with the visa application?"

"I want to write a letter that endorses you like a job recommendation. The more I know, the better," I said and then began to put the pen and paper back in my purse. "But if you don't want—"

"No, no, it's great," she said, but I knew things had changed.

I pulled out the pen, and she continued to give me answers, but they were more carefully constructed, cagey responses.

After we were done, she hugged me goodbye and said again how happy she was that I would help her. "It means so much that you believe in Andy and me," she said.

At that moment, I realized that I probably could be a spy. Or maybe not a spy, but an undercover agent, like in the movies. I had done exactly what Frank wanted and hadn't been caught.

Like any great agent, I waited until I was home to text Frank. I wasn't sure whether it should be a secret or not, so I decided to try to talk in code.

Frank, I'm bored. Can we meet for coffee to talk about children?

His response was immediate.

Sure, see you in five minutes at the café. I'll bring pictures of mine.

In fact, his response was too immediate. That meant he was close to my location. And not only Frank was nearby. Once again, I saw Don Dorlyn, the new guy at the embassy, in his golf shirt and khakis, hanging outside my apartment, having a smoke. This time, the Audi was a block away.

I didn't have time to think about Don, so I shook off the sighting and wrote all Natasha's information on a clean sheet of white paper and put it in my purse.

Ten minutes later, I slid the neatly folded piece of white paper to Frank.

"That was faster than I thought," Frank said, discreetly pocketing it. "Great job."

"Now what?" I said, anxiously awaiting my new assignment.

"What do you mean? You texted me to come talk about children," he said. "I love children. I brought pictures."

"You're kidding, aren't you?" I said, cocking my head to the side in disbelief. "I thought we were a team."

"Right now, there's nothing else to discuss. You focus on your bazaar or festival or whatever it is, and I'll keep doing my job." He stood up to leave a tip on the table. Then he smiled and said, "Thanks."

"I'm beginning to hate you," I said, standing in order to emphasize how serious I was, although we both knew I didn't mean it.

"Then you'll have lots of company."

"Just like you may have lots of company, checking up on me," I retorted.

That got Frank's attention, fast. When I mentioned who I thought was stalking me, Frank seemed shocked at my news for the first time ever. In fact, when I showed him my phone picture from several weeks ago of Don lounging in his Audi in the sweltering heat outside Zach's and my apartment building, he was downright speechless. Who, if not Zach and me and perhaps Andy, was he watching?

"Oh, and he was there when I left, but I bet he's gone now," I said. "He isn't there full time. Just appears in the evening or at lunch or odd hours."

Frank mumbled something to himself before speaking to me. Then he looked once again at the picture. "I'm sure it has an innocent explanation. But good job on noticing it and not saying anything to him."

"Teamwork, right?" I stood up straight and held out my hand.

"Yeah, we're still a team."

I wasn't so sure Frank meant what he said because he accompanied the handshake with a shake of his head, but I felt relief that I hadn't been formally cut from the roster yet.

CHAPTER THIRTY THREE

It was a characteristically sunny day in Sofia for the NGO's international bazaar. I knew that meant we should expect a good turnout.

The cavernous warehouse had been transformed into a mini EPCOT Center. Each country's flag was displayed, in alphabetical order, at the entrance, lending pomp and pageantry to the event. Colorful banners flew from the rafters above, swaying under the breeze from the massive air conditioning ducts, as if to fan those below. Each country's team of volunteers was buzzing around, transforming plain white tables into works of art—a traveling exposition of music, costumes, and food. Enlarged glossy pictures and professional videos of stunning landscapes were carefully situated around the tables, each vying for the most attention.

The morning hours of the bazaar were deceptively peaceful. I even had the time to greet several ambassadors, including the US ambassador. He and his wife appeared for a few minutes to thank the volunteers at our red-white-and-blue table.

As the ambassador was leaving, a security officer pulled me to the side.

"The president of Bulgaria and his wife have arrived. What do you want me to do?" he asked.

"I'll introduce them, and they can say a few words to the audience," I said to the president's assistant. "While they are on stage, I'll thank the donors and volunteers. Then we have a small surprise."

Paka had arranged for the president's favorite performer to sing the Bulgarian national anthem.

At first, it all went according to plan.

The president's wife wore a prim and proper blue suit and matching heels, as if she was attending church. She wasn't worried in the least about the crowd, and she didn't want to sit in a crummy chair by an empty stage until I introduced her to the audience; she wanted to shop.

So I went shopping with the president's wife—sort of.

The first lady of Bulgaria walked around the great hall at a slow and dignified pace, from one booth to another, with a bevy of aides behind her. At each booth, she would smile and daintily pick up items that interested her, asking a question or two about the country. When she moved on, an aide would rush in and buy the items he assumed that she liked the best.

It wasn't what I wanted to be doing, but I soon realized that if no one else had come to the bazaar, this group alone would buy enough to make it all worthwhile. I took my place by the bodyguards and silently thanked Rosa for her salient advice of inviting the politicians.

Sadly, it was only a minute or two before I retracted that thank-you.

I heard the sound of the microphone on the stage being tested. Then it crackled, as if it was being moved. Then it dawned on me: someone was getting ready to speak, and it wasn't someone with AIC.

I looked down at my watch. I began to hyperventilate. I had made a terrible mistake. It was well after noon, and I should have been up there, starting the program, at least fifteen minutes earlier. I could see people seated and waiting expectantly, wondering where I was.

Now, as punishment for my inattention, there was Maya, bigger than life, waving to the crowd like a beauty queen, with spotlights illuminating the shine of her ink-black hair. There was no way someone as politically ambitious as she was would miss a golden opportunity to woo an audience composed of voters on both ends of the political spectrum.

Immediately, I left the shopping line and ran across the room, jumping over small obstacles as if I were an airline passenger about to miss a flight. I made it to the front of the stage, just as Maya started to talk.

Quiet descended upon the audience the moment her voice boomed across the metal building. She almost didn't need a microphone. The president's entourage turned toward the stage in disbelief. The main assistant glared at me as if I were some kind of traitor. My volunteers shook their heads at each other in confusion and wondered why I wasn't on stage, doing my job.

The crowd, which merely came to shop, eat, and hear some music, suddenly found themselves witnesses to something unexpected and exciting— it looked like the president was going to be upstaged by the wife of his nemesis.

"*Hello, everyone!*" Maya exclaimed, like a ringmaster in a circus. Then she leaned her ample bosom forward and cupped her hand around her ear for them to respond *hello* to her. Incredibly, everyone did as she instructed.

"I would like to thank AIC for inviting me as a very special guest to this event today and to thank all the wonderful volunteers for all they have done to make this truly important day a success." She spoke in perfect English and swung her arms out like an opera singer, as if to embrace everyone. Then, like a great performer, she hesitated for a second, waiting for the applause to begin. And it did, once again from all across the room.

I knew the president's wife couldn't understand a word Maya said.

As if Maya could read my mind, once the applause died down, she translated into Bulgarian what she had said, to be sure the president's wife and the majority of the crowd could fully understand it. I could see the president's wife frown as she assessed the positive reception that Maya was receiving from the audience.

"Do something!" the assistant hissed in my ear.

Until that moment, I had been immobilized, mesmerized by Maya's presence. The president's assistant's sharp words sent the fear of some unknown political repercussion into my consciousness and caused me to leap onto the stage, surprising even me with my sudden dexterity. I popped up erect, like a jack-in-the-box, my face right next to Maya's.

Then, as smoothly as possible, I held my hand out for her to give me the microphone.

She didn't.

I sweetly reached over to take it from her, but she still wouldn't let go. She had the audience in her hand and wasn't going to willingly walk away.

It was obvious to me that the crowd below us had to know something was wrong, but I continued to pull on the microphone, even when I heard someone ask, "Why's that American woman being so rude?" I still didn't stop.

Maya smiled like a broadcast news anchor throughout the tug-of-war. She looked in total control, even using her free hand to wave to the audience. When Maya began to speak again, it enraged me further. I decided to end the matter for good.

I raised my voice as loudly as I could in order to drown her out and took over my rightful role as master of ceremonies. "Thank you so much for your kind words, Maya," I said, bending my face down awkwardly to the level of the microphone. "We are glad you were able to speak. Now, if you would be so kind as to stay, I have a special seat right there in the front row for you to enjoy the event. Everyone, give Maya another round of applause for helping me out."

The polite audience responded with applause while I hissed at Maya to leave the stage. "*Now!*" I added.

Either because of the applause from the president's entourage or my demand for her to sit down, Maya was caught off guard. For a moment, she released her grip on the microphone, and when she did, I pulled it away from her.

Unfortunately, my snatching of the microphone caused her to lose her balance, and she begin to fall backward. Horrified, I turned to help steady her, but instead, I caught my ankle in the microphone cord. Before I knew what was happening, it had constricted around my leg like a viper. When I attempted to move—with one foot already off the ground in forward momentum; the other restrained—it meant only one thing could happen. I fell to the ground.

In the end, it was Maya who was left upright, her smile intact, and I was on the floor, clinging to the now-inoperable microphone and hoping I could disappear. Everyone had rushed to stop Maya's fall, leaving no one to witness mine, except the crowd right below and the photographers, who snapped a treasure trove of photographs of me on the stage floor.

It was while I was lying on the floor, face toward the audience, that I saw, for the first time, both Frank and Don, standing a short distance away from the stage but far from each other. I turned my head back to the stage and then saw the psychic, back near the curtains, once again making a threatening gesture toward me. It is amazing the clarity of mind that you have in moments of humiliation. Then, I focused on Leo, not terribly far behind the two men. Why would Leo be there? Perhaps I had hit my head on the way down. I shut my eyes tightly, and when I opened them, they all were gone.

The chaos created by wannabe medics and heroes who were soon fawning over me was too much for Maya. She left the bazaar by the front door. There was also no more need to worry about the president or his wife. By the time I was standing again and had disengaged myself from the black cord, they were exiting the side door. I felt sure the other invited politicians were not foolish enough to risk being on stage with me either.

Before I could think of anything to say to the stunned crowd, some wise soul ordered the national anthem to be played, signifying the end of the program. I slunk away, wondering what in the world I had done, while the audience proudly stood and sang their country's song.

Paka was there for me at the stage exit with an amused smile on her face. She told me not to worry about the fall, and she was glad I wasn't hurt.

"If anything, it took the spotlight away from the politicians. I bet your fall will be the picture on the front page of the newspaper tomorrow," she said, smiling. "We'll get even more publicity and money."

"Ha-ha," I said, groaning with the realization that she was right.

"I also have a message from the president's assistant," she said. "He wanted me to tell you thank you."

I wasn't sure he really meant it.

Then, I decided to look around for signs of Frank, Don, Leo, or the psychic. There were no signs, and I wondered why any of the four actually would be there. It wasn't their cup of tea. It must have been a knock on the head that made me see things.

Behind every fortune there is a crime.

✗

—Honoré de Balzac

CHAPTER THIRTY FOUR

It turned out the president's assistant did love me.

The first video clip on the news the next day came from the president's favorite TV channel. In a remarkable feat of splicing and dicing, the editing department managed to produce a tape that showed Maya pushing the host—me—down to the ground at the charitable event, outraging the early-morning anchors and viewers.

I forced myself to turn on the opposition party's TV channel. Their editing department took a less subtle and probably more accurate approach—they continuously replayed one or two seconds of me grabbing for the microphone and Maya tumbling backward with fear on her face. It wasn't clear that she never actually fell, and they never showed my fall, but it was another masterful work of art, meant to enrage the viewers.

"Quit watching it, Jeni," Zach said as he came into the room. He handed me a chocolate croissant and kissed me on the cheek.

"Oh, I'm so mortified," I said. "I'll never go out in public again."

"Just wear a hat and dark sunglasses," he joked, not realizing I had already planned to do just that. "Didn't the bazaar make quite a bit of money?"

"Yes. Maybe enough to keep our budget for the rest of the year."

"Then don't worry. Do a press release, and thank the president and his wife for attending the bazaar. Mention the other politicians and ambassadors who came, and then spend the rest of the article talking about how much money you raised and how wonderful AIC is. They'll move on to another story in a matter of hours."

"I'm not so sure," I said, still stinging from embarrassment. "The good news is that I can quit the AIC now. They'll be thrilled."

Plus, as hard as it was to believe, I had less than a month left in Sofia. Three months had flown by.

After Zach left, I clicked on the news on the internet, resigning myself to finally looking at all the photographs that had been taken the day before.

Although there were dozens of photographs, it was a tremendous relief to see that in each picture, my face was turned away from the cameras and toward Maya. In fact, I was indistinguishable. I looked again at the news videos and saw they were the same. The cameras were all primarily focused on Maya, and I was a blurry afterthought.

Realizing I would no longer would be mobbed outside the apartment, I finally laughed at the pictures of me falling to the floor, wrapped in cords like I had been hog-tied.

The horror of the previous day was beginning to subside. I took a sip of coffee and sat back in my chair, casually scrolling through the photographs.

Suddenly, I sat up straight and moved closer to the screen. When I'd been on stage earlier that morning, the psychic—or her evil twin—could be seen standing in the rear right corner of the stage, half in and half out of the drawn curtains. Her face was partially obstructed, but from what I could see, her deep-set eyes were focused entirely on me. *So I had seen her.*

There was a connection somewhere, but this time I wasn't going to rush to call Frank or Zach. I was going to think and try to figure it out myself.

I pulled out my chart and studied it. The women at the top of the chart— the female suspects of some unknown crime—were Natasha, Zlata, and the psychic. I added Maya's name because she was Lasarov's wife—and who knew what he was involved in?

Then, there were the men: Zlata's husband, Igor; the politician Volkov, aka the Wolf; and Maya's husband, Lasarov Panov. Lasarov's sole connection was that he was Igor and Volkov's boss and had told Leo to stay away from me. For good measure, I added the mysterious man at the psychic's house, only because Frank had shown a passing interest in him.

I realized, a short time later when I walked past the TV, that I had forgotten to add one of the players—the bank manager who had been arrested. However, it turned out that I didn't need to. The breaking news on TV announced that the bank manager supposedly had killed himself after he was arrested; his body was discovered when he failed to show up for a hearing on his case.

Suddenly, it was if the all the energy in my body left me. I sat on the couch and stared at the TV as it repeated the news over and over again. There was no doubt—it was the Vorbank branch manager who was now dead. I could rationalize one banker dying but two—along with missing money and missing treasurers and extravagant homes in Cyprus? Maybe I should have ignored my lost savings account. Maybe the feeling that I got from the young man in Veliko Tarnovo was right—this was way bigger than me and the AIC, and I could be in danger without knowing it.

I called Zach, fingers shaking as I punched the keys. "Zach," I said, "can we get together for lunch? Now?"

"Sure. Is something wrong?"

"Maybe. I don't know. We'll talk about it."

We agreed to meet at a local restaurant at noon.

Incredibly, by noon, the bank manager's death was no longer huge news. I doubted they understood the connection with Oleg, given the passage of several weeks. And Oleg had been hit by a car anyway. Those deaths made something click in my mind, and it returned to the dead body in the Black Sea. Why no more news on him?

"For sure," I told Zach at lunch, "it doesn't speak well for Vorbank's HR Department that employees are dropping like flies."

"I heard about his death this morning," Zach said about the manager. "He's rumored to have been skimming the accounts. That's not unusual, even in the US, so he might have committed suicide to avoid shame and a jail sentence."

"It makes sense that he was the one who embezzled my money. Who else would it be? Maybe Oleg? But even if he had, I doubt very seriously he would have killed himself over my tiny account."

Then I remembered the attempt to take my money from the savings account at home. If the information was true, and he had killed himself immediately after the arrest, he would not have been the one to try to take the funds from my bank account. He was already dead when my bank had called from the States.

I reminded Zach of the recent news about all the mysterious deaths linked to Vladimir Putin that we had read about recently. In one story, four men, critics of the Russian leader, had committed suicide. They were linked to a Moscow land-transaction business. That seemed like a lot of coincidental suicides to us, but no charges were ever brought. It creeped me out.

"No one seems to just have a heart attack or stroke in Eastern Europe," I said. "It's either a gory death or violent suicide."

"And a message to those who cross paths with the powerful and corrupt," Zach added.

We talked it out until we decided that given the bank manager's death and Oleg's death, we might never know the truth about my account, even though I told Zach I would never give up trying to find Zlata and the AIC money. He just rolled his eyes, knowing that was all too true.

Our food arrived at that point—perfectly prepared chicken, smothered in mushroom gravy, with homemade fries. A basket of bread and small salads rounded out the warm dinner.

"Dietetic." I laughed. "Bon appétit!"

As we finished the meal, I returned to the other topic on my mind and pulled out a copy of the picture from the morning's news.

"Very flattering," Zach said with a laugh, seeing me wrapped in cords and lying on the floor.

"My position, as well as yours, is that the woman on the floor isn't me. It's someone else who looks like me and who wore a similar dress," I said. "No one can see my face, so how would they know the difference?"

"Because you're a bad liar."

"I'm getting better," I retorted. "Anyway, I brought them to show you that the psychic from Rupite was there on the stage." I pointed out her shadowy figure in the curtains. "This time, though, she never said a word, nor did she approach me."

Zach studied it. We both agreed that if it was her, she looked very disheveled and out of place. Her random appearance on stage was bizarre. Maybe she did have dementia. For now, it seemed to be another unsolved mystery.

"Have you heard anything about Natasha's visa application?" I asked.

"She's scheduled for her interview in two days," he said. "I hope, for Andy's sake, she's legit."

His phone beeped, and he checked his message. Turning back to me, he said, "Good news. I have plans for you this afternoon. Frank wants you to meet him at his office"

"Really?" I said. "Now why would I want to do that?"

"Because, Jeni," Zach said, looking squarely into my eyes until I averted them, "you can't help yourself. You're too curious and can't wait to hear what Frank has to say. I know you, and you're still a bad liar."

He was right.

"I need a favor," Frank said when I entered his small cubicle, full of files and loose paperwork, much of it with his indecipherable handwriting. I was surprised that he had no real office and no support staff.

"Sure, a favor. What is it?" I asked. There was no *hello* or *how are you doing?*

"If you don't mind, I need you to go to the Vorbank and get some information for me."

"Why me?"

"They know you," he said, "and I don't want to act like this is a big deal—an American in a suit wanting information."

I focused my attention on Frank's cluttered desk and didn't say anything else while I considered the request. I wondered how he could find anything in that mess. I thought about saying no, but I waited too long. My hesitation to answer was yes to him, and he began to explain what I should do.

"Go tomorrow and speak to the girl at the front desk—the new account manager," he said, keeping his eyes on me while he spoke. "Ask her if there are any updates on your account and the AIC account. See if anyone else has been asking questions about either account. Just like you normally do. Ask her anything you can think of. Got that?"

"That's simple enough," I said, although I felt sure he wasn't really interested in my money.

"That's not all. I want you to get brochures of all the products they offer and try to find out who else they do business with—like other companies, LLCs, etc."

"I thought they were a branch bank," I said. I was confused.

"It's complicated. They're a stand-alone bank with some big investors. Get her to talk about them…if you can—who owns what. Just chat."

"OK. I'll try …" My voice trailed off with uncertainty about the second task, undermining my usual confidence.

"One last thing—here's a taping device to put in your pocket. I want you to turn it on while you are there." He slipped me a small silver listening device, about the size of a large pearl earring. Then he showed me how to turn it on.

Now I really was anxious—not only about the fact that Zach might not know that Frank was wiring me up but about potentially losing the unquestionably expensive toy.

"Don't try to take notes," Frank said. "Also, go after two in the afternoon. It's very slow then, and we can tell that she gets bored. She's likely to talk longer."

"Why do you care about Vorbank? Why the taping?"

"Just closing up some loose ends on something," he said. "Probably nothing there. The taping is for my files, to show what you did. It's easy documentation without more paperwork." With that, he pointed to a particularly large pile on his desk. "I hate to type."

It sounded like an awfully sketchy explanation, and I briefly considered telling Frank no, but once again, my curiosity got the better of me. There was zero chance I wouldn't go to the bank. Suddenly, Agent Jeni was back in business.

CHAPTER
THIRTY
FIVE

It was raining the next morning, so I stayed in bed and outlined my questions for that afternoon. The kitten once again climbed under the covers and nestled at my feet, happy I was in bed and not at the desk.

I listed the topics to be covered, thought up coherent questions, and then made up mnemonic rhymes—those little cues to help me remember key words—so that I wouldn't forget anything, just as if I were taking a test.

I took it as a good omen that the rain stopped when it was time to leave. I dressed in my nicest casual clothes and walking shoes. My plan was to act as if I had happened to walk by the bank and just dropped in.

Like most days, I waved to the guard outside the bank—a familiar face every time I walked down my street. Once he saw me, he smiled as I pretended to hesitate, thinking about the direction I was going to take. I used the momentary stop to turn on the device in my pocket. Then, as I saw Frank do, I tapped on my head as if I'd had a sudden random thought, and I turned back to walk inside the bank. The guard continued to smile.

I was not expecting the same account manager that Rosa and I met to still be working at the bank. In fact, given the life expectancy rate of the bank employees, I would have given her chance of survival a very low probability.

But there she was—happy to see me and happier to have someone relieve the boredom of the afternoon. I couldn't blame her. The sun was at that late-afternoon angle where it streamed through the windows across her desk. It would make anyone want to curl up on a sofa and take a nap.

"I guess you found out about Oleg," she said, pushing aside her work.

"Yes," I nodded sadly. "I was sorry to hear about it."

"The bank took up a collection and gave it to his mother, although I'm not sure it helped too much. She was very upset."

"I'm sure it did," I said. "I was walking by the bank today and hoped you might be here. Have you learned anything about my accounts?"

"Not really," she said and sighed. "My best guess is that the bank manager took it."

"Oh well," I said, slipping into the chair opposite her at the desk. I brought up the lost charity's money.

"Yes, someone mentioned it to me in the breakroom," she said. "The bank manager must have taken it as well."

"You know, another person asked about that money yesterday," she said, as if she could read my mind.

"Oh," I said. "What was her name?"

"No," she said. "This was a man, not a woman." She could tell I was surprised by the answer. "Yes," she said. She lowered her voice to add, "It was a politician on the board of directors!"

"Who?" I asked.

"Mr. Volkov. He wanted all the AIC bank records—the originals."

"Did he get them?" I asked. My heart began to beat harder at this disclosure.

"Yes, but not from me. He got the bank president's permission to see them, and he took them to his office. I haven't gotten them back yet."

"So Mr. Volkov is on the board and has the AIC financial statements?" I said, loud enough for my voice to be heard on the recorder.

"Yes," she replied.

"Who's the bank president" I asked, leading nicely into the whole bank-hierarchy questions.

She told me that the president was a Russian who currently lived in Amsterdam, where he operated a string of LLCs involved in banking and finance. I feigned ignorance on how that worked so she explained that this bank was owned by an LLC, and it was connected to other LLCs based in Moscow. The owners sounded as if they were all Russian. It made sense. It was a Russian bank. But it made me wonder about Natasha and her "business" in Amsterdam.

"Is this the only Vorbank in Sofia?" I asked.

"Yes, it is the only branch in Bulgaria." She said that Vorbank operated in other countries, but that this branch operated independently and, in general, only reported its investment earnings to the main office. In fact, she said the officers or owners had a closer relationship with an LLC that was registered in the Netherlands than with Moscow.

Once again, I thought, *Amsterdam*.

"I know that because they get a lot of mail from there," she said, pointing to an in-box on her desk. "It's part of my job to distribute mail." Then she leaned over and said she hated that part of the job, and she was glad she was leaving the next day for a new position in London.

"Is there a Vorbank office in London?"

"No," she said, "my new job is with a large financial corporation. But the bank does have some connection to an LLC in the US—I think in Virginia, near Washington, DC, which I would *love* to visit—plus an LLC in Cyprus. Then again, who doesn't have an LLC in Cyprus?" She smiled brightly. "The bank president receives express mail weekly from both places."

I wasn't sure what to make of that information and had no ready follow-up questions. I could surmise wrongdoings about Amsterdam, Cyprus, and Russia but the US?

There was a lull in the conversation, so I returned the subject to my lost account. She was willing to help with anything I needed and began handing me internal bank memos with routing numbers that might help find the lost money. She even went so far as to print off some obviously confidential data about the bank that might come in handy for Frank and his team.

I could tell she wasn't worried about being fired. Talk about fireable offenses in an American bank. I wondered for a second if I would be in trouble for taking the data but then concluded that a bank customer couldn't be at fault.

"It must be interesting working here—at least some of the time," I said, finally committed to exploiting what I presumed was her naivety. Now was the time to fish for more interesting stuff.

"It is," she said. "You can't believe the people I see."

"Like who?" I asked, leaning in as if to receive juicy gossip.

She rattled off the names of several local celebrities and famous people.

I then held out my cell phone and scrolled through pictures of Natasha from the AIC bazaar. "This is a friend of mine—she's a well-known Russian model. Have you met her?"

"She looks familiar, but that other woman in the picture—she comes in here a lot." She leaned over the desk to get a better view of my phone. She pointed to the picture of Maya that I had screenshot from the news.

"Oh," I said. This was unexpected news. "Does she bank here?"

"She makes large deposits once a week," she said, "but I don't help her. She speaks Bulgarian and Russian, and she always goes to the same Bulgarian teller who is fluent in Russian. Sometimes, I give her a package of mail that's addressed to her from Dulles, Virginia. I guess she has a business here or there."

"She's not very friendly, is she?" I said.

"Not at all!"

I went for broke and also showed her the picture of Zlata, hoping she knew the missing treasurer. She said that they hadn't met. I told her that it was OK—Zlata had left Sofia before she began to work for the bank.

"I'm curious now. How does this bank make money in Sofia if it's only at this location and doesn't have a lot of clients?"

She shrugged her shoulders. "I'm not sure. They have a few wealthy Russian and Ukrainian clients who make large deposits, but, like I said, I don't usually help them. They all go to tellers who speak Russian. Most of the time, I sit here doing nothing."

"Not a lot of English-speaking clients?"

"No," she said. "I hate it because it means I don't make much money or practice my English. I only get a bonus for new clients."

"That's a shame," I said.

"The money the branch makes goes to Moscow, and that's all connected to the government, somehow or another. I think they must make money off the large deposits that are made, even though there are only a few of them. But they make it somehow or another because last month, the bank president bought a new black Mercedes with tinted windows. He drove here from Amsterdam to show it off at the board meeting."

Once on the topic of men, she became even more chatty. The pretty young account manager told me the recently arrested and now-deceased bank manager was slimy and sexist, and it was hard for her to feel bad for him. "I wouldn't think he'd have the guts to kill himself, but he and that woman in the picture—"

"Maya?" I asked.

"Yes—he and Maya had a big fight near my desk a week or so ago. She called him a thief and said she was going to get even. It was ugly, but she didn't threaten to kill him. I think that maybe he killed himself because he was scared of her; he was a coward."

"Did he take her money?" I asked.

"I don't think so," she said. "She's not on the list of known accounts that disappeared." Then she added, "Maybe it's under another name. Oh, you know what? I need to give you that list as well."

Now I was confused. *That can't be legal. Bank information is one thing, but giving me other customers' personal data ...* I wondered if she was setting me up and decided it was time to leave.

Until then, I hadn't known that other customer accounts had disappeared; I hadn't known about the bank manager's fight with Maya *or* about the president from Amsterdam and his new car *or* all kinds of other disturbing things that she was discussing. Surely law enforcement had to know something. I kept wondering how this bank was even in operation.

"No, that's OK," I said. "Maybe I'll come back tomorrow. I need to head out now." I stood to leave, stuffing the papers in my purse.

"Go ahead and take it. Here it is." And, as if reading my mind, she added, "Don't worry. It's OK. The names should already be in a police report." Then she shoved the list into my hands and threw in some more brochures that I didn't already have.

Despite my misgivings, I took them, my purse overflowing.

She smiled and reclined in her chair. "I'm so glad you stopped by the bank to see me before I left town! What a coincidence."

I stood there with my mouth open, speechless, and I could have sworn that she winked.

"The new person will help you open another account when you decide you're ready!" she almost shouted, as I turned and walked out the revolving glass door.

CHAPTER
THIRTY
SIX

My phone beeped with a text as soon as I exited the bank.

How about coffee at your favorite place? Frank

Despite my misgivings at the bank, I was in a good mood after I left. I wasn't sure what Frank wanted, but I had a lot of information. In fact, I was so optimistic that he would be pleased that I began singing a song that was playing outside a restaurant I passed, almost twirling around with satisfaction.

Frank was waiting for me outside the restaurant when I arrived a few minutes later, ready to open the door for me. As I walked inside, he whispered into my ear that I was to follow his instructions because someone from the bank just walked by, and he didn't want to flaunt their records—not that he had anything to hide, he told me, but it might unnecessarily alarm her. I looked around, and sure enough, a woman wearing a shirt with the bank logo was leaving with some pastries. I recognized her as one of the tellers.

"Thanks for coming," he said as we sat at the table. Then he pulled out a book from a plastic bag, the type used at grocery stores. "I wanted to give you a book on sailing for Zach. I won't be in the embassy for several days. I told him that I would lend it to him, and I am running out of time. He asked me to drop it off with you." It was lame but as good as any other segue for the next event. "Do you have anywhere to put it? I hate to be rude, but your purse seems to be overflowing with trash. Here—if you want to, put the trash in this bag. I'll throw it away for you."

I did as instructed, wadding up the papers and brochures from the bank, along with other old receipts and envelopes. I am sure I looked suspicious, but I felt like an undercover agent.

There was one last hand-over. It only made sense that Frank would spill his coffee in my direction and lean in toward me to clean it up before speaking his final words.

"Jeni, pass me the recorder," he said, barely audible.

My face turned bright red as I remembered I'd forgotten to turn it off after I left the bank. Frank and the whole world would hear me singing to myself—not only off-key but not even knowing the right words. I slipped it into his hand, and he put it into his jacket pocket. At least I hadn't lost it.

We talked about his hometown in Virginia for a while, and I asked if he lived near Dulles. He didn't. By then, our coffee had grown cold, and Frank was ready to leave. He seemed happy with my assistance but gave no indication of why he wanted my pile of brochures and answers to rather basic questions.

Despite the day's success, many things about the day nagged at me. For one, the young woman at the bank was obviously expecting me.

"Zach," I said over my cell phone when Frank was out of reach, "we need to go to dinner tonight."

I was dressed up with purse in hand when Zach arrived home. We went straight to our favorite local restaurant, with dim lights, red upholstered chairs, and the right mix of American and Bulgarian music.

"Zach, I'm worried that I did something wrong," I said. Then I proceeded to outline the entire day's events. "Frank does work for the US government, doesn't he? I didn't do anything wrong, did I?" I was apprehensive about what Zach's answer might be. "I didn't get anything illegal. Actually, Frank didn't even ask for most of what I got. Plus, I don't understand why he suddenly cares about my bank. It's weird."

"First answer—yes, he works for our government," Zach said, "but not with me on my project. I only deal with getting countries to cooperate over law enforcement."

"So?" I asked. "Why did he involve me?"

Zach looked at me and put his hand over mine. "Jeni, I'm sorry. Frank told me what he needed and asked if you would do it. You're the only person we know who banks at Vorbank, and it was an easy enough task for you to ask questions, given you're a lawyer." He shrugged his shoulders sheepishly. "It's my fault. I told him you probably would enjoy it and might even learn more about your account. Sometimes, the ex-pats hate to bother the Bulgarians in the office with small jobs that anyone could do, and they often help each other." Then he squeezed my hand in comfort. "Now I can see that you are worried, but please don't worry. It won't happen again."

"It's *over*?" I almost choked on my drink.

"Yes," he said. "I'll let him know. No more worries."

Well, that wasn't what I wanted to hear. This didn't go well. I wanted to either expose Frank as an international criminal *or* become a full-time undercover agent with Frank—nothing in between. I definitely didn't want to go home and sit out the excitement, if there was some to be had.

Before I could protest the end of my work as a volunteer agent, Zach told me that Frank was leaving Sofia before us.

"Really?" I said.

"He just heard—he's expecting his first grandchild. He's decided to go home as fast as possible. His case is ready to be closed."

"That's great news," I said, even though I didn't mean it. It looked like my espionage gig was up. "But what's his case? What's he doing?"

Zach gave me one of those patronizing looks that he gives when I ask a question that I know he can't answer.

"I know, I know. You can't tell me anything," I said, mimicking his facial expression and serious voice. Then I smiled at our favorite waitress as she poured me a glass of wine. "So, change of subject—have they told you exactly when we are leaving?" This was always the hardest part—the excitement of new places tinged with sad departures.

"Maybe sooner than we first planned. We've already been here over three months, and I'm very close to getting all the approvals we need on the agreements," he said. "So probably not long after Andy leaves. Three weeks or so. Why?"

"Can you take a few days off before going back to work in Bucharest?"

"I should be able to take a week off," he said. "Plan something, if you want."

"Thanks," I said. "I'll start working on it. Try to get me the exact dates."

As Zach instructed, I spent the next morning planning a vacation so he could firm up the dates with his office. My first call was practical—to the States to find out the balance in my bank account from Uncle Bob's bequest and some travel reimbursements I had just received. The good news was that it was still there.

$3,532

Um, I thought, *not a lot of money left.* There would be no honeymoon trip to Auckland or Burma or even Disneyland. But it would buy us a very nice trip to somewhere in Europe, with a little shopping along the way.

The travel agency near our house was almost identical to those found in the States, stuck in the middle of a strip mall of offices. I scoured the large posters plastered on the front window, with enticing packages to places like Greece, Istanbul, Italy, and other exotic locations.

A Danube cruise would be nice, but I lived in Romania. I had been over, around, and alongside the river from one side to the other, through the legendary Iron Gates separating Serbia and Romania, to its vineyard-laden banks in Germany. Plus, it was at the upper end of my budget.

Then I saw it—the perfect one-week trip for Zach and me. We would rent a barge in Ireland and navigate the locks, stopping in small villages, if and when we wanted. Weather would be cooler; the price was perfect; and it was something no one else we knew had ever done. I rushed inside the office. I told the agent that I wanted to book a trip away for three weeks, after Zach finished in Sofia and before we returned to Bucharest.

"I'm sorry, but all the barges are rented well in advance," said an agent with a sign on her desk denoting she spoke English.

I was crushed.

"What, then, would you recommend?" I asked. "Something nice for a second honeymoon—but not where it's too hot." Then I reluctantly added, "I have about $3,000."

"Paris?" she suggested.

"Paris can be hot at this time of the year," I responded.

"That's true." Then she sat back in her chair and perused the walls of her office, seeking inspiration. "I'm at a loss for something special on such short notice in high season," she said.

"I was afraid of that."

"OK, this is what I recommend," she finally said. "You've waited too long to get a good deal on a dream vacation. I think you need to wait for someone to cancel a trip because they are sick or something else occurred that prevents them from traveling. I know it sounds awful, but it always happens, and when it does, I can call you and put you in their place within your budget."

"What if nothing comes up?" I said.

"Then it will be Paris," she said. "Don't be dismayed. I'll be able to do something really nice in the most romantic city in the world on that budget."

I sure hoped so. I craved a vacation alone with Zach—and the sooner the better.

CHAPTER
THIRTY
SEVEN

WHILE I WAS STILL WITH THE TRAVEL AGENT, PAKA SENT ME A TEXT AND asked if I could meet her for coffee and go over the new financial data for the AIC. We agreed to meet at the Hilton at nine the next morning.

She was the first to arrive and was sitting at a table in the corner, with a stack of file folders in front of her.

"Jeni," she said, beaming with pleasure. "I have great news. We made a little over $40,000 from the bazaar, when you add in the sponsorships and the donations. It definitely will fund us through the end of the year if we're careful."

It was incredibly good news. Now that we had a clearer picture of the charity's financial situation, we went through the stack of requests for funds, prioritizing the ones we could help. I wished more members had been there to help.

I knew it would be hard for Paka to handle everything once I left, especially when her only helper was a new Italian member who was not yet immersed in the details of the operations. But Paka had been with AIC for much longer than me—over a year—and she was better qualified than me for my role.

"I promised Zach I would only stay through the bazaar," I said. "After all, we will be leaving in a few weeks." I had also promised Rosa, but it was unlikely she would ever know I did quit.

Paka stared at me for a moment with her large brown eyes wide open, until she took a breath and relaxed, also confident she could replace me. "Thanks so much for all you did," she said. "It has been a nice three months."

"Anymore feedback about the Maya incident?" I asked.

"No, I think everyone felt sorry for you and AIC, not the president and his wife or Maya," she said. "Bulgarians are used to this tit-for-tat fighting between politicians, but they didn't like to see it at your event. On the other hand, the publicity did increase our donations."

I smiled at her kindness and then quickly moved off that subject. "Let's meet one more time before I leave. I'll try to come up with another fundraising idea," I said. "Until then, you probably need to recruit a *lot* of new board members."

After we parted ways, I proceeded to the lobby newsstand, which held papers in every language imaginable. I paid for the English-speaking version of a prominent Bulgarian newspaper—auto-translated, of course.

Paka went to the elevators and extracted a room key card from her Chanel purse. I knew she couldn't see me and perhaps she wouldn't care, but nevertheless, she was being awfully reckless. It didn't help that a tall, good-looking businessman accompanied her, his hand on her lower back.

Knowing there was little I could do or say, I turned my attention to the day's news. The Vorbank branch manager's death had finally made the front page. It wasn't news that he'd committed suicide, as that had happened sometime ago; rather, the article was about his connection to the politician Volkov. *So, the Wolf has reemerged in the spotlight.* I thought back to the first time I'd seen him on the television—in Sunny Beach, when he was defending the innocence of the now-dead criminal bank manager.

The paper reported that, according to anonymous sources, Volkov had recommended the hiring of his childhood friend, the deceased bank manager, over other more-qualified prospects. They said the manager had no credentials, other than that he spoke Russian and Bulgarian fluently. Before he took the bank position, he had worked in a trucking business, mostly as a driver on routes between the two countries.

Volkov was supposedly on the board of directors of the bank, a fact that was mentioned in the conversation I'd had with the young lady at the bank. A disgruntled Bulgarian who had probably lost his money, like me, told the reporter that Volkov was corrupt and a Russian agent. The reporter had done some investigating and discovered pictures of Volkov in Cyprus, partying with Russian politicians. Those pictures were now plastered in the newspaper.

At first, I was inclined to give the politicians the benefit of the doubt—maybe they were just having a conference. But the truth was, although the men—in their custom-made suits; their shirts unbuttoned halfway down; thick, gold chains hanging on their broad, hairy chests as they lounged on leather sofas, smoking fat cigars—might not be guilty of stealing *my* money, they looked like they were definitely guilty of stealing something.

To make things more complicated, I was almost sure one of the women in two of the photos was Zlata, but it was very blurry.

Once home, I pulled out my pitiful chart from the closet, cut the pictures from the paper, and taped them to the page. Then I put an extra line between Volkov and the bank manager and another between Volkov and the Vorbank itself.

I stepped back to survey my work. It had become a mishmash of crisscrossed lines everywhere, like a loose weaving. But the lines were beginning to paint a picture. The question was, what was the picture that was emerging?

Maybe, I thought, *I need to be more analytical.* It was then that I noticed the one person who had no lines—the psychic at the bottom of the page.

It was so odd. I had nothing to connect her to the bank, my money, or the AIC. Other than being present at the bazaar, her only connection to the AIC was me. I couldn't link her to a single person on the list. But her warnings—they had to be about this matter. They were so specific. Oleg, Vorbank ...

"I give up," I told the kitten who had begun to play with the edge of the chart. That momentary distraction made me pause and regroup.

Zach could be right. The psychic had a strange obsession with me that began in Rupite and continued today. If, indeed, her daughter moved her from her home in Rupite to Sofia against her will, then she probably associated me with the loss of her home, and even I would want to kill someone who put me in a home for old persons.

What about the other suspects, if I could even call them that?

Natasha? Other than banking at Vorbank, like me, and being on the AIC board, she didn't have connections to the bank. The worst thing I could say about her was that she had connections to the same condo in Cypress where Zlata was photographed sitting on the cushy blue-silk sofa. And she loved my cousin Andy. And she was Russian.

Lasarov also hadn't done anything bad, to my knowledge, other than to tell Leo to tell Rosa to mind her own business. On the other hand, his wife was Maya, and she had threatened the bank manager who died. But, truthfully speaking, I would have threatened him as well about stealing my money, if I had known about him. Forgetting Maya's threat for the moment, I wasn't sure that merely banking at Vorbank was enough to condemn her.

Zlata? She'd been out of the picture since I arrived. And if the bank manager stole my money and the AIC's, that meant Zlata was clearly innocent and that I had wrongfully accused her.

As time passed, the rash of supposed suicides was looking less like a deep-state conspiracy and more like a sad coincidence. Maria's paper was just an academic paper, and young men often take life too seriously. Maybe Maria broke Oleg's heart, and that's why she left.

It was funny how the passage of time worked—in hindsight, all those things and people that seemed so suspicious the night before had a perfectly innocent, if not rational, explanation. It wasn't like anything else had happened—other than, of course, the bank manager's death, and the fact that Zlata was still gone, and my money still was gone, but nothing else *really* was new.

My musings were interrupted by a knock on the apartment door.

I took a quick look through the peephole on the door and was relieved to see the magnified red nose and forehead of the property manager, peering at me from the other side. Of course, he had keys to the gate and to the front door.

"Hello, Mihai," I said.

"Someone left this package for you at the front door of the building," he said, handing me a large brown envelope with my name crudely written on the front. There was no return address or other writing on it.

"Hmm, I'm not expecting anything," I said. "Did you see who left it?"

"No," he said. "It's been there for a while … dirty … someone kicked it out of the way of the door." He was right. I could even see someone's partial shoe print on the front.

"I guess that means it's not a bomb," I said, smiling to let him know I was kidding. He didn't return the smile. "Is it another kitten?" I joked, knowing better.

"No. It's soft on top—maybe clothes," he said. Like most Bulgarians, my sarcasm was lost on him.

"Thanks, I really appreciate you bringing it up to me," I said.

He left without another word, retreating to his dark space in the basement.

I looked at the package, now on my coffee table, not knowing what to do with it. Something told me to call Zach before I opened it.

"OK, Jeni," he said. "Let me get this straight. It's already been stepped on, kicked, and then brought up to your apartment by the property manager, who has squeezed it. It's soft to the touch but tightly packaged."

"Yes."

"Then it's probably not a bomb. But if you suspect that it is a bomb, you can take it to the embassy or call the local police. Use your best judgment."

I contemplated my options and decided that calling the police didn't seem to be the right one.

"Jeni, do you want to call the police?" Zach asked, still on the line.

"No, I don't think it's a bomb," I said, beginning to feel quite ridiculous.

"OK, if you think it's safe, then open it while I stay on the phone," he said.

I put the phone on speaker mode.

I took out some scissors and carefully slit the tape holding the envelope closed. There, stuffed inside, was a white cloth wrapped around a large item. It took a hard tug to loosen the contents from the thick manila covering.

But when I did, the cloth erupted. Flying into the air and raining down all over me was paper, startling me so much that I inadvertently yelped.

I looked around and found that I was surrounded by piles of Bulgarian money, like Midas with a pile of gold—but paper gold.

"Jeni? Jeni?" a worried Zach shouted into the phone. "What's happening?"

"Zach, I think you need to come home fast. It's not clothes. It's … it's … it's money."

"Money?" he said.

"Lots of it."

"Don't touch anything," he said. "I'm on my way."

In less than fifteen minutes, Zach and Frank entered the apartment. Frank was at the office when I called.

"I'm surprised that you're not happier, sitting here surrounded by all this money," Zach said, smiling when he saw me frozen on the couch, afraid to move. He then wandered around the room, looking down at the money and the envelope on the floor, touching nothing. "You can move around after Frank takes photographs. Frank, are you finished?"

I hadn't noticed what Frank was doing until that moment. He nodded yes.

"Tell us again what happened," Zach said, once I moved to another chair.

I did as he asked, but I could tell the answers were not all that helpful. We all agreed that the source of the money was a question we couldn't answer at that moment, so we needed to make sure it wasn't stolen money, accidentally sent to me. I dutifully went to my kitchen to get some plastic storage bags, along with a black Sharpie pen that I handed to Frank.

"I know you, Jeni," Zach said, as we looked around the room. "You're a great estimator. Have you already figured out how much money is here?"

"This is going to sound crazy, but I think it's the $9,000 that was stolen from me. I think it's my money."

Frank and Zach started talking at the same time.

"What do you mean? Nine thousand US dollars? You lost $9,000?" Zach almost yelled—and he never, ever yelled. "You never told me it was that much! Not even close!"

All the while, practical Frank was ruining what otherwise could have been a great day. "Right now, it's not your money, Jeni. At least, not until we know more. It's evidence. I've called my Bulgarian police counterpart to come to fingerprint and process," he said, although he assured me that I would get the money back if no legitimate owner claimed it.

Before I could plead my case further to either man, Frank put on plastic gloves and began bagging up the "evidence," and I heard a siren in the background.

I looked from one to the other of them, exasperated. I wanted to tell Zach that he'd never asked how much money I had lost, but it seemed bad timing.

"You know I could've been blown up," I finally said.

I wasn't so sure they cared.

CHAPTER THIRTY EIGHT

ANDY ARRIVED AT THE SAME TIME THAT FRANK AND THE BULGARIAN OFFICER were finishing up counting and bagging the money.

"Why didn't you call me?" Andy said. "I think I'd have a better idea of what to do with all that cash than those two guys."

We all laughed. I had to admit it—I was going to miss Andy when he left.

"What's on your agenda?" I asked him, once Frank had left with my money, and Zach had returned to work.

"Natasha said she had a meeting today and that she'd have a big surprise for me when we met tonight for dinner," he said. "I hope it's $9,000 in cash!"

"Oh, you don't want it. You'll either lose it, or someone will take it from you," I said. "Face it; we weren't meant to be rich."

"No, but we *are* Americans and meant for good bourbon," he said. "The good news is that I got just what I needed at the corner market. I finished my projects and got paid again, and I intend to celebrate."

I sipped on a glass of Bulgarian red wine while he sipped on his bourbon and Coke. We spent the afternoon watching sappy, English-subtitled French movies on the TV.

As time slipped by, I noticed Andy was watching the clock. Natasha had not called. His jovial mood was slowly disintegrating.

"I wonder what's wrong?" he finally said.

Something had to have happened at the embassy to delay her arrival, but I didn't want to say anything. I might be wrong.

Zach was home from work when Andy finally received a text from Natasha.

He didn't read it to me, but it satisfied him.

"It looks like I'm on my own tonight," he said. "How about I take you two out for dinner? Work is looking up, and I can pay." Andy picked up the kitten who was playing by his feet and spoke to it. "Even you will get a special surprise—I'll bring home new treats after dinner."

Until then, I had not realized that Andy and the kitten were fast friends. It made me smile. The kitten was a people-cat—affectionate and fun. There should be no trouble finding it a new family, but the offers were not coming in.

We spent the evening at a neighborhood café, planning the trip to Shumen the next week.

Shumen was a pretty city about an hour east of Sofia, where the rolling hills would be full of sunflowers or golden hay at this time of the year. All we recalled of our uncle's story was that he was taken by bus to the officer's POW camp in Shumen near the end of the war, and it was in the summer.

When I was a child, Bulgaria evoked images of bleakness. Until the 1980s, the only film clips of the region that we saw were reminiscent of the gray, grainy images of the 1940s. The occasional news of an athlete escaping Eastern Europe during the decades that it was sealed off from the rest of the world by Communism didn't help its image.

Even after Communism fell, I never saw Bulgaria in full color—no yellow flowers, blue rivers, or green fields; just gray—until I went to Europe. How wrong I was.

It was at dinner that Andy and I realized how little we had listened to our uncle, and we knew little about what questions to ask. The story we heard was the war hero being shot down and taken as a prisoner in a dark, ugly place. But his story was more than that—much more. It was one of falling in love in the summer when the Bulgarian skies were deep blue and the fields of wildflowers were in bloom. It was the story of a dashing American pilot who miraculously survived a plane crash and had a new, free life waiting for him in the United States.

"What have you learned?" I asked.

"The POW camp was at the top of the hill, across the railroad tracks leading to the main city," Andy said. He had found military articles that described the placement of the camp but not the exact address. "Uncle Bob told Mom that the bar or restaurant—whatever it was—was directly across the railroad tracks from the POW camp, down a steep hill. I get the sense that the city proper is on flat land in a valley, and the POW camp was in what is now a residential area that rises above it."

A Tripadvisor search led us to two potential eating or drinking establishments that had been in business for decades. We decided to find them and ask the owners for any information they might have on the history of the place.

"We'll spend the night there," he said, "if that's OK with you."

"Why not?" I agreed.

As the evening progressed, I noticed Andy once again looking surreptitiously at his phone for messages or emails. I could tell by his furrowed brow that there were none.

"What are you doing tomorrow?" I asked Andy.

"Not sure at this point," he said.

"I'm going to the mall. Do you want to go with me?"

"Not a chance," he said.

I should've have known he wouldn't go. If I didn't have to buy some items for the apartment, I would have passed on it as well.

"I'm going to rent a bike and enjoy the great weather," he said. "The low humidity here in Sofia makes it awfully nice."

Andy was right about the weather. It was a spectacularly beautiful day when I woke. Zach and I made plans to grill out on the balcony that evening, and he promised to be home on time.

"Mind if I invite Frank?" he asked.

"Are we adopting him?" I said and then smiled to make sure he knew I was kidding. "Sure, that's great." Then, I couldn't help myself. "I can check out his clothes to make sure he hasn't been shopping with my money."

At that moment, the kitten mewed in agreement, causing us both to laugh.

"That reminds me," I said. "Any news on the kitten? Has anyone called you from the embassy?"

"Two bites," he said. "I'll know more tomorrow." He reached down and scratched the kitten behind the ears. "We'll get you a good home—just wait."

I hated to go to a mall on a pretty day, but I had delayed the trip long enough. We needed charcoal, special light bulbs, some computer parts, socks, and a long list of other boring items.

As I walked past the McDonald's, I wondered how Rosa was doing. I missed her friendship so much that it hurt. It was so unfair. I couldn't seem to get in a shopping mood; I even skipped the delicate chocolate macaroons at the French kiosk at the entrance.

The mood didn't lift until I'd finished shopping, including a stop for wine and steaks for the grill. When I was driving back into the garage, I began to plan how I would marinate the steaks for the barbeque that night. I loved dining al fresco, and the view was breathtaking on a clear summer night. Plus, there were rarely any bugs.

It was just what Zach and I needed—a small dinner party. Perhaps Natasha would be able to join us. Andy would think I was amazing for helping her get an expedited visa. I was so eager to begin preparations for the evening that I literally sped into the garage with the groceries.

Each apartment owner had a storage unit where everything that was rarely used could be kept until it was time to leave the country, at which time they held a garage sale and sold everything to new ex-pats, who happily bought things from them. It would continue like that, owner after owner, until some wise soul said "I don't want this garbage" and threw it out.

The storage unit was also a great place to store charcoal and grilling utensils. I decided to pick up what I needed on my way to the elevator.

I put my shopping bags with my new purchases on the garage floor, fished out the storage unit key, and then opened the door, leaving the key in the lock, as I always did. Otherwise, I would probably leave it somewhere in the storage unit and have to call the embassy for a new key, which they definitely didn't like.

The push from behind was just hard enough to cause me to tumble into the darkness of the unit. I tripped over a snow shovel and a bucket before I fell into the shelves holding suitcases. I caught myself, but by then, the door had been slammed behind me, and I heard the sound of the key as it was removed. At first, nothing but dark and quiet surrounded me. Then, I heard the shuffling of feet on the concrete outside my door. The feet slowly walked out the garage entrance until I could hear them no more.

This was getting ridiculous. I wasn't sure who it was, but if it was the psychic, "This time," I said under my breath, "she made a critical miscalculation."

When the sound of steps ended, I slowly counted to ten and turned on the emergency light. Then I turned the knob and cracked open the door.

What she didn't know was that in the United States, we take safety seriously. The astute State Department figured that, eventually, one of its employees or their children, more likely me, would accidentally lock themselves in the ventless, square, concrete space, which was roughly the size of a tomb. Our government required that the owners of apartments who rented to diplomats install door knobs on storage units that opened from the inside without a key. Luckily, I had previous experience in seeing that the government's plan actually worked.

Once I peeked outside the door, I saw my attacker on her way out of the garage entrance, and this time, she didn't stop to shut it.

Just like that, I knew the tables had turned. I would follow her, instead of the other way around. I dropped my groceries in the storage unit and shut the door.

It was the one thing Frank had not forbidden, although he probably would have, if he actually had anticipated I would follow a demented psychic.

"Who is the stalker now?" I taunted her under my breath.

CHAPTER
THIRTY
NINE

Following the woman was shamefully easy. She obviously assumed I was still locked in the storage unit, so she ambled away without any urgency. I followed her for several blocks, periodically hiding when she glanced back.

She turned off the main road which led to my apartment and into an expensive older neighborhood with large, white-stone homes with red-tile roofs; overflowing window boxes; sweeping, manicured lawns; and security guards in tiny boxes at the end of their drives. The lack of random, unkempt brush or brick walls made it hard for me to find cover off the broad sidewalks.

When the woman finally stopped outside a stately home with wide terraces; short, fat columns; dark-brown trim; and blue-glazed pots full of red geraniums, she stood looking toward the windows. That is all she did—just stood in the front yard, looking at the house—until the security guard approached her and kindly told her to leave.

His request agitated her. She shook her head no; she wouldn't leave.

Perplexed by the situation, the guard returned to his four-by-four black box, which contained nothing but a stool and a tiny TV on a stand. He placed a call and then waited.

It was an impasse that continued for so long that I finally sat down on a curb, out of sight, to await its resolution. I stood when I heard the front door of the home finally open, and a woman exited.

It was Maya. The world was indeed very small. Or at least Sofia was.

Maya walked toward the old woman with a scowl on her face, and they began to argue, loudly and passionately. They clearly knew each other.

I heard Maya tell the woman to leave, but instead, the old woman grabbed Maya's arm and attempted to pull her away from the house, trying to lead her somewhere. Maya became angry and shoved the woman with such force that it almost knocked her down. When that did not deter the woman, Maya yelled for the security guard and motioned for him to remove the irritant from her drive.

The psychic was beside herself, but before she could act further, Maya was back inside the home, having slammed the door behind her.

It was already a mind-boggling scene, but then, the craziest thing happened. The psychic sat down on the curb not far from me. She lowered her head into her hands and sobbed—big, heaving sobs that caused her shoulders and heavy breasts to rise up and down. She was completely distraught.

I didn't know what to do. The woman had just locked me in my storage unit and had attempted to poison me on at least two occasions. I elected to keep a lot of space between us. She was as angry with me as she was with Maya and was totally unpredictable. I finally slunk away, like a voyeur when the show was over.

Before leaving the scene, I made a mental note of the address, although I felt certain Maya's home address was not much of a secret; it was probably in every house-and-garden magazine in Sofia.

It was a long walk home, but despite the unfettered time to think, I couldn't come up with an explanation for what I had just witnessed, other than the possibility that we had both been to the psychic for a reading in

Rupite. Maybe she was harassing Maya too. *That might explain the encounter, but ...*

It was odd of Maya not to phone the police, given the circumstances. Maya didn't exactly come across as the kindly lady next door. *So, why didn't she?* I shook my head in confusion.

When I arrived at the apartment, I was slammed for time to get dinner together. I knocked on Andy's bedroom door to see if he was there.

"Yeah," he said. "I'm in here. You can come in."

"Great. Is Natasha coming to dinner?"

"Beats me. I haven't heard a word from her."

His voice told me all I needed to know, and I didn't think lying on his bed, looking at the ceiling, was doing anything to help his mood.

"Can you lend a hand with dinner?" I asked.

I could tell that staring at the light fixture was exactly what he wanted to do, instead of considering the implications of Natasha's sudden lack of communication. But after a few seconds, he came to the door.

"Sure," he said, shrugging his shoulders.

As we prepared the meal, I babbled about everything I'd seen that day, other than the psychic, trying to fill the cavernous void that Natasha's lack of communication had created.

"Jeni, do you think she's hurt or in danger?" he finally asked.

"Is there any reason she would be?" I chose the great lawyer tactic—answering his question with a question.

"No," he said, seemingly resigned to the knowledge that he most likely had been dumped once again.

"I'm sure she'll call," I said.

"I don't think so," he said, his voice flat. "There's something off with her, and I can't figure it out. I'll probably never understand her."

After that philosophical moment, he popped open a Bulgarian beer while I poured a glass of wine. We toasted each other and went to sit on the veranda to wait for Frank and Zach.

They came in one cab, Zach with some flowers, and Frank with a bottle of wine.

While Zach was barbequing, I took the opportunity to tell the men the story about my encounter with the psychic.

"I've never been stalked. Now I understand how creepy it is," I said. "You begin to feel like you're losing your mind."

"Why didn't you call the police?" Andy asked. "You call them for everything else." He didn't need to remind me about the time I accidentally reported him for unlawful entry into my dorm suite, forgetting that I told him he could crash there for the night.

"I can't explain it, but this time, I was so mad that I wasn't as afraid," I said. "It sounds ridiculous—by all appearances it seems like she wants me dead. But I don't think that's it. I don't think she's a killer. She just wants me out of here—to leave Bulgaria. Go figure." I put my index finger to my head and made circles above it and rolled my eyes.

"Did she know you were following her?" Zach asked.

"No, not at all," I said. "I don't think she would have wanted me to witness her fight with Maya, and she definitely wouldn't knowingly allow me to see her cry."

"I agree with that," Frank said. "I'll have someone with the police look out for her, and they can make sure she's on her meds, if that is the problem."

It sounded like a good resolution to me. I started preparing the table to eat dinner.

"Andy," Zach said, as he helped me set the table, "you don't seem yourself. Is something wrong?"

"Nah," Andy said, putting on a great fake smile. "Natasha's off the radar, and I'm wondering why, but you know women."

Frank and Zach looked at each other intently and came to some telepathic understanding.

"Andy," Zach said, "we have to talk."

CHAPTER
FORTY

"Jeni, turn on the music, and keep the volume up, if you don't mind," Zach said. Then he pulled our chairs close together on the veranda, far from the apartment walls, which we assumed always heard every word we said. Living with the knowledge that your home is bugged by the host country is a reality for all ex-pats, but as long as you live the life of a Boy Scout and don't take home classified information, you're pretty much OK. They're not interested in ordinary husband-and-wife stuff—I hoped, anyway.

This news, I could tell, wasn't going to be ordinary.

"I need to talk about Natasha," Zach said. "She's not coming back."

Andy stared at him in disbelief. "Why not?"

"It's a long story, so lean in, and I'll tell you what I can," Zach said.

It turned out that Natasha wasn't just an ordinary, beautiful Russian girl with eyes that could turn misty on demand. She had been trained in Moscow to work in intelligence. Sofia was her first posting, an easy one because most people spoke Russian. Her job was to make friends with a lady in the AIC and report what she learned to Moscow. They wanted some compromising information—something bad about her married boyfriend— for use in negotiating an oil agreement.

The fact that I appeared at the AIC meeting was a complete surprise to Natasha, and without anyone's knowledge, she decided that it would help her career to become friends with the wife of a US diplomat and get some useful information.

"Who was she originally supposed to spy on?" I asked.

"Paka," Zach said.

"Paka? You have to be kidding!"

"Paka's husband and his partner work in the oil industry and are trying to get a big contract in Bulgaria," he said. "Paka may have been having an affair with the partner."

I nodded that it was true—or at least, it looked that way to me.

"They are always looking for any information to compromise someone, whether they use it now or later."

"OK, I suspected as much on Paka, but why would Natasha bother with me?" I said. "I don't know anything, and, *for the record*, I'm not having an affair."

Zach laughed. "*For the record*, you know lots of things, just not government or corporate secrets. And that's where Natasha messed up."

She had one assignment, and it wasn't to surveil a novice diplomat's wife who knew nothing of importance and had no power or political muscle. It also wasn't to get involved with Andy, but once again, she couldn't help herself. Either it was blind ambition or Cupid's love; it didn't matter. She strayed from her job and made mistakes.

Although none of us knew it, Bulgarian intelligence officers were monitoring the calls between Natasha and her contact in Amsterdam. I guessed then that she must have wanted him or her to meet me on our girl's weekend in Amsterdam, and who knows what trouble I would have gotten into.

Apparently, the Bulgarians had known about Natasha since she arrived in Sofia but had done nothing because she was such a minor player. It wasn't much of a secret.

It was when my name came up and they overheard her discussing Andy that the Bulgarians contacted our embassy. I wanted to laugh when Zach said they demanded to know whether Andy was a spy as well. It was all a big mess, so Frank offered to do some cleanup work with his Bulgarian counterparts.

"Once we knew she intended to visit the States with Andy, and we knew she wanted an expedited visa, we set it up in order to get information from her at the embassy interview," Frank said. "I'm afraid that she got an F in truthfulness."

Apparently, Natasha had made up her college information, her background, and even her birthday.

Once the interview happened and the diplomats compared notes, the Bulgarians couldn't let her stay in Sofia any longer. They arrested her as a spy—or whatever they called it.

"Where is she?" Andy asked. "Is she in jail?"

"No, she's on a plane back to Moscow, probably first class," Zach said.

"You've got to be kidding!" I said, trying hard to keep my voice down. "She's a *spy*! Don't they hang spies?"

Even I knew that was a truly stupid question. Of course they didn't. They *expelled* them, like the bad kid in school.

Andy was quiet as he heard the news. "OK," he finally said. "Are you telling me that I might have slept with a Russian spy?"

"I hate to agree with that," Zach said, "but yes."

With that, Andy stood, slapped his knees, and laughed. "Well, that's the best thing ever. I mean, how cool is that?"

Immediately, Zach pulled him back down by his shirt sleeve so that he was very close to Zach's face. "But you can't tell a soul—*ever*," Zach said, his eyes staring into Andy's, letting him know just how serious he was.

"I know. No one would believe me. Face it; we don't even believe Uncle Bob." Zach let go, and Andy stood back, still with a smile on his face "But what a memory. I knew we weren't going to last, but I couldn't figure out the end game. Now I know. It'll be a far better story when I'm a senile old man than Uncle Bob's POW experience."

"Conversation over now?" I asked, ready to eat.

"Yes, for now—and for the next thirty years," Frank said.

Our voices went back to normal, joking and laughing about Frank's attempt that morning to rent a bike and ride it around the city.

"I think I'm too old for that now," he said. "It's time to be a grandfather and teach the grandkids how to ride."

Later that night, Zach took me out on the balcony to see the full moon and give me a lingering kiss.

Then he pulled me tightly to him in a hug and whispered in my ear. "Jeni, you still have to be vigilant—more so now."

It wasn't what I was expecting, and I wondered why it was so urgent.

"Please be wary." Then he kissed the top of my head. I was totally confused as to what he meant, but before I could ask, Andy joined us to let us know the details of his flight itinerary for the trip home.

Later that night, Zach's admonition was still on my mind. I pulled him close to me in bed, and this time, I whispered to him. "Zach, are you a spy?"

He smiled. "No, sweetie. I'm sorry, but you're not sleeping with a spy."

"I just don't know what you do all day, and all this Natasha stuff—"

"I'm doing the same thing in Sofia that I always have done—get police officers from different countries to work together and track terrorists, traffickers, launderers, and other ordinary criminals," he said. He only found out about Natasha because she was a foreign national who dated Andy, and Zach was required to report to the embassy that she was in close contact with us.

"Then why did you warn me to be careful?" I asked. I quickly scanned through the last weeks in my mind. "The only weird thing I have seen lately is the guy Don, who wanders around our apartment building at least once a day, talking on his cell phone. Oh, and the stalking psychic."

I wanted to joke that maybe they were one and the same, but it wasn't joking time.

"Because I hear things," Zach said. Then he thought more about his answer. "I probably shouldn't have said anything at all. Don't worry about him. Be careful, like, normal careful." Even he knew that sounded lame, but I got his drift.

"Well," I said, "that's a relief—that you're not a spy, that is."

"And why is that?" he asked.

"We only need one undercover agent in the house."

"Really?" He pulled himself up on his elbow to look me intently. "Does that mean I'm sleeping with a spy?"

"Couldn't tell you if I knew," I said, borrowing Frank's infamous answer to anything important.

CHAPTER
FORTY
ONE

"WHAT'S YOUR PLAN FOR THE DAY?" ZACH ASKED AT BREAKFAST.

"Andy is going sight-seeing to places I've already been," I said, "so I thought I'd try to go for a jog or long walk to clear out my head."

"Sounds good," he said. "Just don't go too far from the apartment. Remember what I said."

"Any other instructions or prohibitions?" I asked with a smile.

"None," he said as he kissed me goodbye.

It was a hot morning, and I realized quickly that it didn't invite a walk in the park, so I decided to head to the neighborhood grocery store instead.

Shopping for food was never easy for me in Eastern Europe, and it was harder in Bulgaria than Romania, as there were less-obvious signals as to the contents of a box or can. I often stood for several minutes before a display until I decided on the most likely candidate for the tomato puree I was seeking.

I was deep in thought over pureed or diced tomatoes when I felt someone eerily close behind me. Perhaps it was a sound, but it also could have been the smell of aftershave. I turned back to check in such a hurry that I actually ran into the person with the edge of my large shopping basket.

"Well, hello, Jeni," said Don, who was wearing an appropriate office suit rather than his usual golf shirt and pants. I almost didn't recognize him. "What a surprise to see you."

The smirk on his face let me know this wasn't a random encounter. I resumed shopping and asked in my best casual voice how he was doing and had he found an apartment.

"Not yet," he admitted.

Then he cut in front of my path and reached over, almost touching me, to pick up a can of tomatoes. "It must be hard to be a diplomat's spouse, shopping in a foreign country," he said as he turned the can around.

I just nodded.

"You don't know the language or the lettering. It's tough, I bet." He sighed and put down the can. "Not only do you have to take care of the house and move a lot and can't keep a job, but you sometimes land into all kinds of trouble." He turned to gauge my reaction.

"Really? Trouble?" I asked, thinking I might as well get to the bottom of whatever he was there for.

"Trouble with money, trouble with people—you know, trouble." He looked at me with a condescending grin, as if he knew something, and I was too stupid to know it.

I wanted to control my temper, but as I stood immobile, looking at him, my fists curled in anger around the handle of the cheap red shopping basket I was holding. *What is he getting at?*

"Not me," I said and took a breath to calm down. There was no need to overreact. "I have no trouble."

"I hope not," he said, turning away from me to peruse the other canned items, "because I'd hate to see you hurt."

I said nothing, remembering Zach's words: *"He is not one of us."* I would hear the guy out and leave as fast as possible.

But then he said, "Or perhaps, Zach lose his job …"

With those words, I lost my resolve to remain calm, and without thinking, I unclenched my fists just enough that I could no longer hold on to the shopping basket. It dropped to the floor so hard that a glass bottle of red sauce cracked, its contents quickly oozing through the basket bottom onto the floor, while the sound of breaking glass reverberated through the store.

I poked my free index finger in his face—something I never do, but suddenly, it seemed so necessary, evidence of how out of line he was. "Are you *threatening* me?"

He said nothing but continued to look at tomato cans.

"I'm not sure what you're up to, but I'm not in trouble, and neither is Zach. How dare you—you person who just arrived and knows nothing. How dare you try to scare me?"

My outrage had no effect on Don. He was calm and collected. "I'm not trying to scare you," he said, finally returning his attention to me and plastering a fake pained look on his face. "I just wanted you to know that I'm here for you if you ever need me. *I can fix things.* That's my job. Just call me if you need me." With that, he dropped a card with a handwritten phone number on top of the food in my basket.

I noticed immediately that it wasn't a government card.

Then, without waiting for a response, he turned on his heels to leave the store, only briefly stopping for a parting remark. "Don't forget to clean up the sauce. You wouldn't want to get it on your clothes."

I wanted to scream at him but held it back.

Ugh! What a jerk and what a terrible mess—not just the cleanup on aisle one but the cluster I'm in with just about everyone in Sofia. Or so it seemed at that moment. And Zach's job? Was I really hurting his position? Wouldn't they just send me back if I was doing something wrong?

I seethed, releasing air through my gritted teeth. I knew I hadn't done anything wrong, and this slick newcomer wasn't going to make me believe I had. I took a deep breath and threw my shoulders back. It didn't seem likely in the least that Don really wanted to help me. He would have called Zach instead. And since when did an FBI agent ever say "I'm here to help you," unless you were a hostage victim? And hand you a personal card?

I wanted to call Zach right then and there, but he was in a conference until late in the day without a cell phone. I'd have to do it later.

By the time the mess on the floor was cleaned and I'd checked out of the store, a misty rain had begun to fall—a problem for me, given that I had no umbrella.

It didn't surprise me when a man outside the store entrance opened an umbrella to shield me from the rain. What caught my breath was that the man holding it was someone I knew.

"Nice day at the grocery store?" Frank asked, reaching over to help me with my bags as he held the umbrella over my head. Now, there was no doubt that he was following me, if any doubt had ever existed in the first place.

"Peachy."

"Anything interesting?" he asked.

I was still angry as I described Don's words to Frank, becoming more indignant as the scene was replayed.

This time, Frank seemed surprised by Don's words. He said he had been watching Don, off and on, after I mentioned his lurking around our apartment. However, nothing happened that was too suspicious, and he was beginning to think that Don had a crush on me. He had no idea it might be more than that.

"You want to help me some more?" he asked, a sly smile creeping across his face.

"I don't know ..."

"How about just a word or two to Don?"

That was about the only thing that I would do, as Frank probably knew.

My instructions were not to call to verbally abuse Don, like I wanted to do; instead, I was to call him and tell him that he was right about my tight finances and that I really needed a job to make some money. Could he get me a temporary position in a legal firm in Sofia? Did he know anyone who could help me? Then I was to wait and see what he said.

I followed the instructions as Frank had given them and called Don within the hour. He was excited to hear from me and told me I didn't need to apologize again for my behavior at the grocery store, which I didn't recall doing. Then I told him what I needed and waited for his response.

"No problem," he said. "I have just the job in mind—not necessarily legal, but it pays really well. It's a short-term, easy government-grant position."

I started to thank him profusely, but before I got far, he made a sound like he was clearing his throat, as if he wanted to say more—perhaps something important. I paused and listened.

His voice modulated to a conspiratorial tone. "But first, I need you to do me a favor, though."

I gulped.

He wanted me to go to the police and tell them that I was now convinced that Oleg had stolen the AIC's money, not anyone else connected to the bank.

"It's not true—"

"Well, it might be true," Don said. "Who knows?"

"How would I even do it? I don't know the police, and why do you care about Oleg or the bank?"

"It's no big deal. I'm just helping friends clear up a misunderstanding," he said. I heard the click of his lighter and could tell he was thinking as he took a drag from a cigarette. "Just go back to the police station where you originally reported the theft of the AIC money, and tell them what I said." I was shocked at how much Don knew about everything I did. "The officer you originally spoke to will know what to do."

"OK, I'll go tomorrow." I hung up the phone and looked up at Frank, who was recording the conversation. I collapsed into the closest chair, my energy suddenly zapped from the stress of making the call. Don was a whole different ball game from the friendly bank-account lady.

What had I gotten myself into? I was crossing some line I knew better than to cross. I just didn't know what the line was. Or if I was placing my trust in the right people. I should have called Zach first.

"What do I do tomorrow?" I asked.

"Nothing," Frank said. "Just wait and see what happens."

CHAPTER
FORTY
TWO

Frank's "nothing" didn't last long.

He caught me outside the apartment later that day, as I was separating the garbage into the correct recycling bins.

"Huh?" I said as I continued my chore at hand. The truth was that I'd figured he wasn't done with me, but to come back this soon ... I needed more time to think and to talk to Zach, who wouldn't be free until later in the day.

"Maybe you should do what he asked," he said.

I knew he meant Don and that I should make the report to the police.

"When?"

"The sooner the better."

I didn't respond but picked up the remaining garbage bin from the ground and signaled for Frank to wait outside.

It wasn't but a few minutes before I returned, wearing a dress and heels for the police station appearance. However, I immediately regretted my decision to help Frank when I saw Don was with him, standing with his hands in his pockets, his back to me, while Frank motioned for me to sit in the back seat. There were no greetings.

"We'll all go together part of the way," Frank said as he opened the car door for me. I half expected Don to drive his Audi, but it was nowhere to be seen. Instead, he turned toward the car and slid in the front seat next to Frank.

Both men wore grim faces and were uncommunicative in words and body language, so much so that I instinctively knew something bad was going on—but what? I bit my bottom lip hard—so hard that I was sure my lip might bleed—in order to keep from asking annoying questions. I had to believe that if we were going to the police station, it was highly unlikely anyone would hurt me on the way there. Still, I couldn't shake the feeling that the car ride with the men was not a great idea.

When Frank stopped several blocks short of the station and let Don out, I felt some relief and freedom to ask questions.

"What's going on?"

"We're trying to figure it out ourselves," Frank said. "Don's up to something wrong, but we don't know who he's helping or why. The fancy new car and his lifestyle are serious red flags. This whole AIC thing is not my matter, but now I'm forced to see why Don cares about it. I wanted Don near the police station, just in case." He turned off the engine in the visitor parking space. "There is not much time to talk. When you are finished, take the Metro to your stop. Don't be surprised if you see Don not far behind you."

When I exited the car two blocks from the station, I saw Don in the distance. I paused for a second, knowing that I was free to leave the men and go home or to the police station and perform as Don requested. I chose the more interesting path.

It was frightfully easy to lie to the policeman. Perhaps it was because he knew I was lying and asked no difficult questions. Actually, I'm not sure he asked anything of me. Each time I said something, he murmured the word *yes* and wrote notes on a yellow pad. When I was through, he solemnly stood to shake my hand goodbye. That was it.

Afterward, I stood at the top of the steps outside the station door and searched for Don. He would have been hard to miss, once again standing behind a tree too small to hide his body. I thought that if anyone had hired Don for espionage, they had definitely wasted their money.

When he saw me exit the station door, he left his position and began to walk down the street in front of me. He pulled out a cell phone and crooked it in the corner of his arm while he lit a cigarette. A few minutes later, he turned a corner and was out of my sight.

The rest of the walk to the Metro was uneventful, and I sighed in relief to be through with the task. By the time I entered the crowded train, I was back to normal, wondering what to fix for supper. I didn't get far into menu planning before I spied Don, snaking his way through a group of high school students and their instructor, along with nannies and children in strollers, professional women and men in suits, and an assortment of other Bulgarians adhering to the general rule of good behavior on the train.

Don stopped right before me, where I sat on a bench, squeezed in between two Bulgarian women with large shopping bags in their laps. In order to maintain his balance, he grabbed an overhead strap in one hand, which caused him to swing closer to me. Once he was up close, I realized Don's shirt was wrinkled, and his pants had a stain on one leg. He smelled of smoke and uncleanliness, perhaps remnants of recent alcohol use. I pressed my body back onto the hard-plastic seat to put distance between us.

Don, seeing my movement, used the hand strap to lower himself even further to see me at eye level. "Hope you're happy," he said and then turned his head side to side to survey his fellow passengers. No one was paying attention to us so he continued. "I'm going home." He wildly swung his hand in a direction that could have been anywhere, but I was guessing he meant the States.

I didn't know how to respond so I didn't, but instinctively, I clutched my purse tightly on my lap, as if he were a purse-snatcher or a thief.

He smirked and changed hands holding the strap to enable his body to swing within an inch of my face. "Bad, bad mistake. And to think that all I wanted to do was help you—"

At that moment, the Metro stopped hard, causing the train cars to jerk and screech. Don could no longer hold on with one hand, and he fell across my body, crushing my purse. I pushed him off with all my might when he went to stand up, which caused him to fall onto a high school student who was too polite to complain. That momentary confusion gave me enough time to exit the train without any more conversation with Don.

When I squeezed through the sliding door, I saw Frank waiting on the platform, along with two other men in suits whom I'd seen before at the embassy. He gave me a slight wave, and I headed in his direction.

Don, on the other hand, after forcing the closing Metro doors open, lit a cigarette in his cupped hand and walked slowly to the embassy men. They pointed for him to enter a nearby car. Once again, no one spoke. They all knew the drill.

That was the last time I saw Don. I would later find out that he was put on a plane back to Washington, having been recalled for questionable conduct.

Frank divulged as little as he could, but it wasn't hard to fill in the blanks. I learned that Don had taken this assignment after some bad decisions he'd made and a claim of sexual misconduct that occurred stateside. His father, a federal judge, asked that his friends in the FBI give Don another chance, and a trip to Bulgaria made sense. Out of sight, out of mind. However, Don was short of cash, and Bulgarian women, like women in lots of countries, liked men with money and nice cars. I felt sure that he—privileged and smooth— must have been easy to corrupt.

Frank said Don said he was offered money to convince me to withdraw my complaint about the stolen AIC money. It took him forever to do it, but he finally did.

"What? That's crazy!"

Don claimed not to know the man's name, only that he was very wealthy. In fact, he could have just paid the AIC money back, and nothing else would ever have been said. So something else was going on.

"I have an idea who it might be," Franks said, "someone who would have enough money to entice someone like Don to help them. Only one thing ..."

He asked if I would be willing to help just one more time.

Of course.

I was thinking about Frank's question when I unlocked the apartment door, went inside, threw my purse on the couch, and scooped up the kitten—it had been unraveling even more of the hem on the living room sofa. I held it in my lap as I logged on to the computer for the daily emails and news. There were no emails, but there was breaking news.

The police had identified the body of the man found floating in the Black Sea. I wasn't terribly shocked when they named the deceased as Igor Petrovia and said they were concerned about the whereabouts of his wife, Zlata, who was also missing. But I was sick to my stomach.

"Anyone with information should call the police."

Three dead bodies, all loosely intertwined. It had to be money or politics. But they were such minor players. And where was Zlata?

I thought I might know.

CHAPTER

FORTY THREE

THAT EVENING, I DECIDED TO PULL OUT MY CHART FROM THE CLOSET AND give it one last look. We were leaving within a few weeks, and I was angry and frustrated that nothing had been resolved—by anyone. Maybe my chart had some answers.

Over time, it had become quite messy, so the first thing I did was use a Sharpie to mark through the names of the deceased men. Then I circled Zlata's name and crossed off Natasha, who was just an accidental character. Then I put her back after remembering her ties to the bank. After a moment of indecision, I left the psychic's name alone on the bottom of the page.

What remained looked like this:

AIC money: Zlata was still missing, but her husband, Igor, was murdered. It was beginning to not look good for Zlata. Igor's boss and Zlata's close social friend was the man I called the Wolf, Volkov. His boss was the powerful politician named Lasarov, and Lasarov's wife, Maya, had an ugly fight with the bank manager before he died. Maya, curiously, made large deposits once a week to the Vorbank. Zlata and Maya didn't seem connected, other than through their husbands.

Question to me: Who hired Don to get me to withdraw the AIC police report, and why? And what was Maya's fight about?

My money: Oleg, the account manager, wrote a mysterious paper that he gave to his girlfriend, and he was now dead, and she was in fear for her life. Oleg's boss, the branch manager (and Volkov's good friend), the man who probably stole my money, was dead—perhaps suicide. Volkov was also on the bank board. Natasha said she knew people at bank.

Miscellaneous: Zlata and Volkov may have been together in Cyprus. They knew Natasha. She knew bankers. Russian bank and condo. The psychic knew Maya. The psychic also warned me away from the bank, Oleg, and Zlata. Then there was the wealthy Russian man in Rupite whom I'd seen in the bank. And who sent me $9,000?

Lots of questions, but a pattern had emerged.

I resolved to take one more crack at figuring out what had happened to my money and the AIC account.

The next morning, I told Zach that I was going back to the bank one more time to see what, if anything, had transpired on the accounts. We both agreed that if all I did was ask more questions, the worst-case scenario was that it would make them mad. Best-case scenario: they would have answers, and I would be satisfied. He knew we were leaving soon, and I would leave Sofia unhappy if I didn't try one more time.

As he kissed me goodbye and headed to work, I promised to stay safe, given Don's vague admonitions. But it wasn't necessary. I would be in a bank with security. What could go wrong?

While I waited for the bank to open, I called a realtor in Cyprus. I found her agency's splashy website on my cell phone and chose her because she spoke English.

Like most realtors, she was eager to know what I was looking to buy.

"My cousin said a top-floor condominium he visited might be coming on the market," I told her, the lie rolling off my tongue as easily as the realtor's equally untruthful response.

"Well, then, I'm the right person to help you!" she said, with that chipper tone all realtors assume with new clients. "Tell me about the condo."

Andy had given me as much detail about the condo's location as I thought she would need.

Not surprisingly, the seasoned agent thought she knew just which unit I was describing. It was, in her words, "magnificent."

"That's wonderful. Is it possible for you to check with the condominium manager and find out exactly who owns it?" I asked. "Maybe get their name and number? Then we can follow up. And if you don't mind …"

"Yes?" she said, champing at the bit.

"Please don't tell them that my cousin told me that it might be for sale," I said, adopting as coy a voice as possible. "He might get mad at me and, you know, he doesn't have to know what I'm doing. He'll just try to talk me out of buying anything in Cyprus, which is stupid because I already have the money in an off-shore account, waiting to be spent."

"I agree wholeheartedly that you shouldn't tell your cousin anything!" the realtor said, loving a secretive and cash-rich client. "He would be rude to even ask—it's none of his business what you do with your money."

"I'm *so* glad you understand," I said. "I think we'll have a great relationship."

She agreed to text me as soon as she heard something.

So far, though, no communication from her had arrived, so I took the opportunity to send a few other texts before I moved on to the more active part of my recently developed strategic plan—circling around the bank like a hawk over its prey.

When the hour hand hit nine—the beginning of bankers' hours—I left the apartment like a soldier headed to battle.

"It's time to get the show on the road," I told the kitten, who responded with a deep mew, almost as if it didn't think I should leave at all.

It was a sunny day, so I threw on jogging clothes, sunglasses, a New York Yankees baseball cap, and my never-used Fitbit watch. I surveyed the result in the mirror.

"Aren't you just a little curious about the bank?" I asked the kitten and scratched its little head, at which time the tiny feline tilted its head sideways, as if to look in my eyes and say, *Seriously, you're asking me that?*

Over the past few weeks, it had become increasingly clear that Vorbank never ceased to be the center of the universe on my chart—all lines pointed to or through it. The people and events revolved around it like planets. I just had to figure out why.

Friday was the day that Maya made her weekly deposits of money, and, according to the information contained within the brochures I had been given by the account manager, this Friday was also the day the board of directors met. That meant that Volkov would be there. It was my last chance to go to the bank and find everyone there before I left the country.

One thing I wasn't sure about was exactly what time in the morning Maya would appear. After mulling it over, my best guess was that she would arrive midmorning so that the deposits she made would be credited that day. No prudent businesswoman would make a deposit after noon on a Friday, which would place it on hold until the following Monday. That made late morning, around ten, my best estimate for her arrival.

When I exited the apartment, my adrenaline was pumping so fast that I tried jogging for several blocks. It meant that I arrived at the bank within minutes so I was forced to continue well past the bank. Should I run very slowly or maybe even walk?

Just when I had decided to run in a different direction, I was interrupted by a familiar voice.

"Hello, Jeni," called out the friendly security guard, who had never forgotten my name from my first visit with Oleg. It was obvious he thought that I had slowed down because I was returning to the bank to do business, and he politely rushed to hold the door open for me, inviting me to enter.

I wondered if I should keep running, but then I stilled my feet, thanked the guard as I walked back toward him, and entered the bank. I decided that if I rudely walked away and returned later, it would be suspicious.

The plan was in action at nine thirty, whether I wanted it to happen then or not.

The latest account manager was finishing up with an elderly woman, providing me much-needed time to waste. I plopped down in a vinyl chair at an empty desk. It was the perfect place to observe the account manager and his painful interactions with the French woman, who was having trouble understanding how to utilize the bank card.

He was a dour-looking young man. It was obvious he wasn't happy with his new job. When I took a loud slurp from a water bottle, he glanced over and glared at me, apparently frustrated that another client was waiting, especially someone who was so clearly an American.

"Can I help you?" he asked when the French woman left. She was still staring at the plastic debit card and shaking her head in confusion as she exited the glass doors.

I looked around the room before I responded. Once the lady was gone, the lobby was empty, other than me and a few employees. It made me wonder how they made any money at all.

"Yes," I said, my voice slightly elevated. "I don't know you, but I'm one of the people who had my money stolen from my account here."

"Uh-huh," he said, his eyes narrowing as he more closely examined me, seeming wary about where this was headed. I doubted he had information on my account so I was prepared for another approach for information.

"I am so excited that it was returned to me! I wanted to stop by and say thanks to the bank," I said. "I'm just surprised it was all in cash."

"Cash?" he said, making a small snort with his nose. "What are you talking about?"

I told him the whole story in a "Valley girl" kind of way, tipping my head from one side to the other and flipping my hair with my right hand.

"I don't think so. It is highly unlikely tha—"

"You mean it might not be the bank who sent it to me?" I erupted in surprise. I scrunched up my face in disbelief, opened my eyes as wide as I could, and leaned my upper body over the desk toward him.

He scoffed and made tiny rolls with his head, as if to release tension in his neck. "Of course not. We don't send *cash* to people." Then, for good measure, he snorted even louder for emphasis.

"I don't understand," I said, moving even closer to him as he inched his chair further back. "Can you please make sure the bank didn't return it to me in cash?"

Not in the mood to be nice but happy to escape, he huffed and said, "I'll ask if anyone in the board meeting knows something about your money. They haven't started yet." He rolled his desk chair back and stood up. "Just sit there." He pointed to my chair as if he thought I would run around the room like an errant child.

He walked across the lobby as if he had an iron rod shoved up his back. Then he knocked on a door with a *prive* sign. Almost immediately, a hand reached around the edge of door to hold it open just enough to see who was there.

Whoever was on the other end of the hand was not about to let the low-level account manager see, much less enter, the inner sanctum of the board of directors. After the account manager relayed my story, the person on the other side of the door began to shake his index finger at him in such anger and disapproval that his expensive gold watch slid and caught on the edge of his French cuff.

I couldn't hear any of the words spoken from across the room, but I could hear the din of raised voices coming from the boardroom while the door was open. The meeting didn't sound as if it was going well. I had been to enough board meetings to know when tempers were flaring and the temperature was rising.

When the door closed, quiet once again descended upon the lobby. I took a breath and relaxed, waiting for the account manager to return.

"No, no," he said, so shaken that he almost missed his chair when he sat down, but he caught it with his hands before it rolled out from under him.

"The bank had nothing to do with replacing your missing money from your account."

"*Really?*" I said, sliding back in my chair like a petulant teenager. "That's so strange. It was exactly the right amount, and I could've sworn it was in a large bank envelope." I let out an exaggerated sigh. "Well, I guess it's not mine after all. Shoot."

He turned to work on other business.

I wasn't ready to leave. "It's OK," I said, perking up. "Don't worry about it. I'll go ahead and open a new account with you anyway."

He looked at me for a moment, his mouth in a tight line across his face and with furrows across his balding forehead, but he complied with my request. He dropped his head down, sighed, and pulled open his bottom drawer for the necessary forms needed to complete the process.

I sneaked a look at my watch. It was only 9:50, and I still had no idea when or if Maya would appear. It easily could be another hour—or not at all. I felt sorry for this new account manager, who didn't even warrant a sign with his name on the desk. If the thought of having to deal with the French woman was rough, he had no idea how many questions a lawyer could ask about a simple fill-in-the-blank form, especially when she had time to kill.

Our interactions began to attract the attention of the other bored employees in the bank lobby—two tellers, one by the front entrance and one in the back. There was also another desk for the account manager for Bulgarians and Russians, but, according to a handwritten sign propped on a desktop, that person was on vacation.

It was clear by their furtive looks that the tellers thought I was a pest, and as time droned on, I began to wonder if I had, indeed, become nothing but a nuisance. But at exactly ten o'clock, I saw the *prive* door open slightly and a head peak around for a look toward the back teller. I wasn't just a pest. I was a great, underappreciated, unemployed undercover agent on the right track.

This time, there in his glory, Volkov peered out like the wolf that he was, ready to eat something or somebody. He looked around the lobby, momentarily resting his eyes on the manager and me. Apparently not finding whatever he was seeking, he made sound of disgust and retreated back into the boardroom. He looked like one of those hunched-over gargoyles carved from stone on the façade of medieval buildings—a creature peering down upon passers-by, ready to pounce on them.

I knew Volkov was bad but not why he was bad. Something about him caused my heart to race. All my instincts screamed that I should flee, but Volkov had never actually threatened me. I wanted quiet time to think things through, but the account manager was anxious to finish with me and pushed more papers across the desk for me to initial.

The buzzer on the desk phone startled us while I was asking a question about subparagraph B3(a). The account manager answered the call, hung up the phone, and rolled his chair back. He then pushed himself up with his arms and hunched slightly forward, as if carrying a heavy load on his back. When almost erect, he excused himself and trudged to the private door. Again, the same hand with the watch reached around the door frame, but this time, the door was opened enough to let him enter.

It was a few minutes before the account manager returned, this time so dejected that he shuffled his feet as he returned to his desk.

Not looking me in the eye, he sat back in his chair. "Our computers are down. You'll have to leave and come back later."

"Oh, no," I said. "I have all day. I'll just wait."

For a second, he just looked at me through glazed eyes, his face expressionless, while I smiled back at him. "No," he finally said. "You must *go now.*" He reached in his desk drawer to pull out a paper bag. "I'm leaving for lunch."

It was just a little past ten in the morning, but I decided not to point out his odd eating habits. I was more worried at being forced to leave. I could go, like he asked, and come back another day, but a little voice inside me said, *No, just stay. No one is going to hurt you.*

Halfway through those competing thoughts and just as soon as the manager stood to leave, my plan began to bear fruit. I wasn't going anywhere.

CHAPTER
FORTY
FOUR

Maya finally arrived, the rustle of her bracelets and sharp click of her heels disrupting the quiet lobby. Without a glance toward anyone, she breezed by teller number one and went straight to the lady in the back, placing a large black designer tote purse on the counter before her.

"OK," I told the account manager, blithely brushing off his dismissal. "I'll just wait in that chair over there for my husband to come pick me up." I pointed to an empty chair nearer to the tellers but out of Maya's line of sight. I didn't want her to see me.

The increasingly dour man glared at me and started to object, but I knew there was little he could do to actually eject me. He too knew he was powerless, and he slowly sat back down in his chair, all the while clutching his lunch in his hands. Then he began to sweat; little beads of perspiration welled up on his forehead.

From my new seat, I was able to devote my full attention to Maya. I watched as she pulled out a yellow envelope, similar to the one left at my door, and then she took out bundles of cash and placed them on top of the marble counter. Unlike the contents of my envelope, these bills were tightly wrapped and neatly packaged, but there were so many of them that I couldn't begin to estimate the value of her deposit.

Neither Maya nor the teller spoke. I was mesmerized by the orchestrated process of counting and verifying, counting and verifying—something they must have finely tuned over time. I looked briefly at the account manager. He too was watching Maya, but his face was white as a sheet, and his body had sunk back in his chair.

There was no doubt in my mind that he had been given an order to get me out of the bank before Maya arrived. He had failed.

Other than the whirring sound of the counting machine, the bank was eerily silent. That is why both the account manager and I jumped in shock when a loud voice near the entrance caused a disturbance.

"*Maya!*" a raspy but oddly familiar voice yelled.

The name took on an ominous tone as it echoed shrilly across the lobby floors and walls.

All eyes turned to the source. The speaker—an old woman—had charged into the lobby, while the guard gamely attempted to keep hold of a loose sleeve in order to restrain her. It didn't work. Her gauzy shirt ripped, and the woman ran to Maya, throwing her arm across the money on the counter and flinging it to the floor.

The psychic? What is she doing here?

Before I could make sense of the psychic's arrival, Maya yelled at the woman to stop, pushing at her to leave. But the old woman ignored the demands. Instead, she grabbed Maya by her arms, almost throwing her to the ground. She seemed determined to kidnap Maya, but the entire altercation was completely insane. Did she think she could literally drag Maya out of the bank? And why was she doing it?

We spectators looked at the unfolding scene in stunned silence as the guard attempted to disengage the psychic from Maya, only to be stunned by the sound of multiple gunshots from the boardroom and the chaotic sounds of screams and furniture moving. I started shaking. None of this was in my plan.

I pulled out my phone and hit the 211 button, but before I could find a place to hide, the *prive* door opened, and Volkov the Wolf came out once again, even angrier than before, if that were possible. The entire room's attention was riveted on him.

Volkov held a pistol in his hand and waved it the air. He appeared ready to use it.

I watched in horror as he pointed the weapon back and forth, switching between Maya and the psychic. Blood streamed down his left arm, where one of the other men in the boardroom must have shot him. He looked like an actor in a B-rated horror show.

"*Where is Zlata?*" he yelled to Maya, who was still struggling with her assailant.

Upon hearing Volkov speak, Maya jerked her body toward him with such force that the psychic fell back, and the guard was able to gain control of her. Maya slipped from the psychic's grasp.

"Where do you think she is?" Maya countered, standing tall and snarling at him. She apparently had confidence that he would not shoot her. I wasn't so sure.

"What did you do to her?" Volkov demanded as he moved forward. He was now less than ten feet from her.

Lest Maya not understand the extent of his anger, he turned and held his pistol against the psychic's head, who was now in the grasp of the confused guard. Volkov said something that I took to mean he would shoot her if Maya didn't respond quickly. When a sound came from the boardroom door, he momentarily spun around, probably to verify that no one would try to stop him.

The guard tried to pull the old woman to safety, but the psychic was having none of it. Crazily, she refused to go.

Maya's face revealed only ambivalence to his threat. She relaxed her body, bending one knee slightly, and put a hand on her hip. She shrugged her shoulders and smirked—in effect, telling him to go ahead, shoot her.

Volkov was in no hurry, so he threatened her once again, and I heard him use the word *maika*. I knew that Bulgarian word. It meant *mother*.

Eureka! Finally, something made sense. Maya must be the psychic's daughter. How could I have missed it? I could immediately see the similarities in looks between the young and old versions of the same person. But the connection forced me to view Maya in an even more sinister light. Did Maya really not care if her own mother was killed? This game of chicken with a loaded gun was too stressful for me.

I heard Volkov click a bullet in place. Maya might not care, but I did. No one was going to kill her mother and my stalker.

"*Stop!*" I screamed, the easiest of the many translations for the word *stop* in Bulgarian and one of the few things I knew how to say. I stood in the middle of the room, drawing all the attention to me. Volkov had to know who I was; he had to know I was a diplomat's wife. That would make him stop. He had to know he couldn't kill us all.

Volkov staggered backward a few steps when he heard me, but he recovered quickly. When he turned and waved the gun in my direction, I began to regret my impulsive decision to enter the fray. His eyes narrowed as he considered me, but then he turned away from me and back to Maya, his right arm straight out, and aimed the gun barrel right at her forehead.

Not a sound was made, not even noises from the boardroom. I noticed that both tellers had dropped to the floor behind the counter for protection. I prayed that they also had called the police, but I assumed they were probably too scared to do it.

Volkov stood only a few feet from me but was entirely focused on Maya. He couldn't have suspected that I had the will to do something as risky and foolhardy as trying to save Maya, but my adrenaline rush took over my good sense. Using a low coffee table as a launching pad, I leaped high onto Volkov's back, knocking him to the ground. He was still able to get a shot off, but it missed its mark. I saw Maya fall to the floor in shock. She must have considered him incapable of firing the weapon.

I tried to keep him on the ground for a few seconds so that the guard could subdue him, but the sound of the gunshot seemed to have energized Volkov.

He jumped up with such force that I tumbled off his back and onto the marble floor. He grabbed me with his left hand, groaning with pain as he did, but he needed an easy hostage, and I was it. I tried to jerk my arm away, but he had a viselike grip. Then he reached down with his right hand to pick up the gun, which had fallen to the ground. I kicked the gun aside with my foot as best I could, but it only spun around in circles.

On his second try, Volkov managed to pick it up, while keeping me in his grasp. The blood from his wound now covered my hand and smeared onto my clothes. When he finally righted himself, he lifted his arm and once again aimed the weapon at Maya. She was scrambling across the floor on all fours, seeking cover in the barren lobby—an easy target for any active shooter.

Maya only stopped moving for a second when we all heard the sound of sirens in the distance. In that surreal moment, the psychic pulled out of the guard's arms and ran toward her ungrateful daughter. In spite of the enormous danger, she still sought to shield her daughter from harm. Freed from the responsibility of restraining the psychic, the guard pulled his pistol and yelled for Volkov to stop. I was pretty sure the guard's gun wasn't loaded, and Volkov knew that as well, but it caused Volkov to involuntarily turn in that direction. When he turned his face toward me, I could see his mouth moving, as if he was mumbling to himself.

Would he decide to let me go or kill me?

The sound of the front window shattering was deafening, and when I fell to the floor alongside Volkov, with blood splattered over me, I wondered if this was how I would die. It was only when his long fingers gripping my arm released, and I heard his groan of pain that I realized that Volkov had been shot, not me. It was his blood, not mine, all over me and the floor.

I lay on the ground, afraid to move, until the police ran into the bank, followed by men in dark suits, carrying badges. While the police and medics handled Volkov, the men in dark suits methodically arrested Maya and put what I presumed to be her and her husband's ill-gotten cash in an oversized

Ziploc bag. Then, they silently paraded the bank board members out of their meeting room, one after the other, past their fallen comrade, to the police cars. I assumed they would be taken for questioning down at the ministry. The gory scene probably gave them lots of impetus to cooperate with law enforcement.

I was finally able to confirm the identity of the Russian man at the psychic's house the day of our visit—he was the bank president; his gold cufflinks shone in the lobby lights. It was his hand that had admonished the bank manager to make me leave the bank only minutes before. He must have been in town for a board meeting to clean up the bank's financial mess. It only made sense that the psychic had told him about me and my questions about Oleg, Zlata, and the Vorbank after I left. That put me on his radar screen, and he must have become concerned about what I was doing.

While I was processing this information, the psychic sat in a corner and wept as Maya was handcuffed and led toward the police car. Just when I was wondering whether she was completely callous to her mother's pain, Maya stopped her police escorts at her mother's side and looked down. She lifted her hands that were cuffed together, wiped away tears that were beginning to form, and said "I love you" and a warm thank-you. Then she blew her mother a kiss.

I observed it all—the sadness and aftermath of chaos—wondering how it was that we were saved in the nick of time.

But I didn't wonder for long.

Frank showed up, ambling into the bank like a tardy guest to a dinner party.

I smiled. "You waited long enough."

CHAPTER FORTY FIVE

"You OK?" Frank asked.

"Yes," I said. "I assume Zach told you I was coming here."

"No, actually, I was with the police, surveilling Maya for money laundering. I just got his message." Frank turned to watch Maya as she left the bank in handcuffs. She had resumed a bit of her dignity and was yelling at her captives that her husband, Lasarov, would have them fired.

"You can only imagine my surprise when I saw you in the bank," Frank said.

"I'm glad you did."

"I know one thing," he said, looking at the carnage around us. "Vorbank is probably a thing of the past."

We both surveyed the results of the mayhem in the lobby. The unhappy account officer was boxing up his personal belongings, including his lunch. He had had a much more eventful day than he'd anticipated, likely a little too exciting.

"I don't understand," I said, as one of the tellers brought me a wet cloth with soap to wash the blood off my arms. "What do you, an American, have to do with all this?"

Frank explained that Lasarov and Maya were laundering money through the Vorbank and using it to buying property in Dulles, Virginia. The suspicious land transactions in the States were why Frank was brought in to investigate the matter. He had been working with Bulgaria's Ministry of Interior all along.

"Dulles, Virginia?" I said. "That's crazy. Near the airport?"

"Yes," he said. "Just outside of DC. When you have lots of new money and explosive growth, real estate development is ripe for launderers."

When she began buying land, the US was one of the few countries that allowed real estate to be held in LLCs and the owners never identified. As long as Congress permitted shell companies with hidden ownership and even more dubious funding to operate in the States without adequate oversight, this was what happened. It is changing now.

"It made the US the largest tax haven in the world."

That was a sobering thought.

"What was Maya laundering?" I asked.

"Most of the money was gained by her husband in the form of bribes and kickbacks—the usual petty, corrupt stuff that undermines confidence in the government," he said. "She was the point person for much of the graft, and that was the source of the cash deposits she made each week."

He went on to explain that the bribes and kickbacks occurred when her husband created the new government agency, and it took control of millions of dollars in grant money from the EU, which was intended to be used for a low-income bank loans in poorer villages. Lasarov and Maya made up fictitious borrowers; the bank helped with the process; and then they used the money to buy condominiums in Dulles through an LLC in Amsterdam. The suspicious activity was detected by a career bank examiner, following a whistleblower complaint in a similar scheme. The activity was also red-flagged by the grant administrator with the EU.

"What was the story with her mother?" I worried about what would happen to her. "Has she said anything?"

"I asked. She told one of the Bulgarian agents that she wanted to protect her daughter from you and Volkov. She insisted that you were the reason that Maya would go to jail and that Volkov would shoot her. She claimed to have seen it in the cards." Frank shook his head in disbelief. "When you wouldn't leave Sofia, she was determined to get Maya to leave Bulgaria so she wouldn't be caught—or, worse, die—but neither you nor Maya would budge."

Poor woman—up against two hard-heads.

I watched a female police officer attempting to console the pathetic woman curled up in the corner. It confounded me now that someone with the wealth Maya had amassed would allow her mother to live in such wretched conditions, while Maya jetted about like a queen, but the complexities of mother/daughter relationships are tough to decipher. Maya was ambitious, and her marriage to Lasarov and their high-flying social and political lifestyle didn't leave room for a disheveled psychic mother with missing teeth.

"Now I feel sorry for her," I said; I worried about who would take care of her if Maya went to jail.

"You can make her life easier," Frank said.

"How?"

"It'll hurt, but it's your choice."

I looked at him intently.

"The money dropped at your door was from the sale of her little piece of land in Rupite. It's all she has—or had." He let that news sink in for a few seconds. They had tracked the envelope, looked at surveillance, and came to the conclusion that she had given it to me, thinking it would make me happy and that I would go away and stop asking questions. "She wanted to save her daughter from prosecution."

It would have worked if Frank had not taken the money to the police.

"Did Maya take my money?"

"No, she didn't take other accounts."

"Ah," I said. "Well, it makes sense, in a weird, creepy way, that the psychic would think it was all about my money." I sat quietly, twirling a loose thread on my bloody shirt, as I contemplated my options.

"Jeni, it's really her money, and I think the police would give it to her if you let them," he said. "It has nothing to do with the money laundering. It's just a reminder of how desperately a mother can love her child."

I looked at him in a new light—a government man with compassion.

"Of course she can have it—if it's hers." I ignored the temptation to rationalize keeping the money, given that she tried to scare me to death.

"You'll be out $9,000," Frank said. "And we have confirmed it was hers. Maybe you can get your money from the bank one day; they are responsible for their accounts."

"I know." I smiled and touched his arm to put him at ease. "I never had it long enough in the first place to get attached to it. Uncle Bob would be the first person to say it's the right thing to do."

"Thanks. Not everyone would do the right thing," Frank said. To show his gratitude, he gave me an impromptu, awkward hug. "Like I said before, you're like my wife—she'd do the same thing."

With that, I tightly hugged him back.

It took until I got home and had showered before I felt truly free of Volkov's blood. I still had a few questions that I wanted answered.

Zach and I were in the living room, looking out of the bank of glass windows and watching a rare rainstorm cross over the city. Zach handed me a glass of red wine, and we toasted to surviving the day, literally.

"How did they finally get the proof to link Maya with the money laundering?" I asked.

Zach had spent the afternoon gathering as much information as he could from Frank and his other colleagues.

"The research paper from Oleg and Maria had the routing and account numbers imbedded within it. Oleg was planning to give them to the police before he died. They matched names and addresses from the papers you obtained from the bank. Then they followed the money and connected the dots."

"Did you find out—was Oleg murdered?" I asked.

"Most likely." He let the sad news sink in before saying more. "Most likely by some of Lasarov's henchmen. The store next door to where the accident occurred had CCTV footage at the time Oleg was hit by a car. It showed they deliberately ran him over with a car they stole."

"And Igor and Zlata? What about them?" I asked, wondering about Volkov's rage at the bank that day. "How do they fit into any of this?"

"First things first: Zlata was found dead in a condo in Cyprus this morning," he said. "A realtor went to see about listing it for sale and saw the door entry had been damaged. She called the manager, and he found the body, which had apparently been there for weeks. Neighbors had been complaining about a smell, but no one would go inside and check."

I smiled to myself. I'd tell Frank about my call to the realtor after I got the rest of the story. "So, who owned the condo?"

"Zlata and Volkov, through an LLC. It turned out that they were an item," Zach said.

"Ah, so that explains all the pictures."

"Yeah. Anyway, they convinced the bank manager to help them skim off the proceeds of the larger money-laundering scheme that Maya, Lasarov, and some other politicians were operating. That's never a good idea. And they also took the AIC money. It was all good until the bank manager decided to go rogue and stole a dozen small accounts—probably yours."

Zach said that the bank got worried about my stolen account and the AIC account because I kept asking questions and went to the police. The board president confronted the bank manager, who spilled the beans on Volkov and Zlata. They thought that also was when the board president began paying Don to keep loose tabs on me.

The bank manager may have thought that someone would eventually kill him, so he committed suicide. The whole mess was too much for the guys at the top of the money chain to tolerate, so they cleaned it up by killing Zlata and Igor. They probably couldn't figure out a way to kill Volkov without drawing too much attention so they removed him from the board, and, of course, they punished him by killing his lover, Zlata.

"Ooh," I said, recoiling a bit at that news.

That was what had caused the gunfight. Volkov had been searching for Zlata, but until he heard the news about Igor, he wasn't sure if Zlata was dead. He went to the bank, knowing there would be a board meeting and he could get answers. And if Zlata was dead, he would seek revenge.

Lightning struck at that moment—a rare occurrence—and I snuggled up to Zach.

That was when the gunfight started. The board president tried to get Volkov to leave, but Volkov was out of control and began indiscriminately shooting in the room—more likely to just scare them. However, one of the board members also had a gun and shot Volkov in the arm, stopping his rampage. But then, he left the boardroom to go after Maya. After all, she was Zlata's friend, and she had let them kill her.

There was one final loose end.

"How did Natasha and Andy end up at the Cyprus condo where Zlata died?" I asked.

"The condo is owned by an LLC out of Amsterdam, one of many; the bank president had a large interest in the building. Natasha knew the president of the Vorbank Board, and he arranged for her to use it when she wanted to."

I thought back, then, to Natasha's offer to "talk" to people at the bank about the missing AIC money and her disclosure that she knew people there.

Then, of course, Volkov was on the bank board, so as long as he was in good graces with the bank president, he and Zlata would have had access to the condominium.

I realized that I would never know if Natasha knew about Zlata's death.

For a few seconds, we both appeared lost in thought, but then Zach continued. "Jeni, they're all connected—people like them, the scammers, the entitled, and those grifters and thieves that latch onto them. In the end, they destroy each other. The worst part is that they usually take innocent people down with them."

I took another sip of wine as I considered that sad truth. "You know, I didn't think anything bad would happen inside the bank," I finally said as I wound my arm under Zach's, pulling him closer. "I thought I was safe there—that I could ask questions, and then maybe take some pictures of Maya making deposits, and see who was on the board, and maybe give it all to Frank to see if we had any leverage to get answers."

"I know," Zach said. "I don't think Frank had any idea what was going to happen when he saw that you'd gone back to the bank. I, for sure, didn't."

We laughed at the amount of paperwork that would be generated as a result of the melee at the bank that day.

Frank had promised Zach that he would file reports on Don before he resigned his position and would disclose Don's dealings with the bank president. Don never was a good federal agent. It was time to end his connections to powerful people. His callous disregard for the rule of law had put my life in danger, the very thing he was supposed to protect.

"Well, I never got my money or the AIC's, but I took Maya, Volkov, and the bank down, so I'm OK with it," I said. "The truth is that all I really want is to have my life back and be friends again with Rosa."

Zach turned me around to face him and smiled. "Well, you'll get your wish, Your Majesty," he said. "I have it on good authority that we are going to dinner with Rosa and Leo tomorrow night."

Apparently, Rosa was so mad at Leo that she had stopped cooking and cleaning house. He was desperate to get Rosa and me back together again as fast as possible.

"And the day after, I'll go with Andy to Shumen," I said, pointing to the old map of Bulgaria on the table. "It's high time we fulfilled our responsibilities. And then, after that"—I paused to give Zach a kiss—"we finally take our honeymoon, even if we find out it is only to Paris, the City of Lights"

Fortune brings in some boats
that are not steered.

✺

—William Shakespeare,
Cymbeline

CHAPTER
FORTY
SIX

THE TRIP TO SHUMEN WAS SPECTACULAR—SUNFLOWERS STILL IN BLOOM ON rolling hills and clear blue skies. Andy stopped several times to take photos, especially to capture a quaint village in the background. It was an easy, peaceful trip, just what we needed after the week we had experienced.

Our hotel was a small inn, located at the foot of a hill that rose dramatically above the city. Massive spires of concrete soared to the sky from the top of the hill. It was visible thirty kilometers away, but until I read a directional sign translated into English, I didn't understand that the unusual structure high above us was the Monument to 1300 Years of Bulgaria, aka the Founders of the Bulgarian State Monument. Built under Communist rule, the most famous monument in Bulgaria was a cubist, sharp-edged, and intimidating edifice, built in 1981 to commemorate the 1300th anniversary of the First Bulgarian Empire.

After we checked into our rooms for the night and stowed our bags, I suggested that we see it before we took off for the Uncle Bob memorial tour. Andy agreed—it was too incredible to miss.

We navigated up the winding narrow road to the top and parked in a nearly empty parking lot. A flat walking path led to the monument, perched on the edge of the plateau, a feat of human engineering. We opted out of the alternative trek of the symbolic 1300 steps to the top.

I stopped in my tracks when I left the sunny walkway and entered its vast interior. The maze of narrow alleys between monstrous concrete carvings of past kings and rulers, religious leaders, and significant events from the past 1300 years of the country—some two and three stories high—was jarring. Stern faces, warring stances, and ominous depictions of the past bore down upon us as we walked through the dark and eerie shadows cast by the monument. The experience evoked in me a sense of time and place, wonder and awe, and an odd desire to submit to authority, which must have been a goal of the architect. It was impossible not to be intimidated by figures who once ruled the region. Most resembled robots in a colossal Transformer set.

Yet there was beauty in the monument—after all, it was a true work of art, even if not warm and inviting, and it was located in a breathtaking setting. Its real problem—what you couldn't avoid if you knew history—was its cost in human toil, including forced labor to construct it.

It was that way in so many of the former Communist countries. Most of the monuments were crumbling due to neglect. They conjured up too many bad memories, this monument being the exception. I, for one, was glad it was maintained.

Neither Andy nor I talked as we walked around and contemplated the often difficult and tortured history of the Bulgarians. How they remained such a beautiful, optimistic people, I did not know.

"That was something else," Andy said after returning to the car. "It's time for a drink."

"Let's try the restaurant you might think is the oldest one in town," I said as I opened the driver's side door and reached for the seatbelt.

"I'll navigate," he responded as he pulled out his phone.

It was easy to find. The sign claimed it had been in business for almost a hundred years.

"I bet the ownership of this place has turned over several times," I said as we entered the front door and sauntered over to the bar.

The walls were full of pictures from decades past—important visitors, athletes, and ordinary diners. No employees appeared to be in the establishment yet, so we wandered around, trying to identify famous people on the wall.

Before I could complete my search of the wall photos, a young busboy came into the room and greeted us. He looked to be college-age and wore an American university jersey.

"We aren't ready for customers yet," he said with a smile as he put down his load of glasses. But in typical Bulgarian style, he told us not to worry and motioned for us to sit at the bar. "I'll find the owner to get you a drink."

A few seconds later, I was surprised to see a perky young woman appear; her long blonde hair was pulled into a ponytail. She was way too young to be the owner.

"I'm not really the owner, although he tells everyone that," she said in perfect English, nodding her head toward the busboy. She walked behind the bar and, without taking her eyes off us, pulled out two large beer mugs and hit one of the dozens of taps with the back of her hand, filling them with the optimum mixture of beer and foam. "My mother owns it, but she doesn't come in anymore. I'm home from the States for the summer and helping out."

"Really? You live in the States?" Andy perked up.

"Yes, I teach elementary school in Boston," she said and slid us each a beer.

As she began to talk about her job, it dawned on us that we hadn't asked for anything to drink, especially not beer.

"How did you know I love this beer?" Andy suddenly interjected.

"I don't know," she said, scrunching up her nose like it was no big deal. It made her look even cuter. Then she asked, "Why are you here? Family?"

Andy took a swig out of his mug and decided to tell her about Uncle Bob's story. As he talked, I saw her eyes transition from the courteous look you give an ordinary customer to the intense gaze of someone listening to compelling information. She had stopped cleaning the counters, and by the end of Andy's story, she was searching the restaurant wall, a smile finally crossing her face when she saw an old, framed black-and-white.

"I think I may have the proof you need," she said as she left the bar and strode directly to a wall on the far side of the restaurant. She reached up and pulled off an old picture and returned to us. On it were two smiling American officers and a pretty young woman at the bar, who didn't look much different than the woman before me. "Is this your uncle?" she asked.

We were dumbfounded. It had to be him—it was him.

"Who took this?" I asked as I looked at the black-and-white images taken with the use of a flashbulb camera that reflected in the old mirror behind the bar.

"An AP reporter after the war ended. My mom got the picture from him decades ago," she said. "That's my grandmother. She told us your uncle's story many times. You know, I think she held a torch for him until she married my grandfather."

We all started talking over each other, laughing at the stories about her somewhat notorious grandmother and bemoaning the fact that Uncle Bob was deceased.

Our hostess told us that her mother had sent her to live with a relative in the States when she was a young child to give her a better life. She was a US citizen now. "I love Bulgaria," she said wistfully, "but my home is in the States with my students."

"Are you married?" I asked, at which point Andy elbowed me in embarrassment.

"No," she said. "Haven't met the right person."

I could tell by her clipped response and the fact that she began polishing the bar top that I'd embarrassed her. For sure, I could tell from Andy's glare that he thought so as well.

No one said anything after that until Andy summoned up the courage to speak again. "It would be great to hear more about your life," Andy said, more tentatively than I expected. "I'm going to have to eat somewhere. Do you ... do you have to work?"

"No," she said and looked up from her polishing. "This place operates without much supervision."

"Would you like to join us for dinner?" he said, a bit sheepishly.

"Maybe …"

I wasn't so sure it was going well until I saw her cock her head sideways and take a peek from under her thick eyelashes.

Then she smiled her cute, crooked smile and asked, "But don't you want to know my name?"

"Of course," he said.

"It's Andrea," she said.

As she walked away to grab her purse, she removed her small apron at the same time. I twirled on the stool in order to watch Andy more closely.

"I guess this means if I love you, I'm dining alone," I said.

"Do you mind?"

I just smiled and threw him the car keys. I could take a cab back to the room.

After supper, I called Zach to check on him and tell him about Andy's latest discovery. "You're not going to believe this, but he's already in love again," I told him. "Natasha's barely landed in Moscow, and he's at dinner with a cute blonde."

"Who this time?"

"The young woman who waited on him at the restaurant today," I said. Then, it dawned on me. "Zach, this is probably the one!"

"Huh?"

"The psychic told him that the woman of his dreams would be waiting on him—see? *Waiting on him*! That's it! She even poured him his favorite beer without him asking for it! And her name is Andrea! Andy and Andrea."

"OK, Jeni." Zach laughed. "I thought you didn't believe in that stuff."

"Think about it, Zach—the psychic predicted it."

"Well, if so, then that means maybe the psychic was right about the kitten," he said, surprising me.

"The kitten?"

"The little thing that is snuggled up next to me on the couch," he said.

"I thought you found somebody who wanted it," I said, trying to recall what he'd told me in the aftermath of the bank shooting. "Weren't you going to take it to somebody while I was gone? And what do you mean that the psychic was right?"

"Oh," he said, "I found out this morning that Maya's mother was seen on the apartment cameras, dropping her off in the gift box. She must have thought you needed a kitten."

"You're kidding," I said. "And *her*? How do you know the kitten is a her?"

"I brought her to the vet for shots before I took her to the new owner's house," he said. "The woman was a genuine cat lady with at least six of them. I knew she didn't need to take on another kitten so I brought her back home."

"I would've done the same thing," I said, sitting on the edge of my bed. I kicked off my shoes one a time at the news.

"So, Jeni, do we keep her?" Zach asked.

I stopped with one foot in midair and waited for a second to be sure of what Zach had asked. Finally, I whispered, "Can we?"

I wasn't sure he heard me. I said it so softly. I couldn't even believe what I was saying or hearing. Although I had wanted the kitten under the car that day, long ago, I wanted this kitten even more, the one who had arrived to me, gift-wrapped, at my door.

"Did you know we had a Siamese cat when I was growing up?" he said, as if he didn't hear my question. "It had the same slightly crossed blue eyes and made the same strange sounds, like it was trying to talk to me."

"No, you never told me." I was unsure of what to say.

For once, I couldn't read my husband of many years so what he said next surprised me.

"What do you think, kitty? Want to stay here?" I heard him ask his new couch companion, and then Zach pretended to mew, which made me laugh. "I think she said yes."

A smile began to grow across my face, so wide that my cheeks actually hurt.

"Oh, Zach, I love you so much!"

It would be a lot of trouble—I knew that—but the psychic was right. I needed a cat that would talk back to me when I was alone and purr when I held it and needed me to feed it and love it.

"Well, if she's staying, then we have to name her," he said. "We can't keep calling her kitty."

"I know—how about Baba, after our trip here?" As soon as I said it, I knew it wasn't the best of names for the kitten.

"This kitten is not a Baba. She's different—more like you," Zach said. "Fun and curious. Still, I agree that her name should remind us of Bulgaria."

We were both quiet for a while, each trying to think of a suitable name.

"Sofia," Zach finally said. Then he asked softly, "What do you think about Sofia?"

"Sofia," I said, letting it roll off my tongue. "Yes. She will be our beautiful Sofia, with eyes that match the blue skies of her homeland."

Printed in the United States
by Baker & Taylor Publisher Services